T0381002

Saving Shelvockwood

Brandy Pasanen

authorHOUSE®

AuthorHouse™
1663 Liberty Drive
Bloomington, IN 47403
www.authorhouse.com
Phone: 833-262-8899

Published by AuthorHouse 05/28/2024

ISBN: 979-8-8230-1401-4 (sc)
ISBN: 979-8-8230-1400-7 (e)

Library of Congress Control Number: 2023916597

Print information available on the last page.

Any people depicted in stock imagery provided by Getty Images are models, and such images are being used for illustrative purposes only. Certain stock imagery © Getty Images.

This book is printed on acid-free paper.

Chapter 1

The Beginning

Many years ago, back when the name Lady Morphana was feared... (for that is a name that should be feared) the land of Shelvockwood was a place of magic and happiness. A land where every magic being could roam free. Shelvockwood was as big as the Earth and held almost the same qualities. It had flowers, plants, animals, & trees, but it held the unique beings that Earth could not. The land was beautiful and had two moons instead of one and the stars in the sky were shared throughout the universe. Magic roamed the land like a warm summer breeze. The land of Shelvockwood has been around for centuries. It is the only place where magical creatures' dwell. The fairies, unicorns, and sprites ran about with not a care in the world. That was until the day Lady Morphana decided to take over Shelvockwood. With a new evil brewing Shelvockwood was no longer safe.

Hearing of her dreadful return to Shelvockwood, the forest committee (made up of a few good seeds) desperately tried to figure out what to do. Lady Morphana was an evil witch. She had long black flowing hair, black as the night with no moon. When she walked, she swept the floor with her black and red velvet cape. Ever since her mother, Queen Vespera was killed & her Aunt Sigcerlaw was thrown out of Shelvockwood, Morphana has wanted to take over. You see, Morphana's mother was good at heart, but she married into evil. Sigcerlaw was Vespera's sister. Sigcerlaw was born pure evil and loved King Empanvic (Vespera's husband). Empanvic was pure evil too, and because he was Sigcerlaw thought that they should be together to rule over the kingdom. She didn't approve of her sister's kind heart, so she killed her in cold blood and blamed it on one of the protectors of the ice crystals, hoping that the king would seek revenge. King Empanvic did seek revenge, but in the process got killed himself, causing Sigcerlaw to run from the kingdom before she too was killed. Having heard of her parents' deaths, Morphana's heart became as black as night, and she vowed to put an end to the protectors for what they had done. Morphana has since returned to the land of Shelvockwood and has taken back her father's castle...the Castle of Terror.

This would not do. If Lady Morphana was back, all Shelvockwood would be at stake. The forest committee held a meeting regarding the return of Lady Morphana.

"If you ask me, she is nothing but trouble. I say we call for help. There is nothing we can do. I am a tiny fairy and you, Aged Sir Oak, are rooted to where you stand. The only one who could stand up to her would be you Sorsha, but I am not going to have you do it alone. The only way we got rid of her mother was with the protectors of the ice crystals, but that was years ago." Queen Lavinia said while batting her tiny wings. Just because she is only a few inches tall and can blend in with any lavender flower doesn't mean the forest committee does not listen to her. They listen when she speaks, for she is the Queen of the forest fairies and sprites.

Turning his branches to face the Queen, Aged Sir Oak said, "I must agree with you Queen Lavinia. I am too old and fragile to try and fight her."

Now the very funny thing about Aged Sir Oak's comment is simply this, he is a tree and trees obviously don't move. Being that he is the oldest and wisest tree in Whispering Wood, he doesn't look it. His branches branch out for miles it seems and he has the brightest leaves of all the trees in the forest.

Facing both Aged Sir Oak and Queen Lavinia, Sorsha said through a worried look, "You are both right. You cannot fight her and I myself cannot handle her alone. How are we to summon the new Protectors of the Ice Crystals?"

"Why Sorsha, if you want my opinion, I think we should summon up the Protectors the way they did in the old days. Make that potion that was left in the book from Anastasia, the one that requires orris root powder and sage. And you must not worry yourself like that; it will mess up your very pretty face." Balfour the village elder said.

He was right though. Sorsha had a very pretty face. A young woman no more than twenty-five, with eyes the color of grass, locks of red hanging down to her shoulders tied back with the best arrangement of flowers that the Hidden Garden can produce, and the prettiest crystal diamond hanging from her neck that Anastasia and left behind for the next oracle to wear.

Glancing over at a rather tall build man, Balfour was returning Sorsha's stare. "You can give me that look of wonder all you want Sorsha, but I think it is our only chance at defeating Lady Morphana." Balfour said with a slight sigh.

"Well alright then forest committee, this meeting is adjourned. Sorsha go summon up the protectors with that potion that Anastasia left for you. By tomorrow they should be in Shelvockwood to save us." Queen Lavinia said with a flutter.

ↂↄ

As the bell rang at 3 o'clock, Piper Taylor walked down the stone steps of Willow High and took a deep breath of fresh air. She couldn't help but smile at the fact that the weekend was here, and she didn't have to wear her school uniform till Monday. The walk home was even pleasant with the smell of summer just around the corner. When she finally got home, she had a note taped to her front door from Decklyn. How was she so lucky to have a boyfriend like him? Not only was he caring to her, but he was very protective of her as well. Decklyn was not tall at all, but average for a guy. Just like Piper was average for a girl. She loved looking into his deep hazel eyes when she had a bad day and being able to have a strong shoulder to cry on when life wasn't going the way she had planned. Most of the time he wore a hat because he didn't want to get a sunburned scalp (he shaves his head you see).

Saying a quick hello to her dalmatian Shenna, Piper headed upstairs. Opening her bedroom door, she threw down her backpack by her desk and plopped on her bed. Releasing a sigh, Piper knew she would get nothing done by just lying there on her bed.

Getting up and walking to her closet she opened it up only to find the mess she left there that morning. Her mother had told her that if her room wasn't clean before she went to school, she wasn't going to spend the time with Tiffany and the boys. So, Piper had done the only thing a normal teenage girl would do, she threw everything that was on the floor in her closet and shut the door. Rummaging through the mess on her closet floor, she managed to find clothes that didn't look like her school uniform. After putting on her faded jeans, a white tank top, and some sneakers, she walked over to her floor length mirror to have a look. Tilting her head to the side she still wasn't satisfied so she grabbed a hair tie and put her hair up in a ponytail. Much better she thought as she glanced back into the mirror at her reflection. One of the rules at Willow High was that the girls were not allowed to wear their hair up unless it was for gym class and then when gym was done it was to be put back down. Besides her hair was something that all the girls wanted; straight, brown, and just above her hips. If that wasn't enough the girls were envious of her baby blue eyes. Finally satisfied, Piper headed downstairs to the kitchen and headed over to the phone. Picking up the receiver, she started dialing away. Eagerly waiting for someone on the other line to pick up, she drummed her fingers on the kitchen counter. Finally, an answer, "Hi Mrs. Darling, this is Piper. Is Tiffany there? Thanks, I'll hold. Hi, Tiffany, how did you do on that History test this morning? Oh, well that isn't bad, I think I got at least a 95. Yeah, my mother told me I couldn't go hiking with you guys this weekend unless I cleaned my room and got an A on the History exam. So, is everybody meeting up here before we head out? Ok, see you all in a bit then. Yup, bye." Piper said as she hung up the phone.

Grabbing a bottle of water out of the fridge and rushing back upstairs to her bedroom, she didn't have much time before the gang would be knocking on her door and she still had to pack a daypack and clean her room.

After finishing a quick clean to her room, she ran back downstairs. Throwing her brown daypack by the door, Piper jumped as the doorbell rang. Throwing open the door she came face to face with Tiffany, Phoenix, and Decklyn. Tiffany was dressed in a puffy sun dress and she had her shoulder length blonde hair done up in curls. Apparently this brown eyed girl didn't know what hiking involved, although she probably didn't care as long as she could show off her super model body. Decklyn and Phoenix were both wearing rough looking jeans and tee-shirts. Phoenix was the same height as Decklyn, but he doesn't shave his hair, he spikes his brown hair.

"Ok kids are we ready to get a move on?" said a very energetic Decklyn.

"Alright dude, but if we are forgetting something because we are rushing out of here, you won't have to worry about an ax-murder. I will kill you myself." Phoenix said with a grin.

They all climbed into Decklyn's jeep after loading it and started on down the road. Piper was staring out the window and looking at all the beautiful willow trees. Their town was named after them and nobody on this side of the northeast would forget it. Watching the Willow High students hanging around outside of the Whispering Willow Pizzeria. Just off Oak and Pine streets some old men were setting on the corner in their lawn chairs, yelling at kids from Winnie Willow Elementary for throwing acorns at the squirrels. The Librarian from Weeping Willow Library was picking the books out of the drop box. Boy, would she miss the library, every weekend Piper spent visiting the library. An hour later they all arrived at the spot Phoenix said was good for hiking. "I think we should set up camp here and hit the hay. We can always get up early and start hiking tomorrow." Said Phoenix.

"I second that, besides I am tired as well from being in school all day and then dealing with my brother when I got home." Tiffany said through a yawn.

So, with that said and done, the tent was pitched, and good nights were exchanged. The sound of crickets put everyone to sleep instantly. As the sun rose the next morning, the only remains of where the kids had stayed was the smoke rising from where the campfire was.

The day started out rather nicely. Among the trees, they saw a few female deer with their fawns and a family of bunnies eating clovers by a shady brook. The hike didn't seem to take long before they all came to their first rest stop among the trees. "Isn't it just gorgeous out? I love being around nature." Tiffany said as she was sunning herself.

Phoenix was just about to tell Tiffany that her view on nature was different than everybody else's, but he caught a glimpse of a dark hole out of the corner of his eye. "Hey guys, I think that is a cave over there; want to go check it out?" he asked excitedly.

"Phoenix what if there are wild animals in there?" asked a worried Tiffany.

"Where is your sense of adventure Honey? Besides even if there are wild animals in there, we have flashlights and candy, we can always throw the candy at them and if that doesn't work, we can always beat them with the flashlights." Phoenix said with a grin.

With that said Phoenix picked up his daypack, took out his flashlight, and started walking over to the cave. Not wanting Phoenix to go alone the other three picked up their things and with worried looks took out their flashlights and followed him towards the cave. Once inside each one of them turned on their flashlights. The cave was dark and damp. Piper and Tiffany huddled close together while Phoenix and Decklyn started wandering ahead. Decklyn was just about to tell Phoenix that he thought he could hear running water when he heard screaming coming from the girls behind him. Turning around in time to see Piper fall from view, Decklyn could only assume that that was where Tiffany and vanished as well. Rushing over to where the girls had disappeared, the boys could hear their slight screams. "Well, we either turn back now or we throw ourselves down there after them." Phoenix said as he glanced down at the blackened tunnel.

"They need us. We are the protection on this outing. We can't go get help and just leave them here. What if there are wild animals down there?" Decklyn said as he gave Phoenix a nervous look.

Taking a deep breath, Phoenix flung himself down the tunnel. Decklyn wasn't too far behind him. Phoenix could tell by the light bouncing off the tunnel walls and by the many grunts coming from Decklyn. Once at the bottom, the boys could hear the sobs from the girls. "Piper, Tiffany, are you guys, ok?" Decklyn asked as he pulled himself into a sitting position.

Holding Tiffany tight, Piper said, "We are both ok. The fall just scared us, we weren't ready for it. Amazing enough we both still have our daypacks, but our flashlights we lost."

"What happened? I mean one-minute you guys were there and we turned around for one second and you were gone." Phoenix said while flashing his light towards them.

7

"I thought Tiffany tripped, but when I was about to go and help her, the floor caved beneath me." Piper said while looking up through the dark tunnel.

"How are we ever going to get home?" cried an upset Tiffany.

"Don't start getting upset Tiffany." Decklyn said, "We will find a way home Maybe there is a way out from down here."

"Ok, well let's get cracking. How many flashlights do we have?" Phoenix asked with a smirk.

"Phoenix, we have just the two of ours, the girls both lost theirs when they fell remember?" Decklyn answered while making sure his still worked.

"Correction Buddy, we have just one. Mine must have been damaged on the way down. It doesn't work." Phoenix said while he hit his flashlight trying desperately to make it work.

"Alright, we can make this work. Tiffany stick with Phoenix and Piper, stay next to me. Hopefully there will be no more cave-ins." Replied Decklyn.

And with that they were off down the dark hole of the cave. It seemed like an hour passed when they all came to a dead end. For the passageway ahead of them looked like nothing but solid rock.

"Just lovely. How are we supposed to get out of here now?" asked an angry, but scared Piper. "We don't even know if the flashlight will last that long."

"Trust me, those batteries are just fine. I put them in this morning." argued Phoenix. He was about to argue with Piper some more, but Decklyn put his finger up to his lips to silence them. When they were all quiet and had given Decklyn their full attention, he slowly pointed to the solid rock ahead of them. The rock wasn't just solid rock. It was a wooden door, but it blended in to look like rock. Probably to hide the fact it was a door. Bewildered beyond measure, the four friends walked over to the door. Taking a chance, Tiffany bravely walked up to the wooden door and pushed it open. Right behind her was Phoenix with the flashlight. Going around to her right side, Phoenix turned the flashlight on and brightened up the room behind the door.

The room was rather small and smelled of hickory smoke. As the four friends crammed themselves into this tiny room the door to the cave slammed shut behind them. "Well, this is just dandy." said an annoyed Phoenix as he was trying to pull the door back open with a lot of force.

"Don't panic Phoenix. We have been through much worse before. I mean look at the whole cave situation." sighed Decklyn.

"Yeah ok, that makes me feel a whole lot better." Phoenix said rather sarcastically.

"Bright side, there is another door behind you Phoenix." Piper coughed while trying to muffle back a laugh.

"I suppose you find this funny don't you Piper? Oh, look at how scared Phoenix is getting. Did you ever wonder what maybe hiding behind the door? Could be a bear or an ax-murderer, but let's just find out, shall we?!" barked Phoenix. And before Piper could even make a suggestion back Phoenix had walked over to the door of the tiny room and shoved it open.

The four of them just stood there amazed as to what they saw. They were no longer in a dark cave, but what looked like a tiny house. Afraid to even move, the friends just stood there staring into the house. Not one of them could tell you how long they were standing there before Tiffany started talking in a whisper. "You don't suppose we fell down the cave and landed on the other side into someone's house, do you?"

"Don't be silly." Piper whispered, turning to face Tiffany. "I don't think that that could....Ahhhhh!!!!" Before she could finish her sentence, Piper was buzzed by a big bug. "EWWW, somebody please kill it!" she screamed.

Scrambling to find something to kill this huge bug, Decklyn grabbed a broom and started swinging. Tiffany was hiding behind a huge barrel labeled unicorn food and screaming as the big bug made a beeline for her head. There was so much going on that nobody took notice of the young woman standing in front of the fireplace. "What are you doing?" the woman shouted.

Everybody stopped. Even the bug stopped and just hovered in midair. Then before any of the kids could say a word the bug spoke up and said, "I was under orders of the Queen my lady to come here and retrieve the protectors. Before I could even speak on the Queen's behalf, they started attacking me. I finally believe that they are impostors and must be working for Lady Morphana, but what I cannot figure out is how they got into the protector's broom closet."

Piper had opened her mouth to reply, but she no more than uttered two words and the pretty lady started talking. "We need to give them a chance to speak Elanil. After all the protectors will be from another world."

Another world? What is this lady talking about? The four friends stood in awe. Not one of them knew what to say. Finally, after much debating in her head Piper spoke first. "Sorry to intrude like this, but my friends and I took a wrong turn and ended up here in your house. If you have a phone, we can use we will be out of here and on our way back home."

A bit confused as to what she had just said the little bug Elanil spoke, "What is she talking about Sorsha?"

"Sorsha? That is an interesting name." Decklyn replied.

"Well, what is your name stranger?" Elanil snapped.

"My name is Decklyn Pruette." Decklyn answered. And turning to his friends he said, "And to my right is Phoenix Lucas, my right-hand man. And these lovely ladies are Piper Taylor, my girlfriend and her best friend Tiffany Coven; A.K.A. Phoenix's girl."

"So good to meet all of you, but it just so happens that I summoned you here to Shelvockwood. Elanil, tis a common mistake, but you must inform the Queen at once of their arrival. I have much to explain." Sorsha said.

"Right away my lady." Elanil replied. With that said he flew out of the window.

"The Queen. Weird names. Disappearing rocks. Bugs that talk. Where are we? And where is there a can of raid when you need it?" Phoenix replied through gritted teeth.

"Oh, Elanil isn't a bug." Chuckled Sorsha, "He is a fairy."

Each one of the children gave her a mouth dropping stare. "He's a what?" asked Tiffany.

"Did she just say a fairy? Like the ones in storybooks?" asked a confused Decklyn.

"Now I am really confused. Where are we?" asked a bewildered Phoenix.

"You are in the land of Shelvockwood. I summoned you from another world to help us in our desperate need of help. You see our land is being taken over by an evil witch. Her name is Lady Morphana. I see by the looks on your faces that there is a lot of disbelief in what I say. Believe me when I say that what I say is true. You saw with your own eyes the fairy that the Queen had sent here. Did you not?" Sorsha asked with a look of certainty on her face.

Whispering under her breath so that only Piper could hear her, Tiffany said, "She does make a point. How else can you explain a talking bug?"

"If you are still having doubts, all that will change when the initiation begins. Till then I can take you over to where you will be staying while you are here in Shelvockwood." said Sorsha with almost a skip in her step.

Grabbing their daypacks and following Sorsha as she headed out the door, they were amazed as to all the weeping willows they saw as they stepped outside. Sorsha's cottage was off to the side of what looked like a forest. Knowing that there had appeared to be some kind of question about where they were, Sorsha said, "This place is called Sorsha's Gorge, named after myself of course and the forest that you see ahead of you is called the Whispering Wood.

You will learn about all the different places in Shelvockwood in your own time." And with that the friends were off on one of the biggest adventures they would have all summer.

ᘓᘔ

Not aware that they were being watched by the evil that was bestowed upon the land of Shelvockwood, the newly protectors followed Sorsha through what seemed to be the shortest walk of their lives. They passed many different types of trees and a field of flowers until they came to a fork in the path they were taking. Stopping at the intersection of the fork Sorsha looked at them with a serious face and said, "Beware that if you are taking a walk throughout the land of Shelvockwood, stay clear of the path on the left. For it leads to the Castle of Terror. That my friends is the place that houses Lady Morphana and her many minions."

As they continued down the right path Piper couldn't help but watch the other path fade away as they kept walking. She could almost sense the danger that was ahead and didn't want to deal with any of that now. The path even looked evil, almost like dark magic would enter your soul if you even set foot on the path. If Piper and her friends had followed that path, they would have seen how dark and eerie the Castle of Terror really was. Lady Morphana lives on top of an ugly hill. There are no living trees or streams near the Castle. Everything is dead and lonely looking. Ugly statues can be found on her property of sprites and unicorns that were taken as prisoners and turned into stone. There is, however, a swamp on her property. If you were to even set foot on her land, she would have one of her ogres, swamp goblins, or giants get you. Then you would be hauled off to either the dungeon or the tower where you would be held against your will and possibly tortured. Not to mention the minute one does set foot on her land; they instantly feel how dark the place is. For it is always cold there and the sense of cold running through one's spine sets the mood for nothing but trouble.

Continuing up the right path the clearing ahead was a sight to see, for they were up on top of a hill that looked down into a tiny village. Pointing towards the village Sorsha said, "Over there just beyond the village is the Hidden Garden. This is where you will live while you are here in the land of Shelvockwood. The villagers have done a fine job at building you a new fort. Inside you will find all the things you will need while here in Shelvockwood."

"I hate to interrupt you, but you said the villagers built us a new fort. What happened to the old one?" Tiffany asked with half a smile on her face.

"The old one was burnt down when Lady Morphana returned to Shelvockwood. I think she figured that if she burned it down, we wouldn't be able to get new help. She was so wrong." Said a somewhat enthused Sorsha.

It took them a bit longer to get to the new fort that Sorsha was talking about, but it was a sight to see. There are rows and rows of flowers of all different sizes and shapes, as far as the eye can see. The unique thing about the garden, however, is the flowers and vines form a huge maze that surrounds the fort. This is what Sorsha called a protection against evil coming to invade their fort. The maze was a sight and a mess to walk through, but it didn't take them long to get to the clearing. And right smack dab in the clearing was the newly built fort. Unfortunately, the fort didn't look new. It looked like an old cabin that had been sitting there for years. Giving Decklyn a little shove, Phoenix said, "This dump is the new fort? I can't wait to see what the inside of it looks like."

Phoenix, however, ate his words when he walked in the door behind Piper. The place was magnificent. When you walk in, there is a table with four chairs in a tiny kitchen. The kitchen had a few cabinets and what appeared to be a small closet next to the sink. Tiffany walked over to the closet and opened it to find an old looking broom and mop. While she was looking around the kitchen, Decklyn walked into the tiniest living room he had ever seen. It was right next to the kitchen. There was no couch, but what looked like bean bag chairs and tons of blankets and throw pillows everywhere. It reminded him of a girl's slumber party. There was, however, a fireplace in the living room. Off to the side of the room was another door. This led to the bathroom. The only bathroom Sorsha said was indoors. Decklyn turned around to tell everybody about the bathroom but walked right into a ladder. Phoenix and Piper were already up the ladder. As soon as they reached the top, they called for the other two to follow. When Tiffany and Decklyn finally got up the ladder to their surprise the entire second floor was the bedroom. There was one set of bunkbeds; well, it wasn't really a bunkbed. There was a bed on the right-hand side of the ladder and above it was a hammock. On the left-hand side of the ladder was another bed, or rather a big mattress fit for two. Covering all the beds and most of the floor were more blankets and pillows. "Isn't this to die for? This is just like camping and having a big sleep over rolled into one!" says a very excited and happy Tiffany.

"Yeah, for girls maybe; give us guys a chance to dirty it up a bit and it will be homey." Phoenix chuckled.

"Phoenix where is your sense of style? This is the best place for young kids to live." Piper says with a smile.

Phoenix still smiling and grinning from ear to ear says, "Yeah, yeah ok, whatever."

Watching them from the ladder, Sorsha says, "Inside that wardrobe are some clothes for you all to change into for the ceremony. Please change before we head over to the Whispering Wood. The committee would like to get the ceremony done before Lady Morphana has any time to react to the fact that you are here. There is a lot to talk about, but again, welcome to Shelvockwood!"

Once Sorsha had descended the ladder, Piper turned to the

wardrobe and opened it up. "I guess the blue ones are for you boys to wear and the lavender ones are for Tiff and I to wear. Let's put them on and head downstairs to where Sorsha is waiting for us."

Throwing the new clothes on and looking into the mirror they all looked like something out of a fairy tale. Smiling at each other they headed down the ladder to meet the magical woman. All four of them were as nervous as could be. Even Phoenix, who says that he doesn't have nerves, was nervous. What was the ceremony going to bring? Let alone, who was going to be there?

∾

The ceremony was to take place in the Whispering Wood. Now the Whispering Wood is a bit scarier than the bright colorful places like Sorsha's Glen and the Hidden Garden. The only thing in the forest that isn't scary is Aged Sir Oak. He has been around for centuries; watching out for all those who wish to seek it. Running through the Whispering Wood is the Shady Brook. This is where all the animals go to drink. And if you were to follow the brook long enough you would come to a beautiful waterfall. The forest committee was ready and waiting for the four chosen ones. Aged Sir Oak was introduced to them as was Balfour. The ceremony took place under Aged Sir Oak. He was decorated with acorns and pinecones that the sprites had gathered and the fairies had sprinkled with fairy dust.

"Pike, will you go away!" growls Aged Sir Oak.

In a hyper chipper voice Pike says, "Oh, come on Aged Sir Oak. You must be excited that we finally have four chosen ones coming to help us."

Pike is a hyper little sprite who loves to bother Aged Sir Oak. "I am as excited as you sound, but you don't see me shaking all my branches now do you? Ah, Sorsha. Glad to see you again my child." Aged Sir Oak says very happily.

15

"Oh, Aged Sir Oak, you worry about me all the time, but I can take care of myself." Sorsha says.

Aged Sir Oak smiles widely and says, "Ah, but I do worry my child. For if anything ever happened to you, I would never forgive myself for letting you go anywhere alone. I would have sent Pike with you. This way he would have left me alone. Ah, are these the four? May I have the pleasure of your name's young ones?"

Piper turned to face the talking tree and said, "My name is Piper." And turning to Tiffany and the boys she said, "And these are my friends Tiffany, Decklyn, and Phoenix. We don't' know how we got here or why we are even here, but we will help in any way that we can."

Phoenix was about to pull on Piper's hair when he was buzzed. "Where is the raid!" he shouted.

Snickering Pike turns to Phoenix and says, "That is the Queen, Queen Lavinia."

The Queen buzzes up to Aged Sir Oak and shouts for all to hear, "Ladies, Gentlemen, and gentle creatures, I give to you the four Protectors of the ice crystals!"

Leaning in so that the others would hear him Phoenix says quietly over the loud roar of the crowd, "Someone ought to put a bell on her, so they know when she is about to buzz them." They all chuckled quietly as the ceremony was about to start. There came a hush over the crowd as the Queen spoke again "My friends, today is a great day. A day of recognition; today is the day of the downfall of Lady Morphana!"

The crowd went wild again. Villagers were screaming with joy, sprites were dancing, and all the fairies were fluttering their wings wildly. As the crowd continued to celebrate, the Queen introduced herself to the four kids and then went and got the crystals that everyone was talking about. Coming from around Aged Sir Oak the Queen placed a box on a wooden stump just beside Sir Oak. Turning towards the four friends the Queen said, "Inside this box there are four crystals from the land of our fellow friends. These crystals have powers that Lady Morphana would die for. Once placed around your neck the crystal begins to transform and take on the inner being that wears it. Don't let me fool you, these crystals are to be always worn, for if they fell into the wrong hands, it would be disastrous for everyone. There are four colored crystals and each one has a different power. I will give out the crystals now and explain what they do as I give them out. The first crystal is the lavender crystal. This crystal when worn has the power of invisibility. Wearing the crystal will allow the person to become invisible whenever they want, and they can make anybody invisible. Tiffany, you are the one who is chosen to wear the lavender crystal."

Not knowing what to say or do, Tiffany just walks up to the Queen and leans her head forward. Nothing happened though when the crystal was put around her neck. So maybe all this talk was just talk and the crystals really meant nothing.

Phoenix was about to say something smart when the Queen spoke up again. "The next crystal is the emerald crystal. This one possesses the powers to heal. Once placed around the neck the person with the emerald crystal has the powers to heal any wounded creature or being. This may sound like a silly power to have, but when in need it will come in handy. Phoenix my dear, I give you the emerald crystal."

"I always knew I had it in me to be somebody that everybody relies on. Guess if you guys get sick you must come to me, huh?" says Phoenix with a smile. And with that he bows his head so that the Queen can place the crystal around his neck.

Again, nothing happened, but the Queen went on, "Every woman wants rubies, but this ruby has the power of protection. The ruby allows the person to protect the other protectors from harms way. It also allows the person to watch over the protectors and use any means to save them in battle. It possesses the power of strength and can make the person wearing it stronger than they appear. It can also detect when something is false. For example, if someone is in disguise the ruby crystal can see right through the disguise. Someone very brave and protective deserves this crystal. I think the one to wear this crystal is Decklyn."

"I am glad you think I am brave, but somehow, I think you only think that because I am so built. I will try to keep up to the expectations that come with this power." states a brave, but unsure Decklyn, as he leans in for his crystal.

Still waiting for some sort of magic to happen, Piper waited eagerly. Wondering what the last crystal held. She was the only one left to get a crystal.

"Last, but not least I give you the shimmering ice crystal. This crystal has the power to freeze. Use it carefully though for if someone or something is frozen too long it will stay that way forever. Piper, we all know you are the one to get this crystal, but it has deeper powers that are unknown to all. The last protector never told me what else this crystal possessed, but hopefully you will find out what it is sooner than later." Queen Lavinia said.

Piper walked over to the Queen and bowed her head so that the Queen could place the crystal around her neck. Walking back over to where the others were standing, Piper was a bit nervous. She knew that some type of magic was about to happen, but she could not even explain what she felt.

Turning to face the kids, Queen Lavinia said, "Now let the magic of the crystals begin."

All a bit nervous still as to what was about to happen, they waited patiently. Suddenly, a light breeze swept through the Whispering Wood. Blowing back leaves on Aged Sir Oak, flower pedals were floating through the breeze as each one of the crystals began to glow. As the crystals grew brighter in color the kids began to slowly levitate off the ground. Only a few feet in the air the crystals exploded with light and then went out just like a candle. The four friends began to descend slowly and when their feet finally touched the ground each of them could feel a sense of satisfaction and ease.

"One more thing I must give you all before you go. This is the Protectors journal. You don't have to write in it for it makes its own words. Always take it with you and the crystals. Record what adventures you go on. So, if for some reason something happens, and you need to remember what happened in a past adventure you can just refer to your journal. Do not let it get into the wrong hands because anybody can read it. Now that you all have your powers, how do you feel?" asks the Queen.

"Well, Queen Lavinia, to tell you the truth. I don't feel any different. Should I look different?" asks a befuddled Phoenix.

"You will Phoenix. In time you will know. When you need to use your power for the first time is when you will know you feel different. Are there any questions before I send you on your way back to the fort?" Queen Lavinia asks.

"Actually, there are a few questions." Piper says while debating on what ones to ask first. "We are obviously in a different world. How does time work here compared to where we are from? I don't want my mother to worry about me. And I noticed the path towards the Castle of Terror. Are we not allowed to walk it?"

"Time here works a bit different than time back where you are from. Thirteen years here is not even a second in your world. Time stops completely in your world compared to ours. For whatever reason you go back to Earth and then decide a year later that you want to come back to Shelvockwood, everyone you knew here would be dead and gone." Queen Lavinia said with a sad tone in her voice. But as she got ready to speak again her tone changed to more of a deeper serious tone, "As for the path leading to the Castle of Terror, it is up to you if you want to take it or not, but I advise you not to. Suspicion only leads to danger. Is that all the questions for tonight?"

The four friends exchanged looks and shook their heads as if to ask no more questions. With that said and done the Queen said, "I present to you the Protectors of the crystals!"

The crowd cheered even louder than they had before. It took awhile before the friends could head home because they had so many new hands to shake. It wasn't quite dark out yet, but by the sounds of things nobody wanted to mess around with Lady Morphana; especially in the dark. So, they said their goodbyes and off they went. They walked Sorsha back to her cottage and said they would see her and the forest committee in the morning. Heading through the Hidden Garden's many mazes, they finally made it to their fort. When inside Piper locked the door while Tiffany went around with Phoenix and shut all the windows.

"This gives me the creeps. I mean what if Lady Morphana has one of her ogres out there watching the place? I would hate to meet one of them." a shaken Tiffany says.

"No worries Tiff. I mean we have the four of us here. We all can protect each other. We said we wanted an adventure when we went on the hike right? Well, I say we got one. Besides, we will all be sleeping upstairs. And the littlest noise wakes Decklyn up. That is probably why they gave him the ruby crystal." says a brave and somewhat scared Piper.

"Don't you find it odd that they all knew a bit about us before they even met us? I mean Sorsha just met us; she couldn't have known what we were like before we got here." Decklyn says with curiosity.

"I agree with Decklyn. How can they know so much? We don't have it tattooed on our foreheads, do we?" Phoenix says jokingly.

Piper being tired from a long day and having to deal with Phoenix's comedy all day, says in a frustrated tone, "Think guys. We are in a magical place. Magical! It doesn't take a rocket scientist to figure out that they used some kind of magic to find out stuff about us. Sorsha said she summoned us by using a potion. Now we all have had a along day. I mean with the whole cave incident and now this. Let's get some sleep and we will talk more about this in the morning."

They all climbed the ladder to the bedroom. It was difficult at first as to who was going to share the bed. The girls won, leaving Decklyn and Phoenix to fight for the bottom half of the messed-up bunkbed. The lights were out, and all was well. At least they thought all was well.

⚬⚭⚬

Watching all of them sleep soundly was something that Lady Morphana loved to do. "Yes, sleep my precious protectors. For you soon will not be sleeping soundly. You will be taking turns keeping watch for me and my ogres, giants, and swamp goblins. Slobbo! Come here! I must talk to you." Shouted Morphana.

"Yes Lady Morphana? What can I do for you?" Slobbo says in a grunted voice.

"See these new protectors? I want you to get your ogres on them at once. For this will be the only night that they get any rest at all. You start at dawn." Lady Morphana says with an evil little laugh.

"Yes, my lady. Is there anything else you would like for me to do?" Slobbo asked.

"As a matter of fact, there is. Fetch me a glass of water. My throat is a little horse. I want you to go and cause mischief and mayhem down in the Hidden Garden tomorrow. Be sure to it that you do or else it will be your head!" shouted Lady Morphana.

"Yes, my lady." Slobbo says.

After he left the room, Lady Morphana said to herself very quietly, "We will teach these new protectors a thing or two. I know that we are going to take over Shelvockwood real soon and this time, Queen Lavinia and Sorsha won't be able to stop me!"

⚬⚭⚬

Chapter 2

Welcome to Shelvockwood

Whether it was because they were in a different place or because of all the excitement that happened the day before, Decklyn, Piper, Phoenix, and Tiffany didn't get a wink of sleep. As they strolled down the ladder to the living room area, Piper said, "We should probably do a bit of exploring to check things out. I wouldn't want to get lost in a new place like this. I mean with all the magic and what not."

"I agree, but at the same time I think we should keep low. What if we run into danger?" asked a worried Tiffany.

"Well, we can't stay locked up forever. I personally would go stir up crazy." Phoenix said while doing a little bounce.

"Then let's get what we need for the day and head off on another adventurous hike." Decklyn said humorously.

With that said and done, the four friends gathered up the remainder of their daypacks and headed out the door. Taking a quick look around they decided to head over to Sorsha's cottage. Once they got there, they were greeted at once by Sorsha. Giving them a slight wave to allow them to enter her home. Once inside the protectors all sat around a tiny little table in her kitchen area. "Would any of you like a cup of tea before we get into all of your questions?"

"I am not really a tea drinker, but I think the girls are." Decklyn said.

Looking over at the girls they both nodded as if to say, 'yes we would love some tea', but Phoenix gave a disgusted look and said, "No thanks, I am more of a pop drinker. But getting down to business, do you happen to know if most of the villagers are friendly? I would hate to run into a few of them who would cause us any trouble while we are here."

"Unfortunately..." started off Sorsha, as she poured the girls some tea, "some of the villagers are working for Lady Morphana. Whether it is out of fear or pure hatred of magical creatures, nobody knows. You see the villagers are non-magical beings. For the most part though the ones that are not on Lady Morphana's side rather enjoy hanging out with magical folk. They find it amusing and interesting to be a part of."

Stirring her tea with a spoon, Piper looked up at Sorsha and asked, "How will we be able to tell who is good and who isn't? I mean they probably all look normal to some extent. Do the ones working for Lady Morphana have magical powers? If she is so evil, I don't see why she wouldn't give them something in return for being on her side."

"Lady Morphana isn't stupid. As you have just made clear it would be stupid of her not to give them something in return for helping her. She, however, doesn't see it that way. If she were to give any of them magical powers, it would be dipping into her own and she isn't willing to share any of hers."

"So basically, what you are saying is she is selfish?" Tiffany asked with curiosity.

Snickering a little Sorsha replied, "Why yes, I guess she is a little selfish. I was informed by one of Queen Lavinia's fairies that Aged Sir Oak would like a word or two with all of you. Not that I am not enjoying your company, but the days here in Shelvockwood fly by quickly. I wouldn't want Aged Sir Oak thinking that something had happened to all of you. Besides, I have a meeting with the Queen about the festival coming up in a few weeks. Lots of planning to do."

The girls quickly finished up the last bit of tea that they had and got up from their seats. Making their way to the door, Phoenix turned around to Sorsha and said, "It was nice chatting with you even if it was just for a little while."

"Why thank you. Now try to stay out of trouble all of you and watch out for spies. Believe it or not they are everywhere and can be things you wouldn't expect them to be." cautioned Sorsha.

Waving goodbye, Piper, Tiffany, Decklyn, and Phoenix headed out in the direction of the Whispering Wood. The journey to Age Sir Oak wouldn't take them as long as they thought it would. As they made their way down the path to the forest Lady Morphana had her eyes on them from almost every direction they could turn.

∞

The sun was shining high up in the sky of Shelvockwood. Decklyn and Piper were holding hands just ahead of Phoenix and Tiffany, who were flirting with each other. Coming up to the clearing in the forest, the protectors came to a halt right underneath the hanging branches of Aged Sir Oak. "Hello, Sir Oak. Word has it on the streets that you wanted to have a talk with us." Phoenix said with a beat in his voice.

"Word has it on the streets, what are you talking about? I asked Elanil to let the Queen know that I wanted to speak with you all. What does that have to do with streets that you speak of?" a confused Aged Sir Oak asked.

"Phoenix you are confusing him. He isn't from where we are from. Can't you see there are no streets around here?" Piper said under her breath to Phoenix. Turning to Aged Sir Oak she said, "What is it that you wanted to talk about?"

"My dears, I just wanted to chat with you all and get to know you. I wanted to explain to you all a bit about Shelvockwood as well because I have been around since Shelvockwood was born. Why I know..." but he was cut off by a loud banging noise.

Coming through the clearing was the little sprite, Pike. He was throwing what looked like bottles of medicine all over the ground. Every time he threw one on the ground it let off a big bang and purple mushroom smoke went floating up in the air. "Pike! I will have the Queen order you to be locked up in the village if you don't knock it off!" yelled Aged Sir Oak.

Before Pike could even reply he was swept up by one of Aged Sir Oak's big branches. Hanging upside down Pike said, "I didn't mean to scare you, but I was just with the Queen, and she was showing me this potion that when you throw it on the ground it creates smoke. Throw this at one of the ogres and you will have a chance to run away she said."

Placing Pike down on the ground next to Decklyn, Aged Sir Oak replied, "I don't' care what it does. You know better than to try new potions out around me." Looking now at the protectors he said, "Don't mind Pike, he always causes mischief."

"Kind of like Phoenix does. I think the two of them will get along just great." Piper said with a slight laugh.

"You know many moons ago, when I was just a young sapling, Queen Lavinia was like a mother to me. She would buzz around my budding branches and give me advice about growing acorns. She was a tiny little thing, but she has the heart of a lion. Anyway, one morning just as the sun started to rise about the hilltops, a dark hooded figure started walking my way. Before I could even utter a word, the hooded figure threw an acorn on the ground in front of me. Purple smoke started to rise all around me, and an evil laugh boomed in my ears, 'Why the sudden shaking of the leaves my dear friend? I can offer you anything you want. You will never have to be afraid of anything again. All you must do

25

is a tiny favor for me. Make sure that you give Sorsha this acorn for me...' Before she could finish, however, Queen Lavinia came out of nowhere. With her tiny wand she threw the strongest ray of light at the hooded figure. Knocking them off balance their hood fell off. I couldn't believe it, but with my own eyes I saw Queen Vespera's sister Sigcerlaw standing there in front of me. She had a look of revenge on her face and an evil smile started to form in the corners of her mouth. She looked a lot like her niece, Lady Morphana. Long midnight hair, dark red cherry lips, and the blackest eyes anyone could ever have seen. Sigcerlaw started speaking some weird language rather quickly and stared at Queen Lavinia, but before she could finish her incantation, Queen Lavinia threw down a tiny bottle of lime green liquid. It burst into flames around Sigcerlaw and burned her alive, or so I thought. There was nothing but ashes left on the ground from where she stood. Queen Lavinia, however, said that she wasn't dead, but thrown out of Shelvockwood. I later asked Queen Lavinia what was in that potion. She told me that it was a potion strong enough to banish witches and that she suspected for a long time that Sigcerlaw was one. Some kind of herb was in it that is hard to find but would give the potion what it needed to make sure that Sigcerlaw was never to come back." Taking a good look at the four serious faces sitting in front of him, Aged Sir Oak knew that his story was one of many to bring concern to the newly found protectors.

"Is that where she got the idea of the cloud of smoke, from the old witch?" Tiffany asked with curiosity.

"Actually..." started Aged Sir Oak, "Sigcerlaw's smoke cloud was dark purple, and it contained black magic in it. Queen Lavinia's cloud turns into a very light blue that has a hint of spring smell in it. Really, they are just clouds of confusion and suspicion to their target. Ways to confuse the mind and soul and make them think things that the other party never would. For example, Queen Lavinia's would make an ogre think he was surrounded by a bunch

11111

of Balfour's crowds with pitchforks. Sigcerlaw would make anyone of you or the rest of us feel like we were on the grounds of the Castle of Terror and surrounded by trolls and evil creatures."

"Is Lady Morphana anything like her aunt was? I mean the apple can't fall that far from the tree, can it?" Piper asked with a bit of concern.

"Lady Morphana is evil and the worst kind of evil. She finds sense of humor and enjoyment in tormenting and hurting others. She does so though by playing weird games, not normal games like the ones you would play in the meadow, but ones that she takes time to think about first and that may not come as quickly to you or I." Pike said as he swung from another one of Aged Sir Oak's branches.

Taking a swing at Pike and missing, Aged Sir Oak said, "For a young one Pike is right. Lady Morphana is just as he said, evil in a humorous way. She doesn't care who she hurts or in what fashion she does it in either. I think it all boils down to how she lost her mother and the revenge that needs to be made in her eyes."

"Is it possible if we can hear other stories later? I understand that we need to know as much as we can about the evil in Shelvockwood, but can't we learn something good about it too and not think about all the bad that we must deal with?" Tiffany said rather quickly.

"We can certainly do that Tiffany. I know it is a lot to take in. Let's see. I could tell you a little about Sorsha and how she came to Shelvockwood. Would you like that? Aged Sir Oak smiles while he asks.

"Yes!" replied the four friends all at once.

"Very well. About twenty years ago when Sorsha was only five years old, she was having a picnic underneath the shade of my tree with her dear mother and father. Her parents were the simplest people you could find here in Shelvockwood. They were both villagers, and rather common folk with no magic in their blood. Her father was a blacksmith in the village while her mother taught

Sorsha how to sew and knit." Seeing the look on the protectors' faces, Aged Sir Oak continued with his story. "Enjoying their picnic and the beautiful day, Sorsha looked up at her mother and asked, 'Can I do magic?' Laughing lightly her mother looked down at her with her big hazel eyes and said, 'No sweetheart you can not do magic.' Little did they know that she did have the ability to do magic. She didn't get it from her mother or her father. No, but she did get it from her great aunt who was half human and half leprechaun. That's where she got her red locks of hair too. Growing up in the village was boring to Sorsha. She would rather have been running through the fields of golden grass in the meadows or playing in the river. Her mother kept her close to her side trying to keep her away from the magical folk. A few years later when she was a bit older, Sorsha snuck out and played with the sprites in the river and unicorns in the meadows. When she turned seventeen, she got her nerve and spoke to Balfour the village elder and asked him about magic. He explained everything to her about Lady Morphana, Queen Lavinia, and even me. Sorsha wanted to help so badly that one day Balfour took her to meet myself and Queen Lavinia. It was after that meeting with us that Balfour and his crew, built Sorsha's cottage over by the meadow. Queen Lavinia also started giving her lessons on magic and it wasn't until a few years ago that she got the hang of it all on her own. Her folks were devastated, but unfortunately that story I must tell you some other time because I already promised Tiffany no more stories like that today. I think I can tell you one more story today before I need to rest my branches. Let me see." Started Aged Sir Oak.

He was shortly interrupted by Pike, "You can tell my story Aged Sir Oak. Oh please. I promise I won't interrupt you. I will let you tell it."

"PIKE! Get off my branches and sit on the ground. You know how I hate it when you are all up in my branches like that." And as Pike took a seat by Phoenix, Aged Sir Oak said, "This is a story about Balfour the village elder and how he found out about the magical creatures. Years ago, when Balfour was in his early twenties, Shelvockwood was in no danger at all. In fact, it was one of the quieter times. Anyway, Balfour was working down at the grocery store as a stock boy. His father was always on his case about working at the Blacksmith's shop because it would make him into more of a man. One day after getting into a big argument with his father, Balfour took a walk towards our woods. Growing up in the village all the children are taught that anything beyond the village in either direction was forbidden because the villagers knew there was something strange outside of their township and they didn't want to know what. Balfour didn't care that day. He was so upset with his father that he thought anything willing to get in his way, good or bad, was just begging for his anger. I myself that day was just enjoying the sun shining through my branches, but when I happened to look down, I saw Balfour sitting just underneath my shade and pulling up grass in an angry manner while talking to himself. I had to chuckle just a bit because he was a rather scrawny looking kid and any one of the fairies could have hurt him just a little bit. As he was mumbling to himself, I said, 'Excuse me son, but can I help you?' Balfour just about jumped out of his skin. It took me almost what seemed like an hour to calm him down. By the time I did he was as excited as Pike usually is. Balfour wanted so badly to run home and tell his father. I told him he couldn't because the villagers would shun him. A few months later Sigcerlaw entered our world and started to make Shelvockwood an unsafe place, even for the villagers. Balfour, even though he was still very young, took charge of a militia that would help put a stop to Sigcerlaw's dark magic. The story I told you about Queen Lavinia defeating Sigcerlaw was true, but she couldn't have done it by herself. You see even though Queen Lavinia is very strong, she is after all still a fairy. In fact, Balfour was the one that brewed up the potion that banished Sigcerlaw. He is the one who gave it to Queen Lavinia to us on her. Even though he was very young and one of the common folks, Balfour learned magic on his own and became very strong in it. Without Balfour, Sigcerlaw would most likely have overcome the land of Shelvockwood."

The protectors just sat there. They were all trying to process this world that they were now in and all the stories that were just told to them. This was just something they had to get used to quickly. Decklyn was still sort of confused as to how time worked in Shelvockwood. Taking a deep breath, Decklyn looked up from the ground into Aged Sir Oak's deep wooden eyes and asked, "How does the time work here in Shelvockwood? I mean when we leave will we have missed much in our world? If we can't get back home for years, will years have passed in our world?"

"I was waiting to see when one of you would have asked me those kinds of questions. The Queen only briefly went over this." Replied Aged Sir Oak. "Shelvockwood has been around for decades, almost 10,000 years. I myself obviously haven't been around that long. Only fifty years or so, but when the old protectors of the ice crystals were here in Shelvockwood they made it back from their world one more time. I asked them when they returned for the second time, about the time change and they said that when they stayed here in Shelvockwood for that long of a time, thirteen years I believe it was, they said that when they went back to their world time stood still. Nothing moved. Everybody stood still. Even the waterfalls they said were like someone had hit pause on life itself. However, they also told me that it didn't stay that way long. Maybe only a few seconds and then they were at the same time as when they had first come to Shelvockwood. Almost as if time rewound itself for a few moments and then caught up with itself. All I can suggest to you, protectors, is that you enjoy the time you have here in Shelvockwood because if you can someday return, everything you have known here and everybody you did know may be gone.

Remember friends can come and go, but the memories you have with them will last forever."

And with those last words from Aged Sir Oak, the four friends got up and said their goodbyes to their newly found friends and headed off down the big hill of the Whispering Wood towards the meadow. They had all decided after talking with Aged Sir Oak that they wanted to go speak to Balfour himself. The meadow was much bigger than they thought it was because it took them over an hour just to get through it, but once they were through it, they were just on the outside of the village. It looked like one of the towns you would find in Germany many years ago. There were cobble stone roads and houses lined up one after the other. It really looked like something out of a story book. There were Blacksmith shops, a Shoemaker's shop, the town grocery store, what looked like an old Saloon, a church, a library, a bakery, and even an old one room schoolhouse. The protectors headed straight over to the Blacksmith's shop because that was where Balfour was working Aged Sir Oak had told them. The shop's doors were both wide open and you could see men in there with hammers and hot pokers. Far in the back of the shop stood Balfour. He was looking over the shoulder of a very nervous young kid who was holding a brass horseshoe in one hand and a hot poker in the other. "Don't be nervous son, I myself have been burned many times by these pokers, but it must be done, and we can't let the women folk do it. They have enough to worry about." Balfour encouragingly said.

Decklyn, Piper, Phoenix, and Tiffany headed over to where Balfour was standing. He instantly looked up at them and the smile that he was wearing on his face became very serious suddenly. Rushing over to the friends, Balfour said in a whisper so that only they could hear him, "Let's go to my house just down the street where we can talk. Hurry we must not be seen."

Walking quickly with many of the men starring at Balfour and the kids, they all hurried over to Balfour's house. Once inside,

31

Balfour locked the door and turned around to face them. "How are all of you today?" he asked with a smile back on his face.

"Fine." Piper said with a somewhat of a concerned tone in her voice. "Why did you rush us out of the shop? Are we not welcome here in the village?"

"Unfortunately, you would be correct my dear. The villagers do not take kindly to newcomers, let alone people who associate with magic dwellers. It was a good thing though that those men didn't know who you were. They probably would have started a riot." replied Balfour. "What exactly can I help you with though my dear friends? I am so glad you did come and see me though."

"We actually just came from seeing Pike and Aged Sir Oak, and he had a few interesting stories to tell." said Tiffany.

"I bet Aged Sir Oak had interesting stories to tell. He has been around for years and knows a lot about Shelvockwood. You know they say that Oak trees are the brightest, I guess whoever said that was right." chuckled Balfour.

"Well Aged Sir Oak did talk about this one potion that you had made and given to Queen Lavinia to defeat Sigcerlaw. How did you make it and what was in it? Was it powerful?" asked a somewhat concerned Tiffany.

"Ah, so that was one of the stories he told huh?" Balfour said while scratching his chin. "I was wondering when that story would be told to you all. I just didn't realize it would be this soon. I can't tell you what was in the potion for if it fell into the wrong hands, it would banish anybody. Someday though when it is called for again, I will tell my secret. All you have to know is that it was very strong, and it worked."

"You can't even tell us what was in it? I mean what ingredients you used?" Piper asked.

"Well..." Balfour hesitated, but then said, "I will tell you this much. I used bark from a tree, but I won't tell you what tree it was from."

"That's not fair! I mean what if we NEED that someday to save our lives?" Phoenix blurted out rather fast.

"I think you will do just fine on your own without my old silly spells. Besides, Sigcerlaw is nothing like her brother-in-law was. King Empanvic was much, much worse. For all your sakes I hope you never ever have to use that spell." Balfour said through lighter sighs. "Another thing you are going to want to watch out for is your journal. I know you may all think that it is not worth keeping track of but trust me when I tell you that Lady Morphana would love to get her hands on it and if she did you all would be in a world of hurt. It has everything in there from what the oldest protectors went through right down to what you all encountered so far."

"Great, not only do we have to worry about creatures and big bugs, but we must worry about a woman! Can this day get any better?!" Phoenix almost yelled.

"Now Phoenix, this is the adventure that we all wanted this summer. And don't give me that look like it isn't technically summer yet because it is to all of us. I am going to enjoy every second I am here not just because it is another world, but it is something I will be able to remember for the rest of my life." said an overly excited Decklyn.

"Well, we really should get going Balfour. We still want to stop over at the bakery and pick something up for dessert tonight." Tiffany said.

"Don't go there. I will pick you up something and swing by tomorrow with it. Trust me, you don't want to have anything to do with the villagers. Some of them are working for Lady Morphana. I will see you all tomorrow and thank you for coming to visit me." Balfour said while walking the protectors to the door.

Once outside the four friends took Balfour's advice and quickly left the village. None of them wanted to have anymore conflict that day. The journey back home to their fort was rather short because they all seemed in a hurry to get there. Once inside the door was bolted and goodnights were exchanged as the protectors headed to bed. Little did they know that up in the Castle of Terror, Lady Morphana was watching them through her crystal ball and plotting her next move.

Chapter 3

A Minor Set Back or Two

I t was a nice, chipper morning in the land of Shelvockwood. The sun was shining in one of the upstairs windows of the fort. Phoenix yawns and says, "Good morning, all. Isn't it such a beautiful day? My aren't we all grumpy this morning. What's eating all of you?"

"If you must know, most of us are not morning people." says an annoyed Tiffany.

"Well, you all better get in the mood fast because we have a ton of exploring to do!" said an excited Phoenix.

As Tiffany, Decklyn, and Piper crawled out of their beds and headed down the ladder towards the kitchen, Phoenix was dancing around the room hyper as can be. Breakfast was some oats and berries that were found in the kitchen. A very light breakfast meant that later in the day food would be a necessity, so Piper began packing a lunch basket. Packing things that were light enough to carry, like berries and vegetables. She also had made a few sandwiches too much on.

While she was doing this Decklyn and Phoenix were lounging about in the living room. Tiffany happened to be in the bathroom when the sun went behind a tree. It got so dark in the fort that candles and lanterns had to be brought out. "I wonder how the sun could have been blocked out by the trees when there are hardly any in the garden" says a worried Tiffany.

"Well, aren't you a whistling Dixie, she is right. There is I do believe no bloody trees in the garden." Phoenix said looking through one of the windows.

Facing Phoenix, Decklyn asked with a funny look on his face, "Since when are you British?"

"Since now. I mean it sounded good in my head. Just go with it man!" laughs Phoenix.

Piper taking another look outside says, "Oh, look the sun is out again. Strange weather in this place don't you think? Probably has to do with Lady Morphana. Well, the picnic basket is packed, and we have our crystals hidden on us, so I say let's get dressed and head out. Tiff don't forget the journal."

Tiffany grabbed the journal and tucked it inside of the picnic basket. Quickly getting dressed in the clothes that Balfour had the villagers make them, they looked like people from the renaissance. Piper and Tiffany were wearing light colored dresses and the boys were dressed in baggy shirts and pants. They would have been out sooner, but the girls did up their hair in flowers from around the fort. The four of them were in the best moods to go out and see what this different land had in store for them. They couldn't wait to go exploring. As they all headed out the door, Piper wiped around and said, "Make sure whoever is the last person out of the fort locks it. We don't want any intruders in there." So, Tiffany locked it up and made sure that she put the key in her pocket.

The sky was a baby blue shade and was as bright as a new shining star. The sun was shining and there was a light breeze which made the day seem to just fly right by. Piper and Decklyn were leading the other two just to be on the safe side of things. They weren't going to take any chances being in a strange new place. As they made their way throughout the maze of bushes, they came across a spot in the garden with a weeping willow tree. "This looks a lot like the ones we have back in Willow." Tiffany says.

"I do agree. Let's have our picnic right here." says Piper.

Decklyn started laying out the blanket that he had brought while Tiffany and Piper started taking things out of the basket and setting them down. Phoenix, however, was getting restless and started walking around the willow tree whistling. The song obviously has a bad effect on the willow tree because it picked up Phoenix by his legs and started swinging him around in circles.

"I think I am going to be sick! Someone please tell this tree that I am not evil and if this tree is evil, CHOP IT DOWN!!!" Phoenix yelled as he was flying through the air.

The other three were so shocked as to what was happening that they all just kind of stood there staring at this miraculous thing happening to their friend.

"I am not kidding around. I am really going to get sick. Don't you all just stand there…some…body…help…me!" Phoenix shouted.

Decklyn is about to get his axe that he had brought with him when he too was picked up by the weeping willow tree and thrown through the air.

"Who the bloody hell has the power to talk to plants and animals?" Phoenix asked while he was being flung through the air.

Piper loudly says to Phoenix, "You are the one with that power Phoenix. Try talking to it."

Phoenix shouts, "Oh my gosh, I'm dead!" As Phoenix reaches for his crystal he yells, "Listen up you no good for nothing piece of wood, let us down or else!"

"Phoenix!!!!" Tiffany and Piper shout. "That isn't going to convince it. That is just going to make it even madder, more than it already is!"

"I'll show you, you ugly ogre!" says the willow.

While Tiffany was hidden behind a bush watching her boyfriend and Piper's flying through the air, Piper was rummaging through all their bags to look for Decklyn's axe. When suddenly, the weeping willow started to say, "I do not know who you people are, but you are on sacred land. This land belongs to Queen Lavinia, and I will not have any of Lady Morphana's minions on it spying on her! Now I want you to bring a message back to Lady Morphana from Will the Weeping Willow. The message is…"

The weeping willow was cut off, for Piper started to talk, "Mr. Willow, we are the protectors of the ice crystals. We just arrived here in Shelvockwood yesterday and we were taking a nice picnic under your shaded branches when you started attacking us."

Phoenix and Decklyn yell, "SO PUT US DOWN!"

"But this cannot be you, for this one (holding up Phoenix) was whistling a tune that only one of Lady Morphana's goons would know." Says a somewhat confused willow tree.

"It figures Phoenix that you would get us in trouble on our first day in Shelvockwood." Decklyn says while hanging upside down.

Coming from out under the bushes Tiffany asks, "What was the song Phoenix that you were humming?"

Phoenix says with somewhat of a chuckle, "Well, funny really. I was just whistling the song from Peter Pan, you know 'Following the Leader' I think it is kind of funny that Lady Morphana has her Ogres singing it. Honestly, Mr. Willow, I thought it just had a catchy tune."

Chuckling now out loud the tree said, "Oh, of course. I can see how it would be funny, but you did give me a start. The only ones who sing that in this land are the ogres and swamp goblins. I guess Lady Morphana thinks it will give them some color. But the only thing it gives them around here is a reputation. I do advise you protectors not to sing that song outside of your fort again. For I am nothing compared to what the villagers would have done to you."

Thinking before he opened his mouth, Phoenix asks, "Well, ok if we can't sing that song what about twinkle, twinkle little star?"

A confused willow looks at Phoenix and says, "I haven't heard of that one, so my guess would be that that one is alright to sing."

Enjoying the rest of their lunch under Will the Weeping Willow, the four protectors began packing up their belongings to head back home. They just about had everything packed up when a unicorn came galloping through the garden. All out of breath by the time it got to the kids the unicorn said, "You must come quick...trouble... near your fort. I saw ogres heading towards your fort. It seems like they are trying to burn down the fort again. I bet Lady Morphana sent them to do just that."

"Thank you for coming to us and letting us know. Normally when one sees an ogre, the reaction would probably be to run away, but you didn't, and we thank you for that. Now guys we have ogres to stop. Let's go before they cause any more destruction!" Decklyn says with confidence.

Heading off in the direction of where the unicorn said he last saw them, the four were bound and determined to get rid of them. They were now where they could see the fort when suddenly something buzzed past their heads. Piper thinking quickly said, "Oh, it is only you, your majesty."

Whispering towards Decklyn, Phoenix says, "Again someone needs to invest the Queen in a bell around her neck."

"I was in a conference with Aged Sir Oak and Sorsha when I heard from Pike that ogres were heading towards your fort. I cannot defeat them now, but I can put a protective spell around your fort. Does that help in anyway?" asks the Queen.

"Actually..." says Tiffany, "it does help us. We were just going to start heading behind our fort and walk towards the back part of the Hidden Garden where the unicorn said he saw the ogres."

Satisfied with what she was hearing and witnessing, the Queen continued by saying, "Excellent! I will start the spell immediately." While flying around the fort, the queen was sprinkling some kind of powder and singing, "Ogres, ogres, and swamp goblins...this magic spell is for you. If you ever set foot around the fort at all you will be turned into tiny troll statues. Ogres, ogres, and swamp goblins...this magic spell is..."

"I think it is safe to leave her and let her finish her spell. We must start heading towards the back of the Hidden Garden. Come on guys, are you ready?" asks an enthusiastic Piper.

Decklyn thinks for a bit while they start walking towards the back of the fort. He then says to Piper, "I don't know if this is a good idea or not, but I think we should split up into two groups and cover more land that way. I mean there must be a lot of land back here and it would go a lot quicker if we split up right?"

Thinking about what he said Piper responds with, "It is worth a try, but I think it best the girls do not stay together. You are strong and I am the guide, so I think it best if Tiffany goes with you and Phoenix with me. Let's talk it over with them. Phoenix. Tiff. We are going to split up and cover more land. What do you think about that?"

Rolling his eyes Phoenix says, "You have got to be kidding me. Our first mission and you two already want to head off together? What is this..."

He was cut off rather quickly when Decklyn said, "For your information, you will be heading off with Piper towards the back right of the Hidden Garden, while Tiff and I will be heading off towards the back left. Is that alright with you?"

"As a matter of fact, it isn't. Who says that you get to go off with my girlfriend? I can protect her just as well as you could!" says Phoenix a bit harshly.

"Oh, for heaven's sake. Phoenix, I am not going to do anything with Decklyn. Besides I see where they are going with this. Piper is the guide and Decklyn kind of is too. They are splitting up the guides. Get over it!" Tiffany says in an upset voice.

"Alright Tiff. Just don't get upset with me. I am only looking out for you." Phoenix says in defense of his pride.

So, they split up. Decklyn and Tiffany headed off towards the left of the fort and were already out of sight of Phoenix and Piper. Being brave, Piper started leading the way through the maze to the right side of the garden. "I think this way looks good." she said.

"You know what I think?" Phoenix says, "I think you have no idea where we are. We are lost, aren't we?" two seconds on our own and you already get us lost."

With a worried look upon her face Piper says, "No, we are heading in the right direction. The ogres must be just beyond this turn."

Upon turning the corner and seeing another dead end to the maze Phoenix just starts laughing. "I knew it we are lost. Going to die in a maze, if we don't get eaten by the ogres first. I bet you anything that they will find us first! Ogre bate...what a way to go."

"Phoenix you are not helping matters. It is my first time out as the guide. So, come on now I am bound to get lost. Give me some kind of break, ok?" Piper says through gritted teeth.

Phoenix takes a deep breath and replies, "Oh alright, but I am warning you. If anything jumps out..."

"You are warning me?" Phoenix do not test me. I am upset at myself and my bad sense of direction. I don't need you harping on me right now either." Piper says in a hostile way.

Phoenix throwing his hands in the air like he was giving up says, "Alright, alright I won't test you. I am just saying that if an ogre jumps out at me, I will probably have a heart attack and you will then be on your own."

Smiling for the first time since their picnic Piper replies, "Yeah, I know you would probably have a heart attack. You fear your own shadow."

"Laugh it up princess, but if I were to die you would miss me."

Phoenix says chuckling. "Let's try going this way, Piper." So off they went following Phoenix's directions this time.

☯

Meanwhile on the other side of the maze were Decklyn and Tiffany. They were having just about as much luck as Phoenix and Piper were. Decklyn was ahead of Tiffany, and he had with him the axe. He was ready for those ogres when he should see one. They had been walking for about twenty minutes when Tiffany says, "Decklyn are you at all upset that your name doesn't start with the letter P?"

Decklyn stopped dead in his tracks, turned around and with a confused look upon his face said, "What are you talking about?"

"Well, it is just that Phoenix's name starts with a P and he is the comic relief in the gang. Piper's name also starts with a P obviously and she is the brave guide out of all of us. What about you and me? We just have names that start with other letters. Wouldn't you think it would be cool to have a name that starts with a P? That way when we are walking around in Shelvockwood or back home in Willow, people can just call us the four P's." says a proud Tiffany.

By this time Decklyn is just staring at Tiffany like she has six heads. Trying hard to figure out what to say to her next without hurting her feelings, Decklyn says, "Tiff, I know now why Phoenix loves you."

The two of them started walking again. This time they were silent for some time, that is until they heard a soft growing noise coming from somewhere inside the maze. At first it sounded like it was behind them, but when they wiped around there was nothing there. Looking towards the sky Decklyn starts to get worried. He turns around towards Tiffany and says quietly, "If we don't hurry up and find these things soon it is going to be dark. I don't want to be out here in the dark trying to fight something that we can't

42

see. Not to mention that we are all split up. The ogres could get very vicious."

Decklyn knew as soon as he said that to Tiffany that he shouldn't have. She looked like a deer when the car's headlights were racing towards it. Before Decklyn could say anything to comfort her, Tiffany jumped in with, "Alright let's start moving faster then. I would rather fight these things when I can see them than fight them in the dark. And while we are at it, we might want to start looking for Phoenix and Piper."

Leading the way through the maze once again, Decklyn and Tiffany headed this time towards the right side of the garden. If they were going to encounter ogres they wanted to be close to Piper and Phoenix so that they could call for some back up.

ॐ

Looking through her crystal ball, Lady Morphana was smiling from ear to ear. "Oh, this is priceless." she says, "The four protectors of the ice crystals split up and now all four of them are starting to doubt themselves. Ha-ha-ha-ha-ha! What will they do next that will benefit me? Slobbo! Come here! NOW!"

Slobbo slowly walking into Lady Morphana's room says, "Yes Lady Morphana, how may I be of service to you?"

"Your ogres are doing just fine distracting the protectors, but I was wondering watching through my crystal ball, when they planned on attacking them?"

"Well, my lady they were waiting for the sun to go down so that it was complete darkness. Then they would attack." says a confused Slobbo.

Just before she was about to lose her head, Lady Morphana stopped and started thinking about what Slobbo had just said. Pacing the floor and muttering to herself she stopped at mid pace and turned to Slobbo saying, "That will not work. For if it is dark out and the ogres start to attack, what makes you think they won't attack themselves? They are as dumb as a box of rocks. I want you at once to go and tell them to start attacking. If possible, grab me one of the protectors. I would love to have one of them added to my collection. Grab me one that is shy and dumb, the braver ones will be harder to get a hold of and grab."

"Yes, your royal meanness. Is there anything else I may do for you before I leave?" asks Slobbo.

Thinking real quick Lady Morphana replies, "No, not right now, but if I do need anything I will yell for you. Now be gone!"

And with that Slobbo walked out of the Castle of Terror and started down to the Hidden Garden. Thinking to himself, Slobbo knew that he must get down there before dark or Lady Morphana would have his head.

☯

Phoenix and Piper had managed to cover a lot of territory since they started. However, they hadn't seen any sign of trouble and it was starting to get dark. It wasn't quite dark yet, but dusk. Not having talked for awhile Phoenix jokingly says, "Dusk is something that isn't fun to deal with. If you ask me, I would rather deal with the dark. Actually, I wouldn't want to deal with that either. The dark you can easily run into something and knock yourself out till dooms day."

"So why don't you like dusk Phoenix?" Piper asks, "I mean you can still see things at least."

"Ah, Piper that is where you are wrong. Dusk is worse because your eyes start to play tricks on you. Make you think you see things that aren't really there." Phoenix says.

Turning around to check behind her, Piper gives Phoenix that looks and says, "Oh great, now we will see things that aren't there." Piper was about to say something more when she heard footsteps behind her. Both her and Phoenix turned around and stared into the maze behind them. Straining their eyes to see if they could make anything out Phoenix says, "See what I mean? I hate this. Whose idea was it to split up again?"

"Mine." says a deep voice.

Phoenix instantly became as white as a ghost. Slowly turning around, he came face to face with Decklyn. "You no good for nothing piece of..." Phoenix starts to say.

"Now, now Phoenix. Be nice. Decklyn and I were lucky enough to find you while it is dusk out. Just think if we didn't find each other before dark. I don't even want to think of it." Tiffany says shivering just a little.

Laughing hard and loudly so that Phoenix heard him Decklyn said, "I thought you weren't scared of anything? You should have seen your face. I wish I had a camera."

"You just wait until we get back to the fort. I swear I am going to pulverize you!" says an annoyed Phoenix.

Decklyn was just about to say something else to Phoenix when Piper grabbed his arm and held her finger up to his mouth. She then pointed towards the direction that the fort was in. As they all turned around to see what it was that Piper was pointing at, they came face to face with an ogre. This ogre was huge. He must have been at least ten feet tall, maybe more and he had the ugliest grin ever seen. His teeth were showing, and they were all yellow and stained In his right hand he had what looked like a club and in his left hand he had rope. Leaning over to Decklyn, Phoenix said, "Now what does an ogre need with rope?"

Thinking fast Piper said, "He wants to take one of us back with him to Lady Morphana! Stay together this time. We must get that rope from him. Try not to get hit with the club."

"Piper, if we stay together, it is a better chance for him to grab one of us. I say we fan out around him. You know distract him." Tiffany says.

"Tiff is right, fan out now!" Decklyn yelled.

Phoenix being the comic relief in a bad situation says, "Lookie what we got here. A smelly old carpet. I say all it needs is a good beating."

"Hey over here you big lug!" shouts Decklyn.

Confused as to what was going on, the ogre swung his club towards Phoenix. Quickly thinking (considering his situation) and dodging the ogre's club, Phoenix yelled, "Look out Decklyn!"

Decklyn moved just in time because the ogre swung his club in his direction. As he ducked and rolled just beyond the feet of the ogre, Piper wiped around and grabbed the axe that was thrown on the ground when the ogre started swinging. Running towards the ogre Piper yelled, "Stop or I start swinging!"

The ogre, not knowing what to do threw down his club and took off towards the castle. "Oh no you don't! Get him!" yelled Phoenix.

"We can't let him get away." Tiffany shouts.

As they were chasing the ogre through the maze something shot out and grabbed Piper. Turning around to see what grabbed her Decklyn yelled, "PIPER!"

She managed to struggle the words out, "They are just vines with thorns on them. Just get the ogre!"

Phoenix giving Decklyn and Tiffany the signal to keep going, he took out his crystal and started back towards Piper. The other two took off as Phoenix headed towards the mound of vines that now had wrapped around Piper. Phoenix pointed his crystal at a section of the vines. He didn't have to say anything for his crystal started to shine a bright emerald. The vines drew back and went back up against the maze wall. He did this for about ten minutes until they were all gone. Piper was lying on the ground in tears from the thorns that were buried in her and the cuts all over her.

"Just try not to move Piper. I will have you all cleaned up in no time." said a sympathetic Phoenix.

Pointing his crystal at the cuts on Piper's body, magically they started to disappear. Then Phoenix carefully pulled out each one of the thorns and healed up the open wounds. He was so proud of himself. "If I do say so myself Piper you will be even better than you were before the vines started attacking you!" he said while chucking.

"Thanks again Phoenix for coming back for me." said Piper.

Smiling down at her Phoenix asked, "What are friends for?"

Making sure Piper could walk alright they both headed off towards their friends and the ogre. Once in sight of them they once again got back into action. Decklyn was on top of the ogre and looked like he was riding a bronco. While he was doing that Tiffany was trying to rope the ogre's feet together but failing.

"Would you like some help with that Tiff?" asked Piper looking a hundred and ten percent better.

"Oh, Piper! I thought you were done for. Yes, we must tie this ogre up and take him to the Whispering Wood so he can face the forest committee." said Tiffany.

Acting like he was a cowboy too, Phoenix shouts, "Alright you ride him little doggie! Yee Ha Decklyn! Let's get this thing tied up!"

While Decklyn was distracting the ogre from looking at his friends and the rope; Piper, Tiffany, and Phoenix managed to tie up his feet. Down went the ogre and Decklyn with him. Getting up and shaking off the grass Decklyn helped the rest of his friends tie up the ogre's arms too. As they all looked down at this ogre Decklyn said something that everybody was thinking. "First off congrats to all of us! Secondly how are we going to get him to the Whispering Wood? And thirdly I thought there was more than one of these things in here?"

"I think we chop down a tree and use the rest of the rope we can all carry him or drag him to the Whispering Wood. As for knowing if there were more of them in here, I thought there were too, but I guess we scared them off when they saw how well we took on their friend here." said a somewhat tired Piper.

As Decklyn and Phoenix went to chop down a tree, Piper and Tiffany sat down next to the ogre and took a deep breath. About half an hour later the guys came back with parts of a tree. The four of them quickly started work on the trunk. Tiffany took out the lantern that she had packed that morning and lit it so that they had some light to see what they were doing. Another half hour went by, and they now had a plank like thing to carry the ogre on. Lifting him up on the thing was a chore. There was a lot of moaning and groaning, but it was done. Piper and Phoenix picked up the front of the plank while Decklyn and Tiffany got the back of it. Making sure they had everything that they came with they headed off towards the Whispering Wood. "We have to almost be there this thing weighs a ton!" Phoenix says in a tired voice.

"We are." says Tiffany. "There is Aged Sir Oak. I can see him from here."

Waking up, Aged Sir Oak looks with tired eyes as to what is walking towards him. Scratching his eyes with his branches for he cannot believe what he is seeing. "What is going on?" he says.

"Good evening Aged Sir Oak. We know that you have a meeting tomorrow with the forest committee, and we managed to catch an ogre. Would you be willing to keep him here with you until your meeting in the morning, so that he can be reined?" asked Decklyn.

"Why of course I can." says a shocked Aged Sir Oak. "You realize that you will all have to come back in the morning to explain how you managed to catch an ogre."

"Of course, we will Sir Oak, but if you excuse us, we must go back to the fort and get some rest. It has been a long day." Piper said.

"Of course, of course. Good night protectors!" replied Aged Sir Oak.

After setting down the ogre and waving goodbye to Aged Sir

Oak, the four friends walked back to the fort. Nobody said anything on their way back because they were all too tired. When they did get to the fort all of them went straight upstairs and crashed into their beds without even changing out of their clothes.

ᗒᗕ

"Slobbo what do you mean the rest of them chickened out? How could you let them?! This is ridiculous. I cannot believe that you would let them leave an ogre behind. Not to mention that that ogre is now in the custody of Aged Sir Oak!" growls Lady Morphana.

"They were a lot stronger than we thought they were my lady. When they split up, we had a chance, but as soon as they were all together again their powers were stronger than ever. Besides Brutus was dumb, we don't need him anymore." Slobbo said with his head hung low.

"We don't need him? Yes, that is true he is dumb, weak, and we don't need him, but he could tell the committee of our plans and ruin everything for us. I don't care what it takes. You get him back here. I want him here tonight! If they can't rein him in the morning, then they won't learn anything about our plans. I will deal with Brutus when he gets here. Now go!"

As Slobbo hung his head he said, "Yes my lady." Slobbo was out the door with some of his ogres and off to the Whispering Wood.

Pacing back and forth Lady Morphana was gripping her cloak so hard that her hands were turning colors. "I promise protectors of the ice crystals, I will get even. I will defeat you. And I will be ruler of Shelvockwood!"

Chapter 4

Tons of Trickery

P iper was up and dressed rather early the morning of the committee meeting. She was more worried about what punishment the committee was going to give the ogre for trespassing and causing so much trouble. Seeing as none of the others were up yet, Piper thought she should do something to keep herself entertained. Getting out pots and pans she decided to make them breakfast.

Rolling over just a little bit too far, Phoenix fell out of the hammock. "Ouch, that smarts. Hey where is Pi...I smell food! I beat everybody to the food!" Phoenix says a he races down the ladder and into the kitchen.

"Good morning, Phoenix. How did you sleep?" asks Piper.

Sticking his nose in the air Phoenix says, "Like a rock!"

"Well, I am glad one of us did. Now dig in before the others come down and eat everything." says an energetic Piper.

Phoenix and Piper were just about to sit down to their breakfast when the other two stragglers came waltzing in. "Something sure smells good." Decklyn said while yawning.

"That was some day yesterday, wasn't it?" Tiffany asks.

"I know it was and if it wasn't for Phoenix here, I would have choked or bleed to death." said Piper.

"Glad I could be of service to you darling. Now there is one thing that I don't get though. Where did those vines come from? I mean they came out of nowhere." Phoenix said through mouthfuls of food.

Grabbing a slice of toast Decklyn said, "Well we can always ask Queen Lavinia or Aged Sir Oak about it. I am sure one of them would know. Let's hurry up and eat because we must get ready to go to the meeting."

They all sat down for breakfast. When they finished Tiffany and Phoenix cleared the table while Decklyn and Piper grabbed things, they thought they would need for the day. After making sure that they had everything packed and cleared off the table they headed up to the bedroom to change out of yesterday's clothes. All dressed and ready to go they all headed down the ladder and out the door. Piper turned back to see if they had forgotten anything. Locking the door behind her and putting the key in her pocket she said, "I hope nothing goes wrong today."

As they entered the Whispering Wood Pike was the first one to run into them. In a very fast and upset voice he said, "Someone took the ogre last night right from under Aged Sir Oak's nose!"

"And you hoped nothing would go wrong today." Phoenix said with a sigh, while looking at Piper.

As they walked over to where Aged Sir Oak, Sorsha, Balfour, and Queen Lavinia where they could see where the ogre had been dragged away. Next to the drag marks there were big footprints. Scratching his head and looking at the ground Decklyn said, "Well to me those prints are about as big as the ogre's feet were. You don't think he walked off and dragged the plank with him, do you?"

"No, if you ask me, I don't think he could have gotten himself untied. We tied him up tight. I think the other ogres that were with him, followed us back here and took him back after Aged Sir Oak fell asleep." Phoenix said as he got on his knees and observed the prints a little closer.

51

Buzzing over to Phoenix's shoulder Queen Lavinia said, "I think Phoenix is right. However, I think Lady Morphana told them to come back and get him so he couldn't tell us anything. Not that we could have gotten him to talk to us in the first place, but we probably could have gotten something out of him."

"Well, that settles it then. This meeting is adjourned. There is nothing we can discuss unless the protectors have something to add." a cheerful Sorsha said.

"Actually Sorsha, we wanted to know something." Piper said. "Yesterday when we were looking for ogres, I was attacked by vines with thorns. Where did they come from so fast?"

"That Lady Morphana drives me crazy as those hunters do!" yells Aged Sir Oak.

Flying up towards Aged Sir Oak, Queen Lavinia says, "Now calm down Sir Oak, or you will uproot yourself." Looking at Piper the queen said, "Lady Morphana has ways of casting spells inside her castle. It is possible that she cast one to try and split you all up so that it would make it easier for the ogre to capture one of you."

"Well, it didn't work now did it. If it wasn't for me going back to save Piper, she may have died." Phoenix says proudly.

"Yes, but that was Lady Morphana's plan all along; was to split you all up. She knows that with you all together your powers are stronger than hers ever could be. Plus, she gets the privilege of sending one of her minions to grab one of you while the others are elsewhere." replies Aged Sir Oak.

"Well, that is the last time that she can try that again. There is no more splitting up ever again!" says Decklyn.

ॐ

Pacing angrily up insider her castle, Lady Morphana was devising another plan of action against the protectors. She was very furious with Brutus. On the other hand, though it wasn't really his fault. He was following orders from Slobbo. Slobbo needed to be punished for his lack of advising the other ogres. Starring at her wall Lady Morphana yelled, "SLOBBO! Get in here NOW!"

"Yes, your royal-ness. What can I do for you?" says a somewhat upset Slobbo.

"You know that you have upset me greatly and have cost me one of the protectors. Go to the tower and tell the guard there that I sent you to be chained to a wall for a day. If you don't go to the tower I will know because I will be watching, you through my crystal ball. Now go!" yelled Lady Morphana.

"Yes, my lady." Slobbo said with his head hung lower than ever before.

Proud of herself and how she handled the dumb ogre, Lady Morphana decided that she was going to take things into her own hands. "I will transform an ogre into a unicorn and have him pretend to be injured. A little bit of fake blood here and a couple of bruises and the protectors will think that something is morally wrong. Ha-ha-ha! I should have thought of this a long time ago. This time protectors I have you for good!"

⚬⚬⚬

While Lady Morphana was plotting against the protectors, Aged Sir Oak was telling Pike to quit causing mischief and go out looking for trouble that Lady Morphana could be causing. "Pike get out of my branches and go see if there is a creature or anybody in need of the protectors help." said an agitated Aged Sir Oak.

Hopping down from Aged Sir Oak's branches Pike said, "I won't let you down Sir Oak."

As Pike jumped and skipped away into the forest, the protectors were coming back from Sorsha's Cottage. "Like I said before, don't mess with the master." Phoenix was saying while laughing and running away from Tiffany's flying arms.

When the four of them got to Aged Sir Oak, however, the smiles went away. The look on Aged Sir Oak's face wasn't good. "Who died?" Phoenix asked.

"Nobody died." replied Aged Sir Oak, "When you four left the forest committee talked about how Lady Morphana is probably up to more mischief. She will probably want to get even with you catching one of her ogres."

Decklyn responded with, "She can try whatever she wants, but she won't get far. We will fight her to the end if we must."

All of them were sitting around Aged Sir Oak and discussing what Lady Morphana might be up to next when suddenly Pike came running towards them shouting, "She has done something, she has done something!"

"Calm down Pike." Piper said. "Take a few deep breaths and then start from the beginning."

Breathing for a bit before talking, Pike started again. "Well, I was doing what Aged Sir Oak was saying I should do and go see if there was any trouble anywhere. I was skipping through the Whispering Wood when I came across the river. Feeling a little thirsty I figured why not get a quick drink. As I headed down towards the river, I saw lying on the ground in a puddle of blood a unicorn! He had bruises and cuts all over him. No doubt about it that it was one of Lady Morphana's ogres that hurt the poor thing."

"Oh dear!" said a worried Tiffany. "We must go help him at once!"

Standing up and grabbing one of the bags on the ground Piper said, "Well we have no time to lose. Let's get going."

After a warning from Aged Sir Oak about not trusting anyone, the four friends followed Pike towards the river. They were all very quiet. None of them knew how anybody could hurt a unicorn. Then again, they were ogres and dumb at that. They got to the river in ten minutes. Normally it would take them twenty minutes, but they all must have been anxious to get there. The unicorn was lying in a puddle of blood just like Pike had said. However, there was something that didn't look right to Piper. As Phoenix was about to go over and start healing the unicorn, Piper grabbed his arm and stopped him.

"What are you doing? The longer we wait the quicker this unicorn is going to die." Phoenix said as if confused.

Piper turned towards Phoenix and whispering said, "Look Phoenix, that unicorn would be dead lying in a puddle of blood. This one is breathing and breathing heavily. When I was tangled in the vines, I had a hard time breathing. You can't tell me that that unicorn would be breathing at all that hard with that much blood."

"She is right." Decklyn said. "That has to be another one of Lady Morphana's tricks." And taking his crystal out Decklyn pointed it at the unicorn, as soon as he did that the unicorn transformed into an ogre.

"Oh, great! Another one of these dumb ugly things to fight off." Phoenix said through gritted teeth.

Phoenix spoke a little too loud, for the ogre heard him and jumped up. Looking down at the four of them and Pike, the ogre let out a huge roar. They all had to cover their ears for his roar was so loud that it was even shaking the ground beneath them. Trees looked like they would be uprooted, the water was splashing up onto the ground, and the rocks were jumping all over the ground. "This ogre doesn't have a club. Always a plus in my book if you ask me." Phoenix says under his breath.

Taking a few brave steps forward Decklyn says to the ogre, "Don't even bother trying to fight us. We have caught your kind before. Go back to Lady Morphana and tell her you have a message for her from the protectors of the ice crystals. Tell her that if she ever tries to hurt anybody in Shelvockwood she will have us at her doorstep to deal with personally."

And with that the ogre nodded his head and started trudging back to the castle of terror. "That was easier said than done

Decklyn. I have a feeling that you may have started an even bigger war." said a somewhat nervous Piper.

"I may have, but I think we can deal with her ourselves." Decklyn said rather proudly.

They all watched the ogre leave until they could no longer see him. Once he was out of sight they all turned around and headed back to Aged Sir Oak to tell him of what happened.

Aged Sir Oak was rather pleased and upset at the same time. He knew Decklyn had done the right thing, but he also knew now that Lady Morphana would be more than upset. She would be furious. After telling the protectors to be careful and be on the lookout, they started heading in the direction of the village. "I think it would be rather nice to go to the village and get some more food supplies." Tiffany said with a bit of a cheer in her voice.

Once they got to the village, they were greeted by Balfour, the village elder. He showed them where they could purchase the food in the village from villagers that didn't' mind magic folk. As the protectors got what they wanted they headed back home to the fort to put things away. "This day thankfully was nothing compared to yesterday." said Piper.

"Yeah, but for some reason I am just as tired as I was yesterday." yawned Phoenix.

Everything was finally put away. The protectors were dressed and ready for the land of dreams when there was a knock at the door. Decklyn opened it and standing there was Balfour and some of the villagers.

"We have gotten word that Lady Morphana may try and attack your place tonight. So, I have brought myself and some of my strong villagers to protect your fort while you sleep." said Balfour.

"Why thank you so much." Tiffany said with a yawn.

As they all said their goodnights to the villagers and Balfour, they headed upstairs to bed. Piper fell asleep instantly because she didn't get much sleep the previous night. Tiffany was out as soon as her head hit the pillow, as was Phoenix. Decklyn, however, was the only one who was restless that night. He didn't know if it was because he knew Lady Morphana was after them or if it was because she was watching them all the time.

෴

Peacefully sound asleep in the fort were the protectors of the ice crystals. Unaware that danger lurked just around the corner. After Balfour and the villagers had left, Lady Morphana had gotten so mad about the whole ogre incidents that she sent the next to the biggest thing she had. Using a spell, the giant was made into the tallest tree ever in Shelvockwood. He was placed right outside the front door of the fort overnight. Lady Morphana had warned him not to make a noise until he saw the sunrise. So, the giant had stood there most of the night until he saw the sunrise. Then he let out the ugliest and loudest howl ever heard. "AHHHHHHHHHHHHOOOOOOOOOOO!"

Piper and Tiffany jumped out of their skin and the bed. Decklyn watched as Phoenix fell out of the hammock again. He made a thud on the floor. Phoenix said rather quickly and a little irritated, "What in the world was that?"

Crawling out of bed, Decklyn said, "I don't know, but nothing surprises me around here anymore."

Dressing as quickly as possible and making sure they had everything for the days work, the four friends ran outside and came to a complete stop. Standing in front of them was the tallest tree they had ever seen. It seemed to go on forever. "You don't suppose that Jack came by and buried some beans, do you?" asked Piper. "As a matter of fact, it looks like it has feet."

Just as Phoenix was about to touch one of the so-called feet, a branch swung around and picked him up by his legs. "You have

GOT to be kidding me!" Phoenix yelled as he was hanging upside down.

The tree turned into a tall giant that was rather gangly looking. Not taking any time to waste Piper, Decklyn, and Tiffany took out their crystals and aimed them at the giant. "Put him down!" They all shouted at the same time.

Speaking in a loud deep voice the giant said, "Lady Morphana wants one of you and I am not leaving without one of you."

"Then you will just have to try and leave with Phoenix. We won't let you." said Decklyn.

"Decklyn, keep him distracted long enough for Tiff and I to run inside and get something." Piper said in a hurry.

While Decklyn was arguing with the giant to let Phoenix go, the girls ran inside and got rope that they had left over from the ogre. Knowing that they couldn't just go outside without the giant spotting them first, the girls went out through a window in the back of the fort. Giving Tiffany one end of the rope she ordered her to tie it to something or hold on to it tight. While Tiffany ran off to do that, Piper snuck behind bushes in the front of the fort so that the giant couldn't see her. As soon as she saw Tiffany reappear with the thumbs up sign, she quickly came out from the bushes and ran as fast as she could towards the giants feet. Piper pulled the rope as hard as she could around the giants feet. Not knowing what was going on the giant went down with a big thud like a ton of bricks. Phoenix had gone sailing in the opposite direction towards the rose bushes. Rushing over to help the girls tie the giant down Decklyn said, "That was brilliant! I can't believe we caught a giant. Where is Phoenix?"

Spitting out thorns Phoenix said, "Over here. I love being thrown from trees. I think its coming to be a part of my daily routine."

"Well complain about it later. Come and help us tie this thing up." Piper said.

The four of them finished tying up the giant and covering his mouth so that he wouldn't be able to scream for help. No telling how loud his voice would be or how far it would carry. Decklyn and Phoenix stayed watch of him while Piper and Tiffany ran to get Balfour, some villagers, and the forest committee. Half an hour later the girls came back with just that. Sorsha, Queen Lavinia, Balfour, and twenty of his friends.

"I don't know how you guys do it, but none of the other protectors that we ever had before could have caught a giant!" said Queen Lavinia with much joy in her voice.

"Yes, I must agree with you." said Sorsha, "But what are we to do with him?"

Thinking the queen said, "Well until we can reign tomorrow morning at our meeting, he must go in the underground dungeon in the village. This way Lady Morphana won't be able to come and take him away."

Leaving the protectors to do what they do best, Balfour and the villagers got to it and quickly made a carrier out of wood. They picked up the giant and carried him off with a lot of huffing and puffing back to the village. Sorsha and Queen Lavinia went back to tell Aged Sir Oak what had happened. After everybody had left Tiffany said "My that was interesting, wasn't it? I don't think I ever want to wake up to that again."

"Yeah, but you are never the one that they go after first. Why is it that they always grab me? I mean come on." Phoenix said.

"I think they grab you Phoenix because they can sense a joker." Piper said with a grin.

Heading back inside talking and laughing at Phoenix's hair (he still hadn't combed it), they all sat down to eat a late breakfast. As they were finishing up their toast and eggs there was a knock on the door.

"What now?" Decklyn said as he went to answer the door.

"Do you hear children crying?" Tiffany asked with a concerned voice.

When the door swung open, sure enough Decklyn came face to face with eight little kids. They were all red in the face and looked like they had been crying for some time. "What can we do for you?" Decklyn asked them.

The tiniest little one said, "We came to you because we didn't know where else to turn. We were playing games out in the meadow because our parents like us out in the open so we won't get attacked. Out of nowhere ogres attacked us! Said they had a message for the protectors from Lady Morphana."

"They wrecked our game." said another child.

"Take us to where you saw the ogres and we will handle them." Decklyn said to the kids.

Hurrying up and grabbing what they thought they would need in a battle with more than one ogre, the protectors shut and locked up the fort and went off with the children towards the meadow. Taking their time getting there the children were playing a game of tag ahead of the protectors. While they were doing this the protectors were talking about how they can defeat the ogres.

"Why does Lady Morphana torture us so? She must enjoy it. I mean honestly what else can she possibly throw at us?" Phoenix said while jumping over a fallen log.

Climbing over the same log, Tiffany whispered to the others, "Well if she is up to no good all the time, I guess that means we can't trust anybody. Even if they are little children."

Decklyn immediately took out his crystal pendant when the children weren't looking and held it up to his right eye. Looking through it at the children his mouth fell open. Wanting to know instantly why Decklyn looked so shocked Phoenix quietly asked, "What is it Deck?"

"Keep walking." replied Decklyn. "Tiff was right not to trust anybody. They aren't children, but swamp goblins in disguise. We mustn't let them know that we know who they are. Go along with what they say. I will start thinking of a plan to fight them. Tiff, I must ask though. How did you know they weren't really children?"

"That's easy. I have worked around kids most of last summer and I know that when they are sad or in trouble no matter what kind, they don't prance around and frolic. And if these kids say they were attacked by ogres, why aren't they still scared? And where are all the bruises and scratches from the attack?" Tiffany said with confidence.

After stumbling out of the Whispering Wood they all reached the meadow. The children stopped running around and said to the protectors that it was in the middle of the meadow where they were attacked. Not seeing anything in the middle of the meadow the protectors went along anyway. Decklyn meanwhile was racking his brain trying to figure out what to do when they go to the middle of the meadow. How were they to stop swamp goblins? Well, they were tiny that was for sure, but there were eight of them, four more than what they had. Think Decklyn, it is up to you to come up with a plan. The others are counting on you. Alright, what do we have with us? We have rope, magic powder, and our crystals. We can do this. How to get the others alone? Why didn't I think of this before? Turning to the children Decklyn said, "If you don't mind, we must get ready for the ogres. Hide in the meadow and we will be right there, ok?"

Looking a bit dumbfounded the children said, "OK, but hurry."

As the four protectors went back a bit into the Whispering Wood the children were getting ready to pounce on them. Back in the forest Decklyn gave out his plan. Thinking it was the best plan they had, everybody agreed with him. "Let's go get these things." Phoenix said with confidence.

All holding hands in a big circle Tiffany took out her crystal and turned all of them invisible. Moving quickly the protectors moved towards the swamp goblins. As they all got closer to them,

Piper began to take out her crystal. Thinking to herself this must work. Seeing them in sight, Piper aimed her crystal at each one of them and quickly turned them all to ice. Just as the swamp goblins turned to ice, Tiffany undid the invisibility by only thinking she wished they all were visible again. The protectors quickly tied up the goblins. When they got the last one tied up, Piper unfroze them and boy were they all in a trifling bad mood. "How is it that you protectors know so much?" asked a very ugly goblin.

"Just give up. You will never be able to trick us." Phoenix said with a snide remark in his voice.

Walking through the meadow with the goblins the four protectors were very proud of themselves. They have managed to capture an ogre (two if one didn't get away), a giant, and not goblins. As soon as the protectors walked into the village, they were greeted by Balfour, the village elder. With a shocked expression on his face Balfour said, "Well I will be darned, if it isn't the protectors with more hostages of Lady Morphana's."

"We have eight swamp goblins to add to our collection we have." Decklyn said.

"Correction" said Balfour, "you have seven of the little buggers."

Counting them again Decklyn held his eyes wide open and said, "He is right we only have seven of them. Didn't we have eight though?"

"Yeah, that must mean that we lost one, but I could have sworn we tied up all of them." Piper said looking confused.

"Great! Now we have one of those little brats running back to tell Lady Morphana that her other goblins have been taken by the mean protectors. How much more crap can we pile on top of this heap of garbage?" Phoenix said out loud.

Taking the rope from Decklyn, Balfour said, "Well we can take these ones down to the dungeon under the village and lock them up for their sentence with the giant in the morning. Thanks again protectors. Sorry that one of them got away."

As they watched Balfour take the seven of them away Phoenix said with a smile, "They kind of remind me of the seven dwarfs."

Laughing at Phoenix's joke helped them not think about losing one of the goblins. Phoenix had joked all the way back to the fort. He knew that it calmed everybody down and made them think about something else. It was an early bed night for the protectors. They had a rather tiring day with all the tricks Lady Morphana threw at them. Who could blame her for trying? As they all crawled into bed Phoenix said, "Let's just hope that we don't get an awakening like the one we got this morning. That scared me half to death and I would like to NOT fall out of the hammock tomorrow.

ᴕᴕ

These protectors were a lot harder to trick than the ones in the past. The ones in the past were easier to catch because they were stupid and naïve. However, these protectors had some brains and would be much harder to trick. Pacing back and forth thinking about how they were not even fooled by her tricks, Lady Morphana had a frown on her face. Is it possible that she could beat them? "Of course, I am Lady Morphana. I can beat a bunch of kids. I have done it before, I can do it again. These kids are just going to make it a bit harder for me to catch them, but I will be able to do it." She said out loud.

Looking through her crystal ball, Lady Morphana watched the protectors sleep soundly. "Yes, sweet dreams protectors. Get some rest for I will throw my worst at you yet. Even if it takes me a long time to think of something. I will win and when I do you had better watch out." she said with a snarl in her voice.

Walking with his head hung low (you would too after being chained to a wall), Slobbo came into Lady Morphana's chambers with the swamp goblin that had escaped from the protectors capture. "My lady." Slobbo said, "Here is the swamp goblin that you wanted to talk to."

"Ah yes, come here. Do not be afraid of me. I am glad that one of my goblins had the common sense to get away before they too were captured like the other fools. You are my head goblin now. What is your name?" asked Lady Morphana.

"Gumbo your royal-ness." snarled Gumbo.

"Slobbo you may leave us. Gumbo, please come over here, have a seat, and do tell me everything that happened earlier today." Lady Morphana said.

And as Gumbo told Lady Morphana everything that happened, she listened with an open mind and her eyes got wide. Nodding every now and then and writing things down she was coming up with a plan to get the protectors if it was the last thing she had to do.

Chapter 5

A Stepping Stone

Rolling over to look at her watch, Tiffany could feel how heavy her eyes were. Seeing that it was only 6:30am she rolled back over to try and get at least another hour of sleep. She had this gut feeling that they were probably going to be doing something today and she wanted to be well rested. It was hard to fall asleep. Phoenix was snoring up in the hammock and Piper was having some kind of weird dream because she kept moving around like she was being attacked. Decklyn was the only one sound asleep: lucky bum. But just as Tiffany was about to doze off, she heard a blood curtailing scream from the distance. The scream was like no other. It went right to the spine and could make someone's hair stand on end.

Hearing the scream as well Phoenix again fell out of the hammock. Getting up from the floor he said, "I know it was too good to be true. I am sick of waking up to someone or something screaming. It isn't even 7 o'clock yet, is it? What could be wrong now?"

"Well, let's get moving. Whatever it is won't go away until we get there." Piper said with a yawn.

"At least it is a good alarm clock. I mean I don't get up when mine back home goes off." Decklyn said through stretching.

They were all dressed and ready to go when there was a knock at the door. Opening it up they all came face to face with Pike. He looked like he had seen a ghost. "Pike what is wrong?" Tiffany asked with a concerned face.

"It is Sorsha. She has a ghost in her cottage and is scared out of her mind. She said that it said something to her that frightened her almost to death! I saw it on my way here to get you. You must stop it." Pike said through breaths.

"Well, there is nothing to worry about Pike. The protectors are here to save the day!" Phoenix said as he held his head high.

Heading out their door at 6:45am, the protectors were off to fight a ghost. They figured if they could fight off ogres, swamp goblins, and a giant that a ghost was nothing. Let's face it, it isn't living anymore. How bad could it be? Piper was wide awake and determined not to let a ghost ruin her friend's cottage. She was leading the way to Sorsha's cottage with the others trailing behind as if scared to come face to face with the ghost. Piper stopped though as she came into sight of Sorsha's cottage. Taking a gulp and being brave she crossed the bridge and opened the door of the cottage. Right behind her was Phoenix. Decklyn and Tiffany were just crossing the bridge. Piper and Phoenix walked into the cottage and started looking around for the ghost or signs of it. The only thing they could see was a mess. There were dishes all over the floor and papers everywhere. Phoenix was just about to tell Decklyn and Tiffany to hurry up when the cottage door was slammed shut in their faces. Piper and Phoenix whipped around and saw the ghost had locked them in!

This ghost really looked like something out of the movies. It was a girl and she had long shaggy matted looking hair. As she was floating in midair her night gown came down just past her ankles. She gave out the loudest and most evil crackle ever heard. Piper and Phoenix were frozen where they stood. Meanwhile outside, Decklyn and Tiffany were banging on the door and yelling to the others to let them in.

"Phoenix this isn't good. It is just the two of us in here. How are we supposed to fight this thing?" Piper said through her teeth for she didn't want the ghost to hear her.

Phoenix looking the ghost straight in the eyes said, "How do you do My name is Phoenix. What is it that we can…"

He was cut off however because the ghost threw him with a mystical power across the room and onto a table shattering it. Lying on the floor where the ghost had thrown him, Phoenix appeared to be unconscious.

Moving quickly Piper dove behind a couch. Grabbing her crystal and thinking how she could defeat this thing; Piper came up from behind the couch. Walking towards the ghost she aimed her crystal at it and thinking of freezing it she instantly froze it. Turning towards the door she opened it and let Decklyn and Tiffany in. Tiffany rushed over to Phoenix while Decklyn ran into the kitchen. Coming back with a tablecloth Decklyn threw it over the ghost and tied it so that it wouldn't be able to leave. Looking at Piper Decklyn said, "We must get this thing to the Whispering Wood. Queen Lavinia must take care of it. Just make sure you don't unfreeze her till we get there."

Leaving Tiffany to attend Phoenix, Decklyn and Piper carried the ghost to the Whispering Wood. Once they arrived there, the forest committee was in session already with the ogre, giant, and swamp goblins. Seeing them from afar Queen Lavinia rushed over. Looking confused as to what they had she said, "I didn't want to let Aged Sir Oak see you for he is in the middle of sentencing Lady Morphana's minions. What have we here?"

"Well, your majesty we have caught a ghost and don't know how to get rid of it. We were wondering if you could." Piper said while still holding onto her crystal.

"That is easy." replied the queen. "All you have to say is this," and taking out her wand Queen Lavinia pointed it at the tablecloth and said, "White thing being held in Purgatory, you have done your share of damage. Now leave this world and be at peace at last."

And with that the ghost and the cloth fell to ashes in front of them. Decklyn couldn't believe his eyes. Confused as well as Decklyn, Piper said, "That is all that must be said?"

"Well yes that and you must have a wand for it to work." said Queen Lavinia.

Decklyn was just about to point out that they didn't have wands for it to work when from a distance he could see Tiffany walking with Phoenix leaning on her shoulders for support. When they got to the others Tiffany told them that Phoenix couldn't heal himself. Even though he had the crystal of healing powers he couldn't in fact heal himself. "Of course, he can't." Queen Lavinia chuckled, "He is the curer and mustn't get himself hurt. If he does, he must come and see me. For I am the only one who can heal the curer."

"How convenient that is." Phoenix said while hanging onto Tiffany.

"You mustn't fret Phoenix; you are in no condition to." Tiffany said.

"How did the ghost come about anyway?" Sorsha asked while standing next to Aged Sir Oak.

"I don't know, but that is something that I am going to have my fairies look into right away Sorsha." Queen Lavinia said buzzing up to her.

"I want to help." Piper said looking at Queen Lavinia. "Do you think I can use the library in the village?"

"Figures you would want to know if you could use it. Why would you want to go read books when we have things to do?" Decklyn said in a cocky way with a slight chuckle.

"For your information, books are these things where you can look stuff up. They also have this funny thing about them. When you read them, you learn stuff and that stuff you are reading may help you." Piper said with a sarcastic tone in her voice.

"I don't see why you wouldn't be able to use the library, Piper. It is right next to the bakery. Go with Balfour. Some of the villagers are still terrified of magic folk." Queen Lavinia said with a smile.

"Very well, you want someone to come with you to this library?" Decklyn asked.

"No, thank you. I can go myself, besides you must help poor Phoenix back to the fort and take care of him. I can do the research myself." a very enthusiastic Piper replied.

As they all went their separate ways. Piper to the library with Balfour and the other three to the fort. They had no idea that they would need one another in a few hours.

Finally getting to the library, Piper began searching for reasons as to why the ghost came about. A couple hours later she had a mound of books on one of the tables in the back of the library. Books upon books on ghosts and the reasons why they haunt worlds. Still having nothing on why this ghost had just decided to destroy someone's home, Piper picked up a book called *Ghosts and the Living*. Flipping to the index she came across a section that interested her. Turning to that section in the book, the chapter was titled *Pleasing a Ghost*. After reading the rather long chapter Piper knew she had to share what she had just learned with the others. Grabbing the book and heading to check it out, Piper couldn't wipe the grin from her face. Thanking the librarian and throwing the book in her backpack, Piper opened the door of the library and headed outside. Walking with a fast stride towards the meadow she couldn't stop thinking of how at first the boys would give her crap on going to the library, but in the end would be thanking her for her newfound knowledge of the ghost incident. Piper was almost through the meadow and in the Whispering Wood when she was grabbed from behind! Kicking and screaming, Piper started to panic. Quickly thinking of a move that Decklyn had taught her back home she quickly used it. Pretending to fall forwards, Piper then with all her might threw her head back as hard as she could towards the person who had a hold of her. Connecting with them she heard them say ouch and immediately they let go of her. Piper's head was throbbing now, but she was free, so she quickly started to run when she heard, "Piper that hurt." Stopping and turning around to see who she had encountered Piper saw Decklyn holding his nose. "I came to see if you needed some help and to walk you home, but I guess you don't need the protection of me, do you?" Decklyn said.

"I feel so awful Decklyn, but you see I thought you were someone trying to take me as a hostage or something. I didn't know what to do so I pulled the move you taught me. I guess it works. Although if it makes you feel better my head is now throbbing." Piper said as she took out a tissue and walked over to him. "Here this is for the bleeding. Let's get you back to the fort and clean you up. I am sorry Decklyn."

"Yeah, no worries at all babes. Phoenix did say that teaching a girl how to defend herself was dangerous." Decklyn said while holding his head up so the blood would stop running down his nose."

Walking back to the fort was a lot faster than Piper thought it would be. As they came in sight of the fort, Piper turned to Decklyn and said, "I did find something interesting back at the library in the village, but I will tell you about it when I tell the other two."

"That's my girl." Decklyn replied with a smile.

As soon as they walked into the fort, they heard Phoenix say, "I told you we should have gone with them. Just look at Decklyn. He was in a fight, and I missed out on it. He may have needed my help. Deck, buddy are you alright?"

"Actually, we didn't get in a fight. I went to surprise Piper, and she head butted me." Decklyn replied.

"Didn't I tell you teaching a girl how to fight would end up being dangerous?" Phoenix said while he was trying to hold in his laughter.

℃ↄ

Back at the fort, the four friends were sitting around the table in the kitchen waiting in anticipation as to what they might learn from the book Piper had checked out. The book lay in the center of the table for all eyes to gaze at. Phoenix was still looking rather beat up and bruised from his encounter with the rather unfriendly ghost earlier that morning. Tiffany had managed to clean him up a bit. Queen Lavinia had told them that she wasn't going to heal Phoenix because he wasn't in need of it, and it was good to learn from what happened. Telling the protectors that someday she may not be around to heal the curer and that they all must learn how to take care of him. So, she sent them back home to take care of him. Decklyn had cut bandages out of an old sheet while Tiffany had got out the first aid kit that Piper had insisted, they bring before they left their hometown of Willow.

"Now I know that you found something in this book Piper, that is why it is lying in front of all of us on the table. I am hoping that there is something in it on why ghosts would destroy homes, but do you think there is an explanation as to why or how a ghost can throw a human across a room?" Phoenix said while looking at his bandaged arm.

Smiling slightly in Phoenix's direction Piper said, "I did learn why ghosts would destroy someone's home, but I didn't look for why or how they could throw someone across the room. I could look deeper into it for you if you would like Phoenix. I myself am a little curious as to why that is possible."

"There could be numerous amounts of reasons Piper as to why or how a ghost could move something solid. I think it is something that we really should consider researching deeper into though." Decklyn said with a serious look on his face.

"Alright Piper, what did you find out in this book?" Tiffany asked looking at the ugly thing lying there on the table.

"There are two main reasons why a ghost would come out of nowhere and want to destroy someone's home. One, they used to live there and for some reason or another are stuck. Second, they were sent by someone with specific instructions to cause mayhem. Personally, I believe the second reason as to why the ghost was in Sorsha's cottage. If a ghost was living, there before she would have seen it before now." Piper said with a very satisfied look upon her face.

"Great! So, we do have a reason to believe that it is Lady Morphana. This woman has no life if all she has on her mind is to cause mayhem." Phoenix said.

"What are we going to do?" asked a worried Tiffany.

"All we can do now is start thinking of a plan to approach Lady Morphana. We already took care of the ghost problem. All that is left now is to just report what we learned to Aged Sir Oak and the forest committee." Decklyn said as he began to stand up from the table.

With that said, Decklyn and Tiffany helped Phoenix up out of his chair while Piper grabbed the book from the table. Making sure that everything was in order and that the doors were locked, the protectors were on their way to Aged Sir Oak.

It was a nice day in Shelvockwood. The sun was out and there was a nice breeze that swept through the maze as the protectors made their way towards the Whispering Wood. Even though Phoenix was still unable to walk by himself, he managed to have his sense of humor with him. Decklyn on one side of him and Tiffany on the other. Phoenix was just loving all the attention. "I must say do you two mind picking up the pace. I am not that heavy, and Piper is almost a whole yard in front of us." Phoenix said with a smile plastered on his face.

"Don't make me hurt you even more than that ghost did." Decklyn said while trying to walk over a log.

Turning around to face her friends Piper said, "We are almost there, but if I must say Phoenix, you look like you are enjoying the walk."

"Well when you have your girlfriend on one arm and your best friend on the other, how much better could life be?" Phoenix said.

Decklyn couldn't help but laugh at what Phoenix had said. Tiffany kind of just rolled her eyes and gave Phoenix a grin while Piper gave a little giggle and kept walking towards Aged Sir Oak.

⚭

Not aware that they were being watched, the four friends arrived at Aged Sir Oak in the Whispering Wood. Glaring into her crystal ball, Lady Morphana was smiling evilly, "Yes, my protectors, tell Aged Sir Oak what happened. Tell him that I sent Sorsha an unfriendly ghost. That was just the beginning of my plan, for I have you protectors exactly where I want you! Ha-ha-ha!" Getting up from her table where her crystal ball was lying, Lady Morphana made her way to her window. Throwing open her shutters she looked out into the darkening sky. Walking the grounds below was Slobbo and her newest assistant Gumbo. She was just about to yell down at them and tell them to go feed the swamp creatures when she had an idea. Looking down towards Slobbo, Lady Morphana yelled, "Slobbo! Come here now!"

Turning away from the window, Lady Morphana made her way towards her throne. Taking a seat just before Slobbo came trudging in, she grabbed her ugly black pointy crown and placed it up on top of her head. As Slobbo approached Lady Morphana, he lowered his head and said, "Yes, my lady. What may I do for you?"

"I was just thinking Slobbo, of how these protectors are much smarter than the other ones. And you know what I concluded?" asked Lady Morphana.

"No, my lady, what did you come to the conclusion of?" Slobbo asked.

"Well, you silly ogre. I concluded that the only reason these protectors are smarter than the last ones are because of their guide." As Lady Morphana said this Slobbo gave her this look of confusion. "Oh, Slobbo, I want you to bring me the guide. I don't want the weakest protectors anymore. I want the strongest, the guide!" shouted Lady Morphana

"How should I go about kidnapping the guide?" asked a confused Slobbo.

Giving him the utmost look of disgust Lady Morphana replied with, "Not you, you twit. Send one of my other loyal minions to do the dirty work for you. But I want her here tonight and if I don't have her here tonight then it will be your head Slobbo!"

Taking a big gulp Slobbo said, "Yes my lady."

Slobbo walked out of Lady Morphana's presence and towards the opposite side of the castle to where the other ogres and swamp goblins were. On his way there two things crossed his mind. One was that he must hurry and send as many of her minions out there after the guide because he wanted to keep his head. Second, he had to keep smiling at the fact that Lady Morphana had considered him one of her loyal minions.

After saying their goodbyes to Aged Sir Oak, the protectors were on their way back to their fort. Not knowing that Lady Morphana was after her, Piper led the way again. Thinking about how much she had accomplished in just this one day made Piper happy. Turning towards her friends Piper said, "Would you guys be alright walking back to the fort in front of Tiffany and me? I would like to ask her something just between us two girls if that is ok."

"Yeah, go ahead Piper. I can carry this bump on a log myself. He isn't that heavy." Decklyn said.

"Who are you calling a bump on a log you no good for nothing creep?!" Phoenix asked while giving Decklyn a slight glare.

As the two boys argued and took the lead in front of the girls, Piper leaned over towards Tiffany and asked, "Do you write in that journal that Queen Lavinia gave you?"

Wondering why Piper had asked this, Tiffany replied with, "I do and sometimes when I forget the journal writes it down for me. Everything is in there on how we beat Lady Morphana. Why do you ask?"

Giving Tiffany a look of concern Piper said, "The only reason that I ask this is because I was thinking that if for some reason Lady Morphana got her hands on it, we would all be in big trouble. It has everything in there about how we have beaten her and how the other protectors have beaten her. If she got a hold of that she would know what to expect us to do. I want you to make sure that you always know where it is and don't ever let it out of your sight. And for whatever reason if something should happen to one of us, don't use it to get us back either ok?"

"I promise I won't use it as leverage, but what made you think of all of this? Did you get a threat from Lady Morphana?" asked a worried Tiffany.

"No, I just have read many books and seen many movies on murder mysteries and kidnappings that I know how evil works. I don't want anything to happen to any of us, but if the journal got into the wrong hands." said Piper.

Once that was settled the girls started talking about how in a few weeks the queen was going to visit the fort with some of her royal friends. Watching the boys walk a distance ahead of them they began planning what they had to do to get ready for the queen and her company. Out of nowhere Tiffany was hit over the head by a big club. Before Piper could react or scream, she was gagged and thrown over the shoulder of a giant! Kicking and moving as much as she could, Piper didn't get an arm free until she was a great distance away from where Tiffany was hit. When she did set her arm free, she grabbed the gag from her mouth. Whipping around in time to see Tiffany still lying on the ground unconscious. Piper did the only thing she could think of. She let out the loudest scream she could think of. "AHHHHHHHHHHHHHHHHHHHHH! TIFFANY!!!!"

Instantly the boys stopped and turned around to find Tiffany a few yards away lying on the ground. Phoenix no longer needed Decklyn's help. His adrenaline was pumping so fast that he bolted towards Tiffany. The boys got to Tiffany just in time to see the giant turn into the Whispering Wood with Piper. Decklyn sprinted after them while Phoenix began healing Tiffany.

Not thinking what he would do by himself when he encountered the giant, Decklyn was moving as fast as his legs would carry him. He seemed to be flying through the forest rather quickly. Still hearing Piper screaming in the distance he knew that he was close to where they should be. Trees were whipping past him left and right. He didn't even notice that it was raining out and that the ground was starting to get slippery. Finally, Decklyn came to the top of the waterfall. Looking out over it he could see down to the village and just beyond that he could make out the Castle of Terror. Heading up the hill towards the castle was a tall figure and he could just make out the small figure thrown over the giants shoulders as Piper.

Chapter 6

Names that Start with the Letter "P"

While sitting on her throne Lady Morphana was wondering if Slobbo had sent out the right giant to get the job done; for he was about as smart as a stone wall. Thinking of who she would send out next after the guide when the giant failed, Lady Morphana was interrupted by the front castle doors being thrown open. It was pouring outside and the clash of the thunder in the background made her feel comfy inside. The thing standing in the doorway was even more breathtaking than the thunder and lighting. Dripping wet and all muddy stood the giant and it looked like he was carrying a sack of potatoes over his shoulder. When he got closer to Lady Morphana, she realized immediately that it was one of the protectors. Not being able to control her happiness anymore Lady Morphana shouted, "Wonderful! Please tell me giant that this is the guide of the protectors."

Standing right in front of Lady Morphana now, the giant stood Piper up in front of her and said through slow talk, "Yes...my...lady. This...is...the.... smart...one."

"What is your name giant? For you shall be rewarded for this." Lady Morphana said with her head held high.

"Don't think for one minute that you will get away with any of this you ugly, horrible, spiteful woman!" shouted Piper.

Not losing her smile whatsoever Lady Morphana replied, "But of course my dear, I have already gotten away with the first part of my plan. I have you here, don't I? And might I add that if I were you, I would be more careful about what you say to me. For I am bound to lose my happy mood."

"You don't scare me at all!" Piper shouted, rather annoyed.

Walking over to where Piper stood, Lady Morphana laughed evilly and replied, "I may not scare you now child, but I will find a way to defeat you and your little friends. I have ways to find out what you fear the most and I will play off that, you can count on it." Turning towards the giant again she asked, "What is your name?"

"Reems....my...lady." said the giant.

"Slobbo, take Reems here to his reward in the tower." said Lady Morphana.

"Yes, my lady." Slobbo said.

As they left Lady Morphana turned back to Piper and said, "May I inquire as to your name protector?"

With an annoyed look on her face still, as if someone had burned a book in front of her, Piper said, "I am not going to tell you anything."

"Suit yourself protector. I have no time for you right now anyways. I must carry out the rest of my plan. When you do feel like talking just let one of the guards know. They will then bring you to me." Lady Morphana said to Piper. And turning towards the door she yelled, "Gumbo!"

Coming into the room was the tiny swamp goblin. He turned to Lady Morphana and said, "Yes my lady."

"I want you to take the guide to the tallest tower. Do not torture her yet for I am not in a bad mood. Let the guard know that if she decides to talk to me to bring her to me at once." After saying that to Gumbo, Lady Morphana turned to Piper and said, "Sweet dreams protector."

And with that Gumbo took Piper and led her to the tallest tower in the castle. Once thrown inside the tower and locked in, Piper had time to think. The room she was in was no bigger than a walk-in closet. There was hay all around the floor and a tiny window to look out of on the floor of the tower. Crawling on her hands and knees over to the window, Piper sat down on the floor and glanced out the window. And for the first time since she had been in Shelvockwood she cried; for the only thing visible out of the window was darkness.

⌒⌒

Back at the fort the rest of the protectors were in no mood to talk. They looked like they had been hit by a train and then taken for a ride through a subway station. Decklyn had sprinted back to Phoenix and Tiffany. After hearing what Tiffany had remembered before being hit over the head, they had decided to go speak to Aged Sir Oak. They all however made a stop at the fort first to retrieve Tiffany's journal. She did tell them the conversation that Piper had with her before she was taken. The boys thought it was a good idea what Piper suggested, not leave the journal alone.

Locking up and heading towards Aged Sir Oak the protectors were silent as the dead. Decklyn looked like he was about to cry while Tiffany had been crying. Phoenix didn't say one word and for the first time looked serious on their walk to the Whispering Wood.

Once they got to Aged Sir Oak, woke him up, and told him what had happened he was furious. "PIKE! Pike, where are you? Come here now!" shouted Aged Sir Oak.

"What is it?" asked a very tired Pike.

"Piper has been captured by Lady Morphana. I want you to go at once to get Balfour, Sorsha, and the queen. We need an emergency forest committee meeting." said Aged Sir Oak.

With a shocked look on his face, Pike was off like a bolt of lightning. Returning in only a half hour with Balfour, a few of the villagers, Sorsha, and the queen, Pike said, "As soon as I told them that the protectors were in trouble, they were all up and ready to go. I didn't tell them what happened though. Sorry Aged Sir Oak."

"Don't be sorry Pike. You did just what I told you to do, and I am thankful for that. Now it is my turn to tell you all what happened." Aged Sir Oak said looking at the forest committee. And with that Aged Sir Oak told the story of what happened to Piper.

"We won't get any rest until Piper is safe back in the Hidden Garden!" buzzed Queen Lavinia.

"How are we ever to get her back though?" asked a worried Sorsha.

"That is easy." Phoenix said, "We are going to take her back."

✆✠✆

Not being able to sleep, Piper sat up on the stone floor of the tower. Not only was it freezing in the tower (probably because the window only had bars on it), but it also smelled of a rotting sewer. Piper had to get out of there. As she was playing with straw she was thinking of a nice warm bath, clean clothes, and a warm bed. Wondering what the others were doing right now (probably finding a way to get her back) Piper started to get sad again. Thinking about that and the smell finally getting to her, she stood up and walked over to the tower door. Looking out through the tiny bars she said, "Excuse me."

The guard on duty was a very tiny ogre. He couldn't have been more then six feet tall. Walking towards the door the ogre said, "What do you want?"

80

Quickly thinking Piper said, "I would like to speak to Lady Morphana."

Unlocking the door and grabbing Piper, the ogre tied up her hands and started leading her down the twisty staircase. When they finally reached the bottom of the stairs there was one door. Unlocking it from the inside the ogre grabbed Piper by her arm and led her through the rather dark and gloomy hallway. They passed the throne room and what looked like a ballroom. Heading now up more stairs, Piper was wondering what Lady Morphana would say when she saw her.

After walking through many more hallways with ugly statues and armor they came to another door. Only this door the ogre didn't unlock but knocked on. Instantly there was a loud shout, "Come in!" from Lady Morphana.

Upon opening the door, the ogre brought Piper into what appeared to be the strangest room she had seen in the castle so far. There was what appeared to be some kind of canopy bed in the center of the room with black lace hanging down from it. Beyond the bed was a dark worn-out dresser that had an old mirror on top of it. The room was very dark and gloomy just as many of the hallways were. There were black rugs, a black cauldron, and what appeared to be a crystal ball sitting on top of the table next to the only window in the room. (This is probably what Lady Morphana used to check up on the protectors and the unsuspecting folk of Shelvockwood.) This window was as big as the mirror was and it looked out onto the village towards the Whispering Wood.

Piper's face must have said enough because Lady Morphana said, "Not homey enough for you protector?"

Facing Morphana, Piper replied with, "I myself wouldn't have thought a lady such as you would be caught dead in a room like this."

"What is it protector that you wanted? The guard tells me that you wanted to speak to ME." snarls Lady Morphana.

"As a matter of fact, I did tell the guard I was ready to talk to you. What is it exactly that you want with me? And if it has anything to do with my friends think again because I would never turn them over to you." Piper said,

"Protector you amuse me." Lady Morphana said with a laugh. "You see I was toying with the idea of capturing Queen Lavinia and putting her in a glass jar so I could be able to read at night. Ha-ha-ha-ha! But you see protector, you amuse me so much more than the queen would. I would so much like to know why the queen would think you to be worthy enough to be the guide of the other protectors; you are the one that got caught by me!"

Holding her head high and giving Lady Morphana a look of disgust Piper said, "I don't know why the queen chose me to be the guide, but I do know that you will never hurt anyone in Shelvockwood as long as I am around."

Still amused by Piper, Lady Morphana said, "Protector, that is why you will be locked away in the tower forever! By the way, what is your name protector? Or am I still unworthy to know?"

"The name is Piper, but you can still call me protector, I would prefer it." Piper said with a hint of sarcasm in her voice.

"Very well, "Piper" if that is the way you want it to be. I shall call you whatever I want to call you because I am Lady Morphana! Ha-ha-ha! Slobbo! Come and take this protector back to the tower. I still must think of a punishment for her. I want her out of my sight." Morphana said with the rudest voice she could think of.

Grabbing Piper by the arm and walking her to the door of Lady Morphana's chambers, Slobbo gave a nod to Morphana. Once back inside her smelly tower Piper had to start thinking of ways to get out of there. There was no way she was going to spend the rest of her life in a smelly tower with an evil woman keeping watch over her.

Meanwhile back at the fort the rest of the protectors were getting ready to go attack Morphana and save Piper. Tiffany was busy packing backpacks with candles, rope, and other things that they might need on this attack. Decklyn was sharpening his axe with a rock, while Phoenix was sketching out the map of the Castle of Terror that Balfour had gotten for him. All busy with doing their own thing not one of them looked like they had gotten much sleep. Suddenly there was a big bang; a big purple mushroom cloud filled the room. As the protectors were picking themselves up off the floor they looked up into the purple cloud of smoke and for the first time came face to face with Lady Morphana.

With an evil tone in her voice (the purple cloud spoke like an echoing through a microphone) Lady Morphana began to speak, "Ah, protectors of the ice crystals, we meet at last. As you may know I have your guide. If you ever want to see her again you will bring me the writer's journal."

Without missing a beat Decklyn said, "Piper told us not to give up the journal for her return. If we don't get her back by tonight, then we are invading your castle at dawn!"

"Silly protector! I will never give her up without something in return. If you wish to storm my castle, go for it, but you will lose, and I will win!" and with that Lady Morphana's face vanished as did the purple mushroom cloud.

"Good going Decklyn! Now we won't ever see Piper again." wailed Tiffany.

Looking towards Tiffany, Decklyn said, "Yes we will. We aren't going to attack at dawn. We are going to attack tonight!"

Thinking that nothing could possibly go wrong with his plan to get his girlfriend back, Decklyn grabbed his backpack and started out the door. Right behind him was Phoenix and Tiffany, making sure that the door was locked as they started heading towards the Castle of Terror.

෨෯෨

"Fools! They don't have any idea who they are messing with." Laughs Lady Morphana.

"What should we do my lady?" asks a confused Slobbo.

"I want your boys to be ready for the protectors. If it is one thing I know about protectors, it's that they do just the opposite of what they were planning to do." Noticing that Slobbo had a confused look upon his face still, Lady Morphana said, "They aren't going to attack at dawn, but tonight. Therefore, what should you be doing right now?" she asked in a sarcastic tone of voice.

"Umm...umm..." wondering what he should be doing Slobbo was interrupted.

"You nincompoop! I want you to get your boys ready for the attack they are planning. Now move!" yelled Lady Morphana.

Slobbo raced from Morphana's presence and headed towards the right wing of the castle where the rest of her minions were. However, before he got there one of Slobbo's ogres came waltzing in the castle with what appeared to be a rather ugly looking sprite.

"What do you have Domino?" Slobbo asked.

Swinging this sprite by one of his legs Domino said, "I found him wandering around outside of the castle. He was leaving a trail of seeds towards the tower that the one protector is in. I think he is trouble."

"You know that Lady Morphana doesn't like us thinking, but if I must say so myself that is good thinking. Put him down Domino, but don't let him out of your sight." Watching Domino carefully place the sprite down on the ground Slobbo turned to the ugly looking creature and said, "What were you thinking roaming around Lady Morphana's property? She could have you beheaded for this."

Giving Slobbo the ugliest look imaginable, Pike turned his nose in the air and said, "I was doing exactly what Lady Morphana didn't want me doing. I was leading the other protectors to their guide!"

"This won't do." Slobbo was muttering to himself. "She will have my head for sure. Unless I take this sprite to Lady Morphana myself and tell her what happened. That is exactly what I will do. Domino, you can go. Go inform the others to get to their battle stations for the protectors are on their way." Domino went one way and Slobbo grabbing Pike started back towards Lady Morphana's chambers.

ⓧ

Dragging Pike by his tail, Slobbo shoved him into Lady Morphana's chambers. Upon seeing an ugly looking sprite being thrown into her room by Slobbo, Lady Morphana asked with a surprising look on her face, "Slobbo what is this ugly sprite doing in MY CHAMBERS?"

"My lady. This young sprite was caught outside on the grounds leaving a trail of seeds outside the tower of the protector. What shall I do with him?" Slobbo asked with an ever so slimy grin on his face.

"Is that so my troubled small friend?" Lady Morphana asked with a grin while looking down at Pike.

"You listen, when Aged Sir Oak finds out what your minions have done to me, he will come after you and not to mention what the rest of the protectors will do to you when they find out you have me and the other protector!" said a very upset and frustrated Pike.

"Ha ha, hahaha, HA-HA-HA-HA-HA! You amuse me that you do. What makes you think Aged Sir Oak will notice that you are missing? He will be thrilled that you aren't running around in his branches. As for coming after me, he would never dream of uprooting himself. HA-HA-HA! And don't make me laugh, but the protectors? HAHAHAHAHAHA!!! They have no chance whatsoever in defeating me!" laughs Lady Morphana. Turning towards Slobbo she says, "Take this sprite to the tower, but do not put him in with the protector. Put him in the room right next to hers."

Nodding his head Slobbo grabbed Pike with some difficulty as he was bouncing all over the room. It took much longer for Slobbo, however, to get to the towers because Pike was making it very difficult for him. After what seemed like hours of struggling with Pike up the tower steps, Slobbo threw him into the room next to Piper's and locked the door.

☙❧

"This is just wonderful! I cannot believe I have a protector and a sprite. What was the things name? Never mind that isn't important. Right now, he is locked away in the tower too?" asks a rather unusually happy Lady Morphana.

"That he is my lady, and I must say he put up more of a fight than the protector did. He was spitting fire about how Aged Sir Oak was going to save him and we were in big trouble." Slobbo replied.

"Ha!" Lady Morphana was saying while pacing the floor of her chamber. "Aged Sir Oak wouldn't dream of taking me on let alone leave the Whispering Wood. I would have him in a pile of wood so fast it would make his branches shiver. What am I to do with the girl though? Now that I have her, she isn't really doing what I thought she would. I expected her to give in and have a meeting for her friends to hand over the journal. This is going to take much more work than I would have hoped for Slobbo. How can I get her to talk let alone get what I want out of her? I need some advice old friend, have any thoughts?"

In shock that Lady Morphana considered him a friend let alone wanting to know what his thoughts were on the matter, Slobbo stood with his mouth hanging open. Before Morphana could comment on this though he started to speak, "Well my lady, if you ask me, I think you should pretend like you are going to have the sprite tortured until the protector talks. You could have one of the ogres say to the sprite that I have come to torture you until your friend talks. If that doesn't work, you could always capture another one of the protectors to get her to talk. Seeing one of her friends in need might make her spill what she knows quicker than seeing a sprite in need."

Thinking for a minute about what Slobbo said and taking it all in, Lady Morphana had to laugh a little bit. "Why Slobbo, that must be one of the greatest ideas you have yet come up with. Why this whole time have you not said anything to me about any of this before? You can't be that scared of me?"

Slobbo just stood there in silence and the silence was enough to answer Lady Morphana's questions. "Very well then. I know right now that that girl won't really be affected by the sprite being hurt. I want one of my minions to go fetch me another protector. I know that they are on their way here, so if one of them gets captured before they get here the other two will have no choice but to head back home for the night. Make haste for I feel that they are near now."

Slobbo ran from her chambers. Heading in the direction of the castle where all the other creatures were, Slobbo got together a meeting of ogres, goblins, and giants. He then sent all of them out in hopes that one of them will be able to obtain another protector.

ꙮ

Not aware that they were being hunted by these creatures, Phoenix, Decklyn, and Tiffany were climbing down the side of the waterfall. They had managed to get that far within a matter of minutes it seemed. Grabbing Tiffany's hand to make sure she wasn't going to fall, Phoenix said, "I hope Piper is ok."

"I am sure she is holding on. You forget Piper is strong. She has three older brothers and two older sisters. Being the youngest must make her strong. We must hurry up though before dawn." Tiffany replied to Phoenix.

"Once we get down off this cliff, we have those hills over there and then Lady Morphana's property. Pike was supposed to leave a trail of seeds outside of the tower that Piper was in. I hope he made it ok." Decklyn said while climbing down off a slippery rock.

It didn't take them much longer to get down off the rocks. After that it seemed like everything went by rather fast. They were at the little hills before they knew it. Before they got to the first little hill though Phoenix was buzzed in the ear. He almost swung his fist in that direction, but stopped because he realized that it was a fairy. Taking time to stop quick they all looked in the direction of the fairy buzzing in midair. "Protectors, I am so glad I found you. I have just come from the Castle of Terror myself. I was told to follow Pike in case something went wrong. Sadly, to report he has been captured by Lady Morphana as well. He is in the highest tower along with Piper. Doubt they are in the same cell though. He did put up a good fight." said the fairy.

"Oh, no! Poor Pike. He must be so scared. We must get him out of there soon. He is a forest creature and needs the fresh air." Tiffany wailed.

Phoenix was not being his normal self anymore. He was now a serious determined Phoenix. "We will get both back. Let's get a move on, we have so much to do. Go alert the forest committee immediately!"

With that the fairy flew off instantly. Trudging onward the three friends had so much running through their minds. Would they be able to rescue their friend and the sprite? However, they didn't have much time to think because just before they got over the last hill they were attacked. Coming from the left side were a few goblins that started throwing rocks in their direction. Taking out his axe, Decklyn started swinging back at the rocks. He hit a few back in the direction of the goblins and managed to hit a few of them. While he was doing that Tiffany was trying to outrun the giants that came from their right direction. She was screaming and running back down the hills towards the waterfall. Phoenix turned to Decklyn and said, "Whatever happens don't let anything happen to Tiff. Help her please." As he was trying to outsmart an ogre. With that Decklyn hit one more rock back and took off towards Tiffany's direction. He was almost caught up to Tiffany when he heard Phoenix yell, "Let's go!"

Turning around in time to see an ogre hit Phoenix over the head with a club and knock him unconscious, Decklyn couldn't help but think things were not going the way he had planned. He had promised Phoenix though that he would take care of Tiffany and she wasn't doing well trying to outrun the giants. Turning his attention back to Tiffany, Decklyn made a beeline for her. Once he caught up with her, he grabbed her hand and sped up, practically dragging her with him. They didn't have to run for long though because it seemed like the giants stopped chasing them. Once they got back to the waterfall Decklyn turned to Tiffany and said, "They took Phoenix. That must be why they stopped chasing us. Lady Morphana must have wanted just one of us, but why I don't know."

"Now what are we going to do?" asked a sobbing Tiffany.

"Right now, we go home and lock up and get some rest. Tomorrow, we rescue our friends with the help of Balfour and the villagers." replied Decklyn.

☙❧

Watching Decklyn and Tiffany walk the long journey back towards their fort, Lady Morphana couldn't help but think tonight she would finally get a good nights sleep. Her thoughts were interrupted by Slobbo and Brutus. Hung over Brutus's shoulder was one of the protectors apparently unconscious. "Just take him up to the towers. Throw him in with the sprite. I don't want the other protector to have any contact with anyone but me. Once that is done tonight, we celebrate friends."

Once Phoenix was thrown in with Pike, Brutus locked up the tower and went back down to the ballroom to join in the celebration with the others. This was the first time in years that they had had two protectors captured and a sprite.

The ballroom was filled with all sorts of weird-looking creatures. Lady Morphana sat at her throne wearing her long black robe and her pointed crown, looking rather pleased for once. Swamp goblins were dancing with hags and giants were shoving their faces with all kinds of nasty looking bugs. The ogres were hitting each other and laughing at stupid things they did that day. Everybody was enjoying themselves because not one of them had ever seen or been around Morphana when she was in a good mood.

Lady Morphana picked up her wand that was leaning against her throne and with one wave of her hand she silenced the music. Everybody turned in horrified looks towards her. Looking at all her minions she spoke with a stern voice, "As you all may know we have two of the protectors of the ice crystals!"

The crowd went wild with screams and grunts. Throwing up her hands to silence them again, Lady Morphana spoke again. "The second protector we caught is the curer. I am considering calling the three of them my 'P' collection because all their names begin with the letter P, but you know what. I have thrown that idea out and I have come up with this name. I am calling them 'The Three P's'. This is a celebration for all of us, but beware they have friends who are on the move and will most likely attack at dawn.

I want you all to get a good nights sleep for we must be ready for the attack."

And with that she sat back down on her throne and watched her creatures go back to celebrating their small victory. But while they were enjoying themselves Decklyn and Tiffany were planning their attack.

Chapter 7

The Rescue

The night seemed to have crawled to Tiffany and Decklyn. It didn't seem like dawn would ever come that fast. They had talked so much when they got back to the fort about what they were going to do. It wasn't' until almost 2 o'clock in the morning that they finally came up with a plan that even Lady Morphana wouldn't have thought of. Grabbing stuff, they thought they would need for the day, they only packed one daypack because they didn't want any extra stuff to carry when they knew they would be running for their lives. Decklyn threw the backpack over his shoulder and turned to Tiffany, "You ready?"

"As ready as I will ever be." she replied.

Heading out the door of the fort the two friends walked side by side with their heads held high. Their plan was to rescue them, but not to do it in broad daylight. Their plan wasn't to attack the castle at all, but to rescue their friends and then plan to attack when they had all four of them together. They weren't going to do it during the day either like Lady Morphana expected. They wanted to make sure that they caught her off guard. To confuse her more, they were going to act like nothing was wrong and go about their business, which was very hard to do because they knew their friends were in trouble and needed help. Taking a stroll through the woods towards Aged Sir Oak, Tiffany and Decklyn walked with a slow pace. Once they got to Aged Sir Oak, they could relax and breathe a little knowing that they were safe. "How are you on this fine day Aged Sir Oak?" Tiffany asked with a chipper tone in her voice.

Looking a bit confused as to why both were happy and in a good mood Aged Sir Oak replied with, "I am alright, but may I ask what is up with you two? Your friends are captured by the evil witch and you both are happy about it? I know I am just a tree, but I am a bit confused by your actions right now.

Leaning in and whispering so only Aged Sir Oak could hear him Tiffany said, "We know Lady Morphana is watching our every move and we want her to believe we are moving on. We are going to rescue Piper, Phoenix, and Pike tonight, but we need her to think we are forgetting about them."

Chuckling out loud now, Aged Sir Oak through laughs said, "Let us move on then my friends. We need to start getting ready for the big festival." Receiving looks from Decklyn and Tiffany of pure curiosity he continued, "The festival is a day we celebrate here in Shelvockwood. It's based on the day that the four protectors before you defeated the evil queen many, many years ago. It is the day the queen died and Shelvockwood was safe from harm."

"Then let us get ready for it. What do we have to do Aged Sir Oak?" Decklyn had asked while standing up from the ground.

ଚାଡ

Meanwhile back in the castle Lady Morphana was in a foul mood. As she paced her floor for the tenth time there was a slight knock on her door. "ENTER!" she shouted.

Entering her chambers with his head held low was Gumbo. Facing the floor, he started to talk, "Sorry for disturbing you my lady, but I heard you shouting in here and I figured you needed to talk to someone about it."

Starring at him in complete shock, Morphana had to close her mouth because it was hanging open just a tiny bit. "In all my years of reigning I have never had anybody ask me if I wanted to talk. Have a seat Gumbo."

Gumbo sat down in a black wooden chair over by her mirror. As Lady Morphana poured her thoughts out onto this goblin, she started to relax a little. It did feel good to get some of her emotions out and not keep everything bottled up inside her. She told him everything she had seen the other two protectors doing this morning and what they were doing last night.

To her relief Gumbo helped her out in a way. He had ideas that she had not even thought of. "You know my lady they may have given up hope, that they cannot win against you. Either that or they are planning a different attack on you, one that you won't know about because they are making it look like they have moved on. You should keep your castle grounds heavily protected from now on. At least until we have all the protectors here."

After their conversation Lady Morphana made sure that her castle grounds were well protected and that the tower to the prisoners was guarded well. Once that was all done, she did something that she hadn't done in years. She put her crystal ball away.

∾

The towers were damp and cold at night, but during the day they were humid and muggy. Piper, however, managed to figure out rather quickly that Phoenix was the other one captured. Once he did come too though the three of them started planning their escape. "Phoenix, are you hurt at all?" Piper asked with concern.

"Just bruised up a bit, but not really hurt. I guess that is a good thing seeing as the queen isn't here to fix me up. Where are we? It smells like my grandfather's old socks." Phoenix said while holding his nose.

"We are in the towers where they keep prisoners." said an angry, but hyper Pike. "I swear when I get out of here, I am going to hit something. I will make sure I get even with all of them for the way they have treated me and talked about Aged Sir Oak like he isn't worth the time."

"Calm down Pike. Right now, we don't need to be excited like that. We need to think of a way to get out of here. I know Decklyn, he will be on his way, but he won't be here that quick. He will want everybody to think about something else. If Lady Morphana thinks he is coming now he won't show up until later. We just need to make sure we are ready as well to help them out in any way we can." Phoenix said while getting up from the floor. "Piper, can you see anyway down from the tower on your side?"

Crawling over to the tiny window on the floor of the cell, Piper looked outside. There was nothing to climb down on, it was all just straight down. And at the very bottom of the tower was a moat. This really was a castle right out of a fairy tale. "No, Phoenix, I have no way out from my cell. How about you?"

The cell Phoenix and Pike were in looked just like Piper's. The only difference was their window was just a hair bigger, but not by much. Crawling over to the window, Phoenix and Pike looked out. Right across from their tower window was a tall gangly looking willow tree and below the willow was what looked like dried moss. Phoenix had to throw his hand over Pike's mouth the instant it fell open. "Pike keep quiet. We don't need the ogres hearing your screams of joy and ruining anything we could do." Walking back to the door and looking at Piper through the bars on the door Phoenix said, "Yeah there is a way. We just need to now figure two things out. How to get out the window and how to get you over here. I can probably work on the window if you can come up with an idea on how to get over in our cell for a few minutes."

"It's a deal Phoenix, I am cooking up a plan as we speak." Piper said while crawling back over to her window. Her best ideas came to her as she stared off into space and cleared her mind of all worries.

∽∞∾

Nightfall came rather quickly. Decklyn and Tiffany thought it wouldn't get there quick enough, but it did. Having everything set and ready for the plan to begin the two friends said their goodnights and headed up the ladder to bed. Once up in the loft they quickly took out two potions that were in tiny vials. They were a dark blue color and smelled something fierce. Looking deep into each other's eyes they both knew what they must do to start their plan. Clinging the vials together they both downed the blue liquid. Tiffany made a face of pure hatred, while Decklyn looked like he had swallowed bad medicine. "Queen Lavinia said it would kick in as soon as we took it and that we only have a good few hours before it wears off. I figure that gives us time till we get the others. It's on the way home that we are going to have a problem with it wearing off." Decklyn said.

"Do you suppose it worked? How will we know if it did or not? I don't like this, Decklyn. What if it didn't' work and Lady Morphana can see us still?" asked a worried Tiffany.

"We have no choice." replied Decklyn. "Let's just get going since we have limited time and see what happens on our journey."

The potion they took was supposed to make it so that if Lady Morphana looked into her magic crystal ball all she would see would be Decklyn and Tiffany sleeping soundly in their beds. But as Decklyn said they didn't have much time because when the potion did wear off Lady Morphana would be able to see exactly where they were and what they were doing. Grabbing their already packed bags, Tiffany and Decklyn headed back down the ladder and out the door. The journey in the dark was unbearable. Queen

Lavinia had also told them that they mustn't use candles because Lady Morphana would still be able to see the lights and that would put up a red flag in her eyes. So, they walked quietly in the dark only a few feet apart from each other, using the moonlight to see.

Once they got to the waterfall though is when things started getting difficult. It was a pain in the butt during the day, but at night it was practically impossible to figure out where they were going. About twenty minutes later both made it down the side of the falls in one piece.

Heading now towards the hills where they were attacked just the other day, Tiffany whispered to Decklyn, "You don't suppose Lady Morphana has any of her goons out tonight do you? I would hate to run into one of them."

Taking a break and turning around to look at Tiffany he replied, "Not tonight. She thinks we are sleeping and knowing her she will want to make sure her goons are well rested for when we do plan an attack on her castle."

Whispering, not only because it was dark out, but because she feared they were being watched somehow, Tiffany asked, "Well do you think the seeds are still there leading to the tower we have to go to?"

"Pike knew what he was doing. Before he left though, Aged Sir Oak told me that he had Sorsha make special seeds for Pike to leave on the ground. The seeds were supposed to vanish and then reappear when water was thrown on them. That is why I brought a canteen of water from home." Decklyn said.

"That is amazing that they thought of that. I guess they all know who they are really dealing with huh? Let's get moving, Deck. I don't want to be out here anymore. I am getting the creeps being out in the dark." Tiffany said while climbing the last hill.

Once they got to the top, they could see the castle gates a few feet ahead. The gate was a big iron gate. It was wide open and one of the sides was leaning. The castle was dark looking. It looked like it was out of a spooky Halloween horror movie. There were even bats flying from one of the towers above. Walking through the gates Decklyn and Tiffany were careful of where they stepped. Reaching in his bag Decklyn took out the canteen. He untwisted the top and started lightly sprinkling the water over the ground. Soon he hit one of the seeds. It lit up a bright lime green color and just as quickly as it lit up it went out. "That must be, so we won't get caught." chuckled Decklyn. They found the trail and were soon standing under the tallest tower of the castle.

$$\infty$$

A little bit before their friends took the long journey to the Castle of Terror Piper, Phoenix, and Pike were figuring out their plan to escape. Piper had come up with the idea of how to get over to Phoenix's cell. The big question now was how she could convince the ogre. Ogres were dumb, it shouldn't be too hard. Leaning through the bars Piper tapped the ogre on the shoulder. As he turned around to look at her Piper started to speak. "I know Lady Morphana has me under strict house arrest, but do you think I could just go and say hi to my friends over there? I won't be long, I promise." She said with a winning smile.

Shrugging his shoulders, the ogre looked kind of befuddled. Taking a quick glance over at Phoenix's cell the ogre shrugged his shoulders again and started fumbling through keys on a chain. Unlocking Piper's cell the ogre grabbed her by her arm and dragged her over to Phoenix's cell. "Say hi." said the ogre.

"Oh, well the way I say hi where I come from is by giving a hug. Can I give him a hug too?" Piper asked.

Still looking rather confused the ogre fumbled again through the keys and took out another one unlocking Phoenix's door now. Throwing Piper in there and locking up the door the ogre said,

"You have till I come back from dinner." And with that he turned down the spiral staircase and was gone.

"Wow, he has to be the dumbest ogre." Phoenix said while throwing his arms around Piper. "I promise you I will get you out of here."

Not really speaking, Pike ran over to Piper and threw his arms around her. He looked like he had been crying a little bit. Piper gave him a huge hug in return. Once they got their greetings out of the way Pike asked, "How are we getting out of here? Even if we do get a few of the bars moved over how are we going to climb out?"

"That's easy Pike." Phoenix said, "All we must do is climb out the window and onto those branches right there. From that point on its down the tree and through the castle grounds."

Looking confused Piper asked, "How are we going to get the bars open enough for us to all fit through them?"

Smiling with his sheepish grin Phoenix turned to Piper and said, "I was doing some thinking while I was in here, cause let's face it that is all anybody can do up here is think. Remember how you felt when we first got here and then how we felt after the crystals took over? It was like a cloud was lifted. I believe if you and I put our crystals together we can create some kind of power that will be enough to move some of the bars. What do you think? Worth a try?"

"It could work, but what do we have to lose?" Piper replied.

Just as they were about to put their crystals together, they heard a small faint noise coming from down below the tower. Running over to the window they all tried desperately to look out. It was rather hard to see anything because it was dark outside. There was, however, enough light from the moon to see the outlines of Decklyn and Tiffany at the bottom of the tower. Throwing her hand instantly over Pike's mouth, Piper caught it in time before he screamed for joy. Looking down at Decklyn and pointing to her crystal, Piper gave the sign of this is what we must use.

At the bottom of the tower Decklyn got what Piper was trying to say. Turning to Tiffany, Decklyn said, "We all must combine our powers together to get them out of the tower. I don't know what we must do, but I am sure it won't be too hard to figure out."

"I think they want to bend the bars. Why don't we all just hold our crystals and imagine the bars being bent?" Tiffany asked.

Giving Tiffany the big bug-eyed look and smiling wide like the Cheshire cat, Decklyn said, "That is exactly what we have to do!" And looking back up towards Phoenix and Piper, Decklyn gave the nod, and they all knew what they had to do. It was like they could all read each other's minds. Phoenix and Piper sat down on the floor of the tower and closed their eyes. Holding their crystals in their hands they grabbed each other's hands and held on tight. Down below the tower the same thing was happening with Decklyn and Tiffany.

The bars on the tower cell window started to slowly bend outward and before long there was enough room even for Phoenix to fit through the window. Hurrying up because they didn't know how much time they had Phoenix, Piper, and Pike climbed through the window and onto the willow tree. It took them only a few minutes to climb down the tree, but once they were on the ground hugs were quickly passed around and then the friends held hands one more time to bend the bars back to what they were before they climbed out of the window. Hurrying up now because they were all still in danger of being on Lady Morphana's land, they ran across the grounds of the Castle of Terror and started their long journey home.

❧

The friends were almost all at the fort when Lady Morphana finally heard the news of the escape from her grounds. Pacing her chamber and talking to herself, Lady Morphana was furious. How could anybody escape from her castle. It was impossible. With all her ogres, giants, and swamp goblins on the grounds it was utterly stupid to enter her grounds or flea from them. Thinking that there must have been something overlooked she stopped pacing and asked, "How exactly did they all get out of their cells again?" while turning to Slobbo and Gumbo.

Both had their heads held low to the ground because they both knew that Morphana would be even more upset when she found out that the ogre on duty let the one protector in the other cell with the others. "Well, my lady" started Slobbo, "Skragter was on duty, and he said that before he went to dinner one of the protectors asked him if it would be ok that they visit the other ones. He's dumb my lady, didn't know what to do and let them all be together before he came back from dinner."

"It wasn't really his fault my lady. He is just a dumb ogre like Slobbo said and didn't know any better." Gumbo replied when he saw the look Lady Morphana was giving them.

Lady Morphana's eyes got as big as acorns, and she instantly lost her temper. "WHAT? WHY WOULD. HOW STUPID IS HE!" Pacing even more rapidly now Morphana looked like she was about to spit fire. "I want someone to bring him to the dungeon and remind him who he needs to report to if there is a question about prisoners. As for you two, you both had better figure out how they all got out of the tower and fix the problem before we get new prisoners. Now leave me!"

Lady Morphana was left alone to peer into her crystal ball at the protectors, finally entering their fort and looking rather happy. They were hugging each other and laughing and playing games. And right before they all went to bed, they had made some hot chocolate. She watched them all night long, it seemed before the last one finally went to sleep. Morphana wasn't going to get a wink of sleep tonight because of what happened on her grounds. She knew she had to come up with a newfound plan. As she was getting ready to put away her crystal ball there was a knock on her chamber door. "Who is it!" she shouted.

And from the other side of her door, she heard a voice that instantly threw all her anger aside and made her almost melt into a puddle on the floor. Before she could utter another word, however, her door was thrown open and standing in the doorway was her long-lost love, Perlangitis.

Chapter 8

The Festival

After waking up and having a nice breakfast the protectors and Pike heard a knock on their door. As Tiffany opened it, standing in the doorway was Balfour. "Oh, my heavens you did rescue them. This is a great day friends for not only is it the day of the grand festival, but we now have cause to really celebrate the return of Phoenix, Piper, and Pike. You must all get dressed immediately. Aged Sir Oak, Sorsha, and Queen Lavinia have been up all night preparing for the grand festivities and you four are the guests of honor. Pike, Aged Sir Oak would love it if you went and helped them, plus he doesn't know that you all are back yet, nobody does. What a wonderful surprise. Welcome home friends!"

Balfour left with Pike while the friends were left to get ready for the big festival. The girls ran upstairs first to go change while Phoenix and Decklyn just relaxed at the table. Once the girls were dressed in their springy dresses (Piper in green and Tiffany in Purple) it was time for them to do up each other's hair the way Sorsha always wore hers. While they were putting flowers in their hair the boys took their turn and went upstairs to change into their outfits. The girls finished their hair just as Phoenix and Decklyn came down the ladder from the loft. Their outfits looked nothing like the girls springy ones. They were wearing long white shirts and brown breezy pants. Satisfied, the protectors headed out towards the Whispering Wood where the festival was to take place.

Once they arrived at the Whispering Wood, they were amazed as to what they saw in front of them. The forest was hopping with fairies, sprites, villagers, and woodland creatures. The village women and girls were all doing their hair in flowers from the Hidden Garden and the men were all laughing and taking out weird looking instruments. Queen Lavinia and her fairies were rushing around sparkling up the place and making sure Aged Sir Oak looked his best. He was covered in sparkling acorns again and lots of ribbons of greens and blues. Sorsha was trying to get the sprites to wear sparkling blue ribbons that the fairies had made, but she wasn't succeeding very well. "Sorsha would you like some help?" asked Tiffany.

As soon as Tiffany spoke there was a hush over the crowd. Turning heads and looking to see whoever spoke, everybody suddenly burst out in a cheer loud enough to shake the ground. For the sight of the four protectors was joyous for all. Villagers came up to them and shook their hands while fairies were buzzing around them sprinkling sparkles everywhere. "Let's here it for the protectors!" shouted Balfour.

"Hip-hip hooray! Hip-hip hooray!" everyone shouted.

Aged Sir Oak's booming voice was heard over everybody's shouts, "Protectors so glad you are all here. I must say I did miss Pike too. Glad you are all safe and sound. We all look forward to your stories, but let's get on with the festival first, shall we?"

Before everybody went back to what they were doing Queen Lavinia had her fairies bring out flower crowns she had made up for Piper and Tiffany. Once they were placed on their heads Piper and Tiffany curtsied in thanks and went to help Sorsha round up the sprites again. It was a difficult task, but once they had on their blue sparkly ribbons, they scampered off to go play with some of the village boys. "Sorsha, you look wonderful today." said Piper.

She was right too. Sorsha was dressed in a long white and pink dress and had her hair all done up in white and pink flowers.

"Thank you, Piper. I really have Queen Lavinia to thank and her fairies because I told them I wanted to look great for the festival today. Was it dreadful in the castle Piper? Was Lady Morphana mean to you?" asked Sorsha.

"It was dreadful, but I didn't let it show. That is what Lady Morphana would have wanted, to see my misery, but I didn't want her to have that satisfaction. And she was no meaner than she usually is."

"Let's go help some of the village women with the food set up and then we can begin the festival of fun." suggested Sorsha.

So, the girls were off to help set up the food tables. The forest didn't look like a forest. In fact, it looked like a wedding reception hall. There was a big table over by Aged Sir Oak for the important members of the forest committee and the protectors. Just next to that was a small stage where it looked like a band was being set up. There were round tables everywhere for the rest of the villagers to sit and the sprites and unicorns just sat on the ground waiting for the festivities to begin. The boys were helping the village men set up the stage for the music and talking about their journey home last night.

Once everything was set up some of the villagers took the stage and began playing the strange instruments. It was a sound that brought about peace and happiness to the crowd around them. Sprites and unicorns began to dance and some of the village girls danced with them.

Everybody was having fun listening to the music and dancing. Piper went up towards the band and was taught how to play the violin. It wasn't as hard as it looked, in fact Piper liked playing the violin now. She was told by her mother that she had to play a musical instrument in high school and that it was either going to be the flute or the violin. Piper had chosen the violin because it was much louder and prettier sounding than the flute. She just hadn't started lessons yet at school. Boy won't her mother be proud.

Taking Piper aside, Sorsha showed her how she could use the violin to bewitch the mind. As she stroked the strings, she began to realize everybody was calmer and some of them were dancing lightly around. Everything Piper was thinking was coming out in the strokes of the violin strings and that was how she could bewitch the mind. She was imagining her music would soon make people cry and it did!

After Piper played the violin Queen Lavinia buzzed up onto the stage and spoke so that all could hear her. "Ladies, gentlemen, and woodland creatures! Today is the day of the grand festival, but it is also a day of joy for we have all four of the protectors of the ice crystals here with us to celebrate!" The crowd went wild, and it took her a minute to calm them down again before she could continue, "Let us begin our fest and then we can continue on with fun games and stories from our new friends."

Everybody began taking their seats. Piper, Decklyn, Phoenix, and Tiffany took their places at the head table by Aged Sir Oak while Pike and his sprite friends sat down on the ground around them. Sorsha took her seat next to Tiffany and Balfour sat on Decklyn's other side. Once everybody had a seat Queen Lavinia took out her magic wand and waved it twice in a circle and instantly plates of food appeared in front of everyone. There was so much food to choose from that it was hard to decide what to eat first. Phoenix, however, was digging into everything. "Phoenix, don't you think you should slow down and chew your food?" whispered Piper.

Through mouthfuls of food Phoenix replied, "I would but this is all so good compared to the bread and water we were getting at Morphana's."

There was really a lot of food; berries and nuts (for the forest creatures) every kind of pie you could think of, salads, and different kinds of meats. Everybody ate until they couldn't stuff themselves anymore. It didn't take long for everything to quickly disappear either. With a wave of her wand again Queen Lavinia had everything moved and picked up. The only thing left was the stage for the band to continue playing their music from the olden days. The men and boys brought out their bows and arrows and began a game of archery while the kids took turns ridding the unicorns throughout the forest. The women of the village were sitting around Sorsha and Queen Lavinia in hopes of learning some new spells on how to clean up their kitchens the way the queen cleaned up the feast.

Tiffany decided she was going to go play hide and seek with Pike and some of his friends. As she took off towards the meadow Phoenix said he was going to go learn how to shoot a bow the old-fashioned way. Decklyn just looked at Piper as if to ask can I go too? She gave him a smile and he took off right behind Phoenix. Piper looked around and decided she needed some time to think about things. She went over and told Aged Sir Oak she was going to take a walk towards the brook, and he said that was fine he just wanted her to take one of the nymphs with her. Looking down towards the ground Piper saw what a nymph really looked like. They were tiny people about the of a Barbie doll. Piper noticed that there were lots of them and that she just noticed them now because they were all dressed in greens that made them blend in with the forest floor. There were small men ones and women ones. The one that came up to Piper was a girl and she tugged on Piper's dress as if to say pick me up. Bending down, Piper held out her hand so that the nymph could climb up. Picking her up and placing her on her shoulder, Piper waved to Aged Sir Oak and headed towards the brook.

Once out of sight the nymph spoke in Piper's ear, "You know some of the nymphs aren't happy about your return."

Looking at the nymph Piper asked, "Why is that? I thought you guys were on our side?"

"Some of us are and some of us aren't. I personally am glad you are all home safe, but my mother who favors Lady Morphana says she had hoped today would be a gloomy day." Said the nymph.

"I don't understand though. Why are some of you on Morphana's side? Don't they know she is evil, and she wants to destroy Shelvockwood?" Piper replied with a concerned look on her face.

"Some of the elder nymphs believe that Lady Morphana will bring back her mother from the dead and they fear that if they aren't on her side, they will die with the other creatures of Shelvockwood. My mother told me I was foolish for thinking that a bunch of kids could save us, but if you asked me, I would rather put my life on the line than to live an eternity under the rule of Lady Morphana." said the nymph.

"Well, I guess you can't change the mind of the elders, but I am glad to know that there are some of you on our side. Are there a lot of nymphs?" Piper asked.

"Yes." said the nymph, "There are tons of us. We hide in the forest floor and come out only to get rations. We dress in colors of the forest floor so that we can hide if we need to. Like I said there are half of us that like you and the other half doesn't like you."

"Well, I guess that is a good thing. Can't you talk to your mother and persuade her? Tell her that we won't let her down?" Piper asked while looking towards the tiny nymph.

"My mother is stubborn. She is set in her ways, kind of like Aged Sir Oak is. He isn't fond of the elder nymphs either. Says they are nothing but troublemakers for Shelvockwood. He doesn't turn the believers away though; says we have potential and courage. By the way, my name is Nefertiti. What is yours?"

"That is a pretty name, from the Egyptians. My name is Piper. Kind of ordinary." replied Piper.

"No, I like ordinary. Lady Morphana must have been really upset and down if she didn't even try to interrupt the festival.

Either that or something happened to take her mind off attacking the festival. That one is even scarier than the her being upset and attacking." said Nefertiti.

"Well, let's just enjoy today then. It isn't every day that Lady Morphana ignores everybody especially if she is mad like you said." Piper said.

The two of them continued their way towards the shady brook. Neither of them had a care in the world and were just enjoying each other's company.

☙❧

Meanwhile Lady Morphana was sitting on her throne looking down at Perlangitis. "Why have you come back? I told you to leave my castle and never come back. Then you show up at the door of my chambers and act like nothing has happened. I told you to leave again and you followed me to my throne. What do you want Perlangitis?" asked a rather upset Morphana.

"Morphana, you don't scare me like you scare everybody else. You try so hard to act like your mother, but deep down you aren't like her at all. Don't give me that look; you and I both know it is true. She tried to make you evil like her, but you are nothing like her. You want so much to be like them down there. That is why you can't hurt any of them." Perlangitis said while pointing to the people in her crystal ball.

Standing up instantly Morphana was outraged. "I do not want to be like them. I never in my life wanted to be like them. My mother had a chance to be like them and she told me what it did to her heart. Almost melted it, can't have that. I need to have my icy heart and you being here isn't going to help it stay that way." she yelled.

"Come on now." Perlangitis said with a smile as he started walking towards Lady Morphana. "I know you don't want an icy heart. I almost had you completely melted too until your mother, the retched woman that she is interfered. That is why you sent me away huh? You know I was trying to melt your heart and your mother warned you about me before she died huh? How did she die anyway? I never did find out in my travels."

Looking rather dumbfounded Lady Morphana simply pointed to the door and said, "Get out!"

"Morphana, I am not leaving. Even if I must go live down in the village and dress like one of them so you won't find me, I will. And believe me I will win." Perlangitis said as he headed towards the door. "By the way, I left you a present in your chambers before I followed you down here to your throne. I hope you like him and take good care of him; you are all he has now."

Perlangitis was out the door. Getting up rather quickly and walking to one of the windows Morphana saw with her own eyes Perlangitis walking on her grounds below and then in an instant he vanished as if by magic. Furious as to his arrival and the whole mishap with the protectors she started running through her castle. Passing goblins who moved in fear and statues of gargoyles. Up the stairs she ran her long black cape trailing behind her. Images of old family passed her on the walls and the big picture of her mother passed as she came to an incredible halt in front of her bedroom door. Taking a deep breath before she opened her door, Lady Morphana turned her doorknob and threw open the door. Walking slowly into her chambers she looked around the room for something odd. Everything looked the same. Dark and gloomy except for her window shades were now drawn open. Looking rather disgusted at the sunlight now pouring into her room she walked over to the window and shut the shades. As her eyes started getting adjusted to the darkness again, she noticed a big egg sitting on her bed with a note leaning up against it.

As she came up to the egg, she noticed that it was spotted rather funny and sort of moving. Grabbing the note, she read:

To my dearest Morphana,

Inside this egg you will find the thing you have wanted since you were little, but your
mother would never let you have. I my love have gone to the ends of the world to
find one for you. When you finally notice the egg it will be in the process of hatching.
Take care of him my love for he is just a baby and you will be the first thing he sees
when he hatches. The old hag I bought him from said he was the last of his kind
and that he will either be nasty or one of the kindest of his kind. I have placed a
spell on him that you will never be able to break. He won't be evil, but will be an
angel and the last of his kind. Please keep him and think of me when he is around
you.
If you decide that you want to work things out and melt that icy heart your mother
has given you let me know. I will be around. Take care my love and remember
you can change who you are. You don't have to be like your father; pure evil.

Sincerely yours,
Perlangitis

Taking the note and stuffing it in the pocket of her cape Morphana looked like she was about to cry. Before she could think of anything though, her thoughts were distracted by the shattering of the egg. Pieces went flying everywhere and standing no more than two feet high on her bed was a tiny brown dragon. He shook off the remaining pieces of the eggshell from his body and lightly coughed a little bit. No fire flew from his mouth, but some smoke came from there. Looking up at Lady Morphana the dragon started hobbling towards her and crying for attention. Bending down and petting his tiny head Morphana said, "I am your mother. I must say you are the cutest thing I have ever seen. Boy wouldn't my mother be royally mad if she only knew what was sitting on my bed. I shall call you Scales."

◎○◎

The festival lasted all day and for most of the night. It wasn't until late when the moon was held high in the sky that everybody started getting weary. Nymphs ran into dark holes in the ground while sprites sprinted off deep into the woods with the unicorns. Villagers were gathering up the children and lighting up torches to see on their journey home. Fairies were heading towards the tree branches and turning out their wings. Once everybody left it was just the four friends, Sorsha, Queen Lavinia, Balfour, and Aged Sir Oak. Pike had fallen asleep on some of Aged Sir Oak's upper branches. Looking up at him, Aged Sir Oak couldn't help but smile. He had missed the little guy. Turning his attention to everybody below Aged Sir Oak said, "I must say that was a marvelous festival. I don't remember ever having one like that before."

"I will agree with you there Aged Sir Oak. Our festivals before weren't as amusing. I loved the story you told Phoenix of Will the Willow. I never knew he had it in him to be like that." chuckled Sorsha.

"I rather enjoyed that story too Sorsha, but my favorite had to be the escape they did last night from Lady Morphana's grounds. Brilliant!" Balfour said while patting Phoenix and Decklyn on their backs.

112

Buzzing up to where everyone would be able to see her Queen Lavinia said, "Yes that story had to be the best thus far. I am worried as to why nobody has heard a peep from Lady Morphana. She must have been furious when she found out and I can't imagine she just dropped it like that. I thought for sure when you told me this morning Balfour that all the protectors were back and Pike too that she would be attacking today. I don't think she just ignored it because of the festival. She wouldn't care."

Turning towards the queen Piper said, "Actually I was talking to a nymph earlier today and she had suggested that Lady Morphana could have been distracted by something that off set her madness towards us." Receiving looks from all the forest committee Piper asked, "Is something wrong?"

"Actually, yes there is Piper. Do you know which Nymph you talked to?" asked a worried Sorsha.

"Her name was Nefertiti." replied Piper.

All of them took deep breaths and then Aged Sir Oak replied, "Ok Nefertiti you can believe. She is one of the nymphs that is on our side. I am assuming she told you about all of that though?"

"Yes, she explained it all rather nicely to me, but I for a second think we should take into consideration that she may be right. Lady Morphana may have had a bigger distraction to take her mind off all of us. If that is the case that is not good." replied Nefertiti.

"Hold the phone." Phoenix said, "What are you all talking about? She is ok cause she is on our side and blah blah blah. Someone explain something to me. What's going on?"

Piper then relayed to everyone her walk to the shady brook with Nefertiti. Once she was done Balfour said, "Well if this is all true, we all must be on the lookout for Lady Morphana now. I would hate to think something distracted her from your escape. Whatever her reasoning for not attacking today cannot be a good thing."

While they were all discussing what needed to be done in preparation for Lady Morphana's plans to attack, Tiffany was still sitting on the ground where some of the villagers were learning small potions and spells. She was mixing some herbs and pretty liquids together in one of the cauldrons. Not really listening to what everybody was talking about, she dropped a small blackberry into the cauldron and instantly jumped when a loud bang was made, and a blue cloud rose from the cauldron. Everybody turned and looked at Tiffany and with shocked expressions seemed to ask what she was doing. "I was just throwing some stuff in the cauldron. I didn't think I would create anything. I don't even know what I did create." Tiffany replied.

Flying over to where Tiffany was sitting on the ground, Queen Lavinia looked down at the stuff in the cauldron and the blue cloud floating in midair just above it. Turning around to everyone she said, "Tiffany has created a potion to look into the future."

Tiffany showed Sorsha and Queen Lavinia everything she threw into the cauldron right down to the one blackberry needed to complete the potion. Gathering up all the cauldrons and potions Sorsha was ready to head home. "Sorsha let me help you with those. I will walk you home too before I myself head home." Balfour offered.

"Why thank you Balfour. That would be much appreciated." Sorsha said.

Once Balfour and Sorsha had said their goodnights and were out of sight the queen said her goodnights and flew up to one of the tree branches and blew out her wings. Aged Sir Oak gently grabbed Pike and with one of his big branches and placed him down on some moss and dried leaves beneath his tree. Turning to the four protectors in front of him Aged Sir Oak said, "Goodnight protectors. I am so glad to have you all back safe and sound. Have a safe journey home and get a good nights rest. I overheard Queen Lavinia and Sorsha talking about throwing a spells and charms sleep over. If that is the case Decklyn, Phoenix you two will be off learning things with Balfour for the night and will be sleeping with Pike under the stars."

Phoenix looked at Decklyn as if to say great and Decklyn couldn't help but laugh. After saying their goodbyes to Aged Sir Oak the four friends were off towards the fort. The walk home wasn't as long as they thought it would be. Once inside, they all climbed up the ladder and jumped into bed. They all fell asleep without changing from their clothes.

Chapter 9

Spells and Charms Sleep Over

The morning of the sleepover had the girls so excited. "Tiff, can you remember the last time we had a sleepover?" Piper asked excitedly.

Laughing just a little Tiffany said, "Piper it was just before we came to Shelvockwood."

"Oh, right. Well, that was just you and me. I am talking about a sleepover when you have a bunch of girls over. This one is going to be different I know it. There won't be scary movies and popcorn, but spells and who knows what else." Piper blurted out.

As the boys made their way down the ladder, they could hear the girls gabbing away in the kitchen. "My aren't we all excited this morning." Phoenix said. Turning to Decklyn he asked, "How come you aren't as cheerful in the morning Deck? Not a morning person are you buddy? Aww come here I will give you a big hug and make you feel all cheerful inside."

Dodging his wide-open arms Decklyn replied, "Get away from me man. I don't need to be that cheerful in the mornings. Besides we have 'manly' things to do today. Balfour said to meet him down in the village bakery this morning. Guess we better get going huh? Sorry to go already girls, but we have manly things to do today."

As Decklyn said manly things, he and Phoenix posed in their

manly stances. It made the girls burst out laughing. "Alright get going then we must get the fort ready for the queen and Sorsha. They have a bunch of nymphs and fairies coming as well and we can't have it looking like you two destroyed it before they got here." Piper said.

After hugging them goodbye and wishing them all the luck in the world the boys headed out the door and were off towards the village. Turning back towards Piper, Tiffany said, "Let's get cleaning then."

And for about an hour and a half the girls cleaned the fort from top to bottom. They started up in the loft and made sure that all the beds were made and that all the clothes were picked up off the floor. Heading back downstairs they picked up the throw pillows and bean bag chairs and made it look homier. After that they headed into the kitchen to pick up the breakfast mess that they had left there. Just as they started sweeping up the floors there was a knock on the door. Tiffany ran over to it and threw it open. Standing outside waiting patiently was Sorsha, Queen Lavinia, some of her fairies in waiting, and Nefertiti and some of her nymph friends. The girls welcomed them in and as soon as the door was shut the queen and Sorsha began their spell of hiding the fort from Lady Morphana's crystal ball. "This is so she can't see what spells and charms we make." said Nefertiti.

Once the spell was done, they all got started on making the fort look like a potions lab. Instead of lots of junk food, sleeping bags all over the floor, and a pile of horror movies there was a black cauldron on the kitchen table (took up most of the table) with candles all around it, spices and herbs lined up ready to use, and all the windows had their curtains drawn closed so that nobody could look in. Not only were there candles around the cauldron, but everywhere you looked there were candles. Once the last candle was placed, Queen Lavinia lit them all with one wave of her wand. The fort looked like something out of a Halloween movie.

Piper and Tiffany looked around the fort and couldn't believe how much it reminded them of a witches house. Piper was just about to comment on it when she caught a glimpse of what was lying on the floor in the living room. She nudged Tiffany and pointed towards what she was looking at. Tiffany turned to look at what Piper was pointing at and couldn't believe her eyes. Lying on the floor of the living room surrounded by all the throw pillows and bean bag chairs was a Ouija board. It didn't look like the ones that Milton Bradley made. It was made from real wood and smoothed over to shine. The Ouija board wasn't shaped like a square either, but mis shaped to add a more unique touch to it. Sorsha must have noticed the looks on the girls faces for she said, "Don't worry we use the Ouija board to ask it specific questions about Lady Morphana. We don't ask it anything dark and eerie."

"So, what do we really do at these parties? I mean do we just sit around and cast spells or gossip?" asked Tiffany.

Chuckling lightly Sorsha said, "We do both. We all learn new spells and teach old ones to protect us from Lady Morphana, but at the same time we gossip too. What is a sleepover without gossiping?"

"Well, I am ready to learn. Let's get this party going." said an overexcited Piper.

And with that they all gathered around the cauldron. Sorsha showed everything before she put it in the pot. She made sure to point out what everything was as well. The first spell she made in the cauldron was used to attract a persons inner nice side. Dumping in the cauldron first was a dash of rosemary. They sprinkled in was a few apple seeds which were followed by a few daisy leaves. Stirring the liquid rather lightly Sorsha said, "All it needs now is a touch of fairy dust and we can then test it out."

"Umm, isn't it a bit dangerous to test it out on us? What if it doesn't work? How will we know?" asked a worried Nefertiti.

"Not to worry dear. It will work just fine." Queen Lavinia replied with confidence.

Once the fairy dust was added the potion turned a light bluish color. Pouring just a bit into a tiny glass Sorsha handed it over to Piper. "Take a tiny sip." She said to Piper.

Giving the liquid a rather funny look, Piper took a sip of it. Rather surprisingly it didn't taste that bad. Tasted like blueberries. Looking up at Sorsha as if to ask what next Piper saw above Sorsha's shoulder a tiny version of Sorsha, but instead of looking pleasant and happy this Sorsha looked miserable and mean. Taking a few steps back Piper gave a look of horror and instantly everybody wanted to know what was wrong. "Piper, what is it? What's wrong?" asked Tiffany while rushing over to her friends side.

Before Piper could reply Queen Lavinia spoke, "You didn't see Sorsha's good side did you Piper? You saw what her bad side would be, if she went bad. Listen up all of you. This potion does show the nicer side to someone if they are bad to begin with. In all our cases if we took this potion, we would see each other's bad sides. This potion not only can show what an evil person could become, but what a good person could become as well. Anybody else want to try it before we move on?"

Tiffany wanted to see what everybody would be like if they became evil, so she took a sip of it as well. Following Tiffany was Nefertiti and some of her friends. The fairies stayed away. Once everybody got a sip, shocked faces went around the table. Piper couldn't help but think that Tiffany could never become the person she saw above her shoulder. Tiffany was just looking at Piper and then back in the direction to her left shoulder as if comparing the two Piper's.

Once the potion wore off (which did take a few moments to do) Sorsha and Queen Lavinia were getting ready for the next potion. Once the cauldron was clean and they could see excited faces around them, the queen began the next spell. This time the queen was putting nasty smelly things into the cauldron. First went in what looked like a few dead worms, which were followed by pepper, basil and a few green leaves. As Sorsha stirred the pot Queen Lavinia turned to her viewers and said, "This potion that we are making is for getting rid of evil from a person's body. And I can see by some of your faces that the smell is getting to you. I know what the next question is. Yes, it is true. Does this potion have to be swallowed to work? The answer is yes, my friends." As she got horrified faces, she went on, "Let's say Piper went evil. Her friends don't want to just give up on her. They don't have to. They simply make this potion and get her to take it. That is the hard part, getting her to take it. Nobody would want to swallow something as vile smelling as this. If Piper did indeed take this potion, she would kill all the evil inside her and would be pure and good again. Any questions?"

Everybody looked sick to their stomachs rather than having questions, but there was one hand that did go up. Nefertiti raised her tiny little hand and asked, "If someone was evil to begin with, could they take this potion and become good?"

Looking at Sorsha, Queen Lavinia answered, "Actually Nefertiti, it doesn't work that way. Why do you ask?"

Looking down to the floor as if she didn't want to say why, Nefertiti replied, "Because my mother is pure evil, and I was hoping I could turn her around."

"It takes more than just potions and spells to get someone's heart, it takes love. If your mother loved you at all that should be enough to break her evil curse." said Sorsha while giving Nefertiti a pat on the back.

As they all started to clean up the mess for the next potion Piper and Tiffany walked into the living room to talk for a bit. They both were obviously upset about the new potions they had learned. "I didn't know we were going to learn things like this. I don't know if I like it too much." said Tiffany.

"I don't like it either, but we must look on the positive side of things. We may need these potions later unfortunately. Who knows if one of us goes evil." Piper said.

Nodding her head in agreement, Tiffany and Piper walked back into the kitchen and positioned themselves around the table to see the next potion. Little did they know that they would need one of the potions sooner than they thought.

ᐁᗄᐂ

Meanwhile Decklyn and Phoenix had made it to the village and were in the process of learning how to get ready for their first goblin hunt. "You see how the blade bends when you throw your weight into it? That is so you don't really cut the goblins but frighten them into giving up. I had the queen and some of her fairy friends put some magic into these swords. I don't believe in violence, just justice." Balfour said while throwing the blade in Phoenix's direction.

Jumping out of the way Phoenix yelled, "What are you mad? I am not a goblin. I am deathly afraid of getting cut."

Laughing Decklyn said, "Phoenix, Balfour just said that the blade bends. Now why would you move out of the way? Watch, I won't move. Go ahead Balfour."

Watching with huge eyes Phoenix observed his friend be almost slashed with the blade of the sword. To his astonishment though Decklyn didn't move at all. The blade did. As if to say I shouldn't be hurting anybody you throw me at.

"I still don't care. Whether it does move out of my way or not. I don't like it. How are we to catch these goblins anyway. Aren't they fast and tricky? They may look dumb, but they are rather smart I think." Phoenix replied.

"Phoenix, I would like you to meet Gabriel. He is one of the

121

newest villagers and used to be a goblin himself." Balfour said while chuckling at Phoenix's reaction.

"How is that possible? He is too tall and doesn't look ugly at all. I mean for a man. I don't get it." coughed Phoenix.

"That is a long story, but to shorten it up some, Queen Vespera." With shocked looks Gabriel continued, "Yes, I said her name. She doesn't scare me now that she is dead. Anyway, I was walking through the woods one day hunting goblins that had disturbed my garden. Out of nowhere Queen Vespera popped up in a cloud of purple smoke. Dark and disturbing she was. Long black silky hair and a long-crooked nose. She laughed with an evil laugh worse than Lady Morphana's. As she talked, she raised her hands in the air. As long as I live, I will never forget what she said as she raised her hands. "You who so desperately threatens goblins shall become one until the day you die." And once she threw her hands back down in my direction I began to shrink down to size and before I knew it, I was an ugly goblin. I probably wouldn't have lived long either amongst the real goblins, they would have seen right through me. After she had left, just as quickly as she had arrived, I was encountered by Pike. He had come from around one of the willow trees nearby. After seeing the whole thing, he walked me to Aged Sir Oak and the forest committee. Explaining everything to them, I was taken into protective custody by the village. After many months of trying to break the curse Queen Lavinia and Sorsha managed to break it. I became a man again and vow to capture every goblin I came across. I was very thankful never to run into Vespera again as long as she lived, but that is another story you will learn someday. Disturbing as it may be." Gabriel said while gathering up his belongings for the journey to the Whispering Wood.

Watching Gabriel with the other men was amusing. Decklyn and Phoenix thought it was interesting to see how he looked like a big football player in high school with all his buddies around him.

Once they were all ready to go out looking for goblins, they headed through the village waving as they passed onlookers. Just outside the village was the edge of the meadow. They had to walk through the whole meadow before they finally got to the Whispering Wood. On their way through the meadow though Phoenix had another question he just had to ask. "Why is the Whispering Wood called the Whispering Wood? Things don't seem to be whispering in there."

"Well Phoenix" Balfour started, "It was a long time ago when everybody was afraid to leave their homes. Queen Vespera was so powerful that everybody feared for their lives. So, for any of us to get anything done, or even plan an attack on her, we had to meet in the forest and for years we all whispered in there so she wouldn't be able to hear us planning anything. Ever since then it was just called the Whispering Wood."

"Oh, I see." Phoenix replied. "Well, let's just get on with this hunt and no more shop talk it is too depressing."

There was not another word until they hit the edge of the Whispering Wood. Decklyn quickly pointed in the direction of the entrance and quietly said, "There is a tiny cluster of them just in there. What do we do when we catch them?"

"We scare them with our blades and then the other men sneak around them and throw sacks over them. It sounds easy enough, but it really isn't. They are fast and tricky. So, we must move fast. Lady Morphana sends them out to do evil work and catch sprites and fairies. Let's get a move on." Gabriel said.

So, with that Phoenix and some of the other men snuck around to the back of the goblin pack while Decklyn, Balfour, and Gabriel had the swords and where ready for some action. It all happened so fast. Swords swinging one way, goblins running the other way and men falling everywhere with sacks. Phoenix managed to grab one and was having a hard time trying to keep the thing from running away while he still had a hold of the sack. It was a funny sight to see. All in all, when they were all said and done, they managed to catch ten goblins. The journey back to the village was a long one. The goblins didn't just give up. They put up a good fight. Once they got them all down to the village it was time to celebrate their victory. Passing by you wouldn't really know what the men in the village were up to, but if you passed the bakery, you would see the fun that was going on inside.

⊘⊘

While the men were celebrating and the girls were having fun at their spell sleepover, Lady Morphana was feeding Scales some meat links that she got from the kitchen. Looking up at Morphana, Scales purred like a cat happy that it got some milk in a saucer. Petting him just under his chin Morphana said, "You are the one thing I have always wanted when I was younger, but my mother would never let me have. I don't know why, but I was forbidden to have a pet dragon. I know why Perlangitis sent you. He is trying to win my heart by sending you to me. It is going to take more than just you to win me over."

Satisfied that she was just petting him Scales gave a little cough and out shot some smoke. He was still too tiny to shoot flames yet, but once he got bigger, he would be able to do just that. Just as he hopped off the bed there was a knock at her door. "Who is it?" Lady Morphana demanded.

"It's just us my lady. Gumbo and myself. We wanted to make sure that you were ok. We heard some noise earlier." Slobbo replied.

"Come in then if you must see with your own eyes that I am alright." Morphana sighed while she descended the bed herself.

Upon entering her chambers Gumbo froze in fear. His eyes became as big as potatoes, and he turned as white as if he had just seen a ghost. "Why what is the matter Gumbo? You cannot tell me you are afraid of this little puny dragon." chuckled Lady Morphana.

Taking a deep breath he replied, "Actually most of my kind was wiped out years ago by dragons. I don't remember what kind wiped us out, but ever since then we all have been afraid of them."

"Well, Scales is just a baby. I can train him to like who I want and hate who I want. It's a good thing you goblins are on my side this time huh?" she said while laughing evilly. "Slobbo, I want you to bring me some more of that meat that you gave me earlier. Scales absolutely loved it."

"Right away my lady. Is there anything else you would like us to do? We will inform the grounds immediately of the baby dragon if you want us to." Slobbo said.

"Yes, let them all know not to anger me for I can train Scales to do my evil bidding now and don't have to rely on ogres anymore. Let them all know as well that I want to keep him a secret for as long as I can." Lady Morphana said with a yawn.

"Alright my lady." Slobbo said. Gumbo and Slobbo were out the door and down the hall quick as a snap. Gumbo didn't want to stick around any longer than he had too and Slobbo just wanted to inform the grounds as soon as possible so they knew not to upset Lady Morphana for they had a reason to fear her now.

Chapter 10

Fun in the Meadow

It was a few weeks into fall before the leaves really started to change throughout the land of Shelvockwood. After the fun time the boys had with the village men and the girls had with the charms party, they were in no rush to jump into anything major just yet. The few weeks that did pass by were just as calm as the Shady Brook on a sunny day. The four friends spent many days walking through the Hidden Garden learning its many passageways. It was on this day though that things began to pick up again.

"What do we have planned today? Anything interesting? I am getting fidgety with all the picnics we take. I need some action." Phoenix was saying to Tiffany.

"I think Piper had us going to the meadow today to watch all the unicorns and children play." Looking at Phoenix's reaction Tiffany went on, "I think it would be good for us to play with some of the village children and let them know that we aren't all as bad as their parents make us out to be. And as for the unicorns they fear their own shadows. Piper seems to think if we make a game out of hanging out with them that they will soon not be so paranoid around us."

The four friends were off towards the meadow for a fun filled day with the unicorns and children of the village. Phoenix had to admit that it wouldn't be so bad playing with them. He did want to run around a bit.

Once they reached the meadow, they all noticed that the children were already playing with some of the unicorns. Running this way and that and laughing the whole time. Just as they were about to enter the meadow one of the children grabbed Decklyn's arm. "I wouldn't just go out and start playing if I were you. My mother always told me to make sure that they really were children I was playing with. She said so many of their children disappeared because they were off playing with other children, and they turned out to be nasty goblins. I don't know if I trust the unicorns either. What if they stomp on me?"

"I wouldn't worry about the unicorns. They are more scared of you than you are of them. And as for the children, I can see your mother's point, but I think that unicorns can tell real children from fake ones. It doesn't look like they are too scared of these kids. Let's ask if we can play with them." Decklyn replied to the little girl. "What is your name by the way?"

"My name is Clara." She replied while turning her foot in the ground and holding her head down.

"Don't be shy of him Clara. He is nothing but a big kid himself." said Phoenix to Clara while he punched Decklyn in the arm.

So, the five of them headed into the middle of the meadow. All the children and unicorns stopped their games to find out who was in the meadow. One of the unicorns spoke up first, "Do you all want to play with us? We were just getting ready to play a game of..." he was cut off however by another unicorn.

"We don't know who they are. Can't ask someone to play games with us if we have no idea what they want. They could be working for her." said the other unicorn rather snotty.

"Pardon me, but we aren't working for Lady Morphana. We are the four protectors of the ice crystals, and this is our friend Clara.

127

Is it ok if we play some of your meadow games with you?" Piper asked while looking at the unicorn.

"If you are the protectors of the ice crystals then show us your crystals. It's not that we don't trust you, its just well. Yeah, we don't trust you. We need proof." said the unicorn.

Phoenix, Decklyn, Tiffany, and Piper took out their crystals to show the onlookers. Stumped and rather dumbfounded the unicorn said, "Sorry I doubted you protectors, but with Lady Morphana turning her ogres into trees and goblins into children it is hard to trust many. My name is Sparuxe, and this is Chanbo. We were all just going to start a game of hide and seek if you all wanted to join us." said Sparuxe.

"How in the name of everything that is holy can you play hide and seek in the opening? Everybody will be able to see where you are." Phoenix said while giving the others a look of can you believe this joker?

"That is easy." started Chanbo. "First, we pick someone to close their eyes and start counting. While they are counting everybody else runs throughout the meadow and finds a good hiding spot. The wheat is so tall in the meadow that it is easy to hide. You just must lay flat on your stomach. It is harder for the seeker to find us because they are searching for us, we can move away from them. With the wind blowing already it is hard to tell if someone is moving away from you or if it is the wind."

"Sounds like a fair game." Decklyn said. "I'm in."

Sparuxe said he would start out being the seeker. Once he started counting everybody went scattering in different directions throughout the meadow. Little did they know that in a few hours' time they would be running towards their homes and the forest for protection.

"Scales my dear would you like to go spread your wings? I haven't let you out once since I have had you and you have grown so much." Which was true. Scales was now the size of a great Dane. "I think its time for you to enjoy the fresh air. Do not hurt anybody though." as Lady Morphana said that Scales hung his head to the ground and she continued, "You can bring home captured creatures though, just don't hurt them or eat them."

After she gave him a good pat on the head and unchained his collar, Morphana opened the stable doors and Scales took off into the sky. She knew he had been wanting to stretch since he was put up in the stable. Poor thing. Just as he was rounding the corner of the sky above Slobbo came running to the stable. "Oh, you let him out. I was going to have someone's head."

"Not to worry Slobbo. Scales needed to be let out. He needed to stretch. Besides I wanted him to get to know the protectors a little bit." laughed Morphana. "Now is your chance to clean up his pen while he is out of it."

Morphana was off towards the castle while Slobbo was left to clean up the mess Scales had left behind.

⟨χ⟩

It was now close to midday, and everybody was still enjoying the game of hide and seek. Piper had just found Sparuxe and Pike when she heard a scream in the distance. Instantly everybody in hiding stood up and looked around to see where the scream had come from. Tiffany was running towards Piper and waving her hands towards the sky. Looking up towards the sky everybody started screaming at this point and running towards the forest. "What is that?" Phoenix asked while standing next to the other three.

All four of the friends appeared to be mesmerized by this flying creature. However, as it started to get closer Decklyn said,

"I think we better start moving. It looks like a dragon!" Picking up a bit of adrenaline they started running as fast as they could towards the forest. Most of the unicorns and sprites made it to the forest because they were faster than the others. But for most of the village children, like Clara, they were still somewhat in the open meadow. The unicorns ran back out into the meadow to pick up the straggling children. Phoenix and Decklyn managed to grab a few of them too on their way to the forest.

Just before they made it to the forest, however, Scales did a dive and almost took out Piper. She and Tiffany were only a few feet behind Phoenix and Decklyn, so they had to throw themselves on the ground to avoid Scales. Getting up as quickly as they had gotten down on the ground the girls were back up and running for their lives again.

Once inside the forest the protectors turned around to get a good look at Scales. He was still hovering over the meadow, but now seemed interested in getting as close to the forest as possible. Running deeper into the forest were unicorns, sprites, and children. Once out of range of Scales, Phoenix rested against a tree and through breaths said, "Now that we all got our exercise for the day, I think that thing needs to invest in a bell around its neck so we know when it is around."

"I don't think we are done. I mean we still have to go home and after we get through the forest the Hidden Garden is wide open for attacks. How are we going to get home?" Tiffany said through short breaths.

Looking in Tiffany's direction Decklyn said, "Did you forget? You have the crystal of invisibility. We can use that halfway through the forest and then the rest of the way home. Let's go inform Aged Sir Oak first of what is going on so he knows that the village children can't get home."

Heading in Aged Sir Oak's direction the four friends walked. They didn't have to worry about the dragon swooping down on them, but it was flying directly above them. Once they reached Aged Sir Oak, they met the other creatures and children that were in the meadow earlier. Apparently, they weren't the only ones that thought of informing Aged Sir Oak first and he didn't seem happy at all. "She did what?! Pike go and get Sorsha but mind the sky. Nefertiti you go get Queen Lavinia and tell Elanil to get Balfour at once, but for goodness sakes watch the sky! This must be by far one of the worst things she has done." Upon seeing the protectors, Aged Sir Oak gave a great sigh of relief. "Friends come forth. There is much you need to learn now in the short time that we all have."

"What's going on? What do we need to know? I mean it is plain as the eyes can see that that thing in the air is a dragon and that Lady Morphana sent it out to play. So, what do we need to do?" Phoenix replied.

"Phoenix there is more to it than just the dragon. You see Lady Morphana, when she was younger her mother Queen Vespera forbade her to own a dragon. That look portrays the question of why would her evil mother not want her to own a dragon? Well, you see dragons can be either good or evil. It all depends on how you train them. Lady Morphana was only interested in a dragon because her love Perlangitis owned one. Queen Vespera forbade Morphana to see Perlangitis because he was trying to change Morphana. He wanted to make her heart pure."

Looking from Decklyn to Tiffany and Phoenix, Piper turned to Aged Sir Oak and said, "You mean Morphana's love wanted to turn her good and her mother wanted her to stay evil?"

"Yes." Aged Sir Oak answered. "There is more. Queen Vespera used to be good and pure. That was until she met Morphana's father, Empanvic. Now he was a man of pure evil. Coming from a family of evil for centuries. He was wooed by Vespera and vowed to make her his. Empanvic's family was furious with him. They believed that Vespera would never turn to their side and that Empanvic was wasting his time. Vespera proved them all wrong. She became

131

as evil as Empanvic and together they ruled Shelvockwood. For centuries we were all under their rule and power. When Vespera gave birth to a little girl we were all in grave danger. For a child to be born under that kind of evil would certainly bring it to the throne. For years they trained her in the evil ways, and she was by far the evilest offspring known to our world. A few years go by and Vespera was now left with her daughter to raise on her own because Empanvic was killed by the protectors of the ice crystals. Yes, my friends. The newly found friends of ours had killed the king and were now bringing Shelvockwood to our hands. The hands of good. Vespera was furious at the loss of her lover and vowed to bring up her daughter in the name of her late husband. As the years went on, she taught her all that Empanvic had taught her when she was first brought to evil. However, when Morphana was seventeen years old when she ran into a young man by the name of Perlangitis. He was rather strange and just by the looks of him Morphana thought he was like her. Only to find out later that he was good like the protectors who had killed her father only a few years ago. That didn't stop her interest in him though. He had managed to start melting her heart of ice. It didn't take long for Vespera to find out that this man was endangering all that Empanvic and herself were trying to overcome. She forbade her daughter to see him anymore and had him banished from Shelvockwood. Perlangitis did leave for his own safety, but he left Lady Morphana a letter to show her that she would always be on his mind. Vespera would have gotten rid of the letter if she knew he had left her daughter one, but she didn't know he did. He left the letter with me to give to her when the right day would come."

"Has Lady Morphana seen this letter from Perlangitis?" Tiffany asked with curiosity.

"No, my child. She hasn't seen it because just after he was banished Vespera was then killed by the protectors of the ice crystals. Morphana lost everything that Perlangitis had taught her and vowed to get revenge on her parents' deaths." After saying that Aged Sir Oak seemed to trail off.

"Is that all Aged Sir Oak or is there something you aren't telling us?" Decklyn asked while looking into the old tree's eyes.

"Morphana became as evil as her parents after their deaths. With the help of her aunt Sigcerlaw she killed them." As he said these last few words Aged Sir Oak saw the looks on the four friends' faces. Continuing he said, "That is another story for when we have time. Right now, we must worry about whether that dragon is pure evil like Lady Morphana or still on the fence."

"I believe the dragon to be on the fence. Not good or evil." Replied Sorsha running up to Aged Sir Oak. Right behind her was Pike and just in the clearing of the forest was Nefertiti with Queen Lavinia and her fairies. Elanil wasn't far behind with Balfour who was running full force with some of the villagers. As they scooped up their children and hugged them Sorsha said, "If the dragon was evil he would have gone after the unicorns first."

"Why of course! I don't know why I didn't think of that Sorsha." Aged Sir Oak said.

"Ok, for those of us who don't know what is going on can we get some sort of explanation please!" Phoenix replied.

"Oh, but of course Phoenix. Unicorns are very pure creatures. Not only does the old scriptures say that, but they are fast creatures which hold immortality. It is very easy to lure a unicorn too. Whisper a good poem into their ear and they will follow you anywhere." said Sorsha.

"And our horns cure illnesses of all kinds. They don't just bring immortality, but any strange illness can be cured with the liquid inside our horns. This is why evil for so many years has tried to kill us off and take our horns." said Sparuxe.

"This can't be the end of Shelvockwood again, can it? What must be done?" Balfour asked.

"Now calm down Balfour. Shelvockwood is in no danger right

now. The dragon is just out stretching its wings. We must though find out where Lady Morphana got this so-called dragon. The only one she knew of who wanted her to have the dragon more than anything in the world was Perlangitis. Could he be back in town?" Queen Lavinia asked.

"If so then we must find him at once. He is our only hope for restoring Shelvockwood to peace. It's taken us many years to get this far, and I would hate to see it end with Lady Morphana becoming eviler than her parents." Sorsha replied.

"Right you are. Ok Balfour I want you and your villager friends to start looking for this man. He should be aged a bit by now, but still looks like a commoner. On your way home make sure you look towards the sky and do keep those children safe." After Aged Sir Oak said that Balfour and the village men headed off towards the village with the children right by their sides. Next Aged Sir Oak turned to Sorsha and said, "While Balfour is doing that, I want you and Pike to watch over the unicorns in their cave. For the most part I want Pike to be kept out of the open for a while. Sparuxe, you need to make sure all your friends know that Pike and Sorsha are coming to stay for a few days. Let them know what is going on and what happened today out in the meadow."

With that Sparuxe bowed down so that Sorsha could climb on his back. Pike was thrown up on Chanbo and once they were settled, they were off towards the caves of the unicorns. Turning towards the protectors Queen Lavinia said, "You all must be careful. I don't want anything to happen to you on your way home. Send me a sign when you get there safely."

After saying their goodbyes, the friends started heading home through the forest. Once they got the clearing of the Hidden Garden, their view a few hundred feet ahead of them is when they all held hands while Tiffany made them invisible. With some difficulty they made it through the maze of the garden to their fort. Once inside they let go of hands and instantly became visible again. As Piper was drawing one of the curtains closed, she noticed that the dragon was flying back towards the castle. "That was an interesting day don't you think?"

"I would say that the story was more interesting than all the running around we did all day long. I myself would rather hear stories than run around." Decklyn answered. "But yes, I believe today was very interesting. We have learned more about Lady Morphana than we wanted to."

"Almost makes me feel for her. To think that her life was more complicated than ours when we came here. To be stuck in both good and evil must be a hard decision to make." Tiffany said while taking off her coat and hanging it up on the nook by the door.

"I want to know more about how she killed the other protectors. That to me says she is pure evil. Who could really take another life?" Piper asked.

"Well, if anything ever happened to people, I loved very much I would probably kill as well." Decklyn answered.

"True, but I just couldn't imagine doing it either." replied Tiffany.

"I am sure we will hear how the other protectors came to their deaths, but I want to know what that letter said. The one that Perlangitis left behind when he was banished out of Shelvockwood. I bet it said something that would have changed Lady Morphana's mind for good." said Phoenix.

"I bet we could read the letter. Aged Sir Oak has it right? I am sure he would let us read it. Right?" asked Tiffany.

"I don't know Tiff. It was to Morphana personally. I doubt Aged Sir Oak read it himself. It's for her eyes only probably which is how it should be. I wouldn't want everybody and their brother reading a letter Decklyn left for me." Piper said through a yawn. "I am going to head to bed though. All this fresh air and running around did get to me. I will see you guys tomorrow ok."

After saying her goodnights Piper climbed the ladder up to

the loft and was sound asleep in a matter of seconds. Decklyn and Phoenix were more awake than they had been that morning and they were more interested in trying to figure out all the events that happened earlier that day. Tiffany stayed up a bit longer and then went to bed herself. It wasn't until much later that the four friends would find out what had really happened to the other protectors of the ice crystals.

Chapter 11

The Spider Crystal

A fter the encounter with the dragon the protectors kept their eyes open to the sky. That didn't stop them from enjoying themselves in Shelvockwood. On a cool fall day, right before everything started to change, the four friend were sitting by the Shady Brook enjoying the weather and having a picnic. Tiffany was doing Piper's hair up in flowers and ribbons, while Decklyn and Phoenix were trying to shoot berries into each other's mouths. As Piper started to do Tiffany's hair Phoenix and Decklyn decided to throw a ball around. Phoenix threw Decklyn the ball and just as Decklyn reaches for it he trips over a small diamond cut rock. Looking down at what he tripped over Decklyn said with some excitement in his voice, "Hey guys I found something over here. Come look at it."

As Piper put the last finishing touches on Tiffany's hair the girls got up and went over to Phoenix and Decklyn. Looking down at the crystal Tiffany jumped back and said, "Eww, there is a spider in that crystal.'

Looking closer the others saw the spider as well. "What should we do with it? I mean what if it is a trap? I think we should take it to Aged Sir Oak. He knows a lot about Shelvockwood and maybe he knows what this crystal is all about." Phoenix said.

Before going right to Aged Sir Oak with it, Piper pulls out a big brownish color, rather old ratty book from her backpack. Flipping through the index she finds what she is looking for. Turning to that page she begins to read. "Created by Queen Vespera the spider crystal is not good or evil. It is very rare and hard to find. Like a four-leaf clover it brings luck to whoever finds it. It's powers thrive on what is truly stored deep inside, good or evil. Queen Vespera created it to overpower her husband Empanvic and take over the throne. She made it from the flesh of a spider and a diamond rock found deep in one of the caves found in the Whispering Wood."

"By the sounds of it this crystal shouldn't fall into the wrong hands. I guess it is a good thing we came across it and Lady Morphana didn't." Phoenix said.

"We should take it at once to Aged Sir Oak and see if we can hide it somewhere. I would hate for Lady Morphana to find out we had it in our possession." replied Tiffany.

The four friends picked up their picnic, bagged up the spider crystal, and headed off towards Aged Sir Oak. Once they reached him, he threw his branches around. It looked like he was grabbing something in his tree. Holding a squirming Pike upside down by his leg, he bellowed. "Pike what have I told you about running around in my branches!"

"Looks like they are at it again. Didn't take Pike long now did it?" Phoenix chuckled.

"Hey look, it's the protectors." Pike said while still hanging upside down.

Placing him on the ground, Pike ran over to the protectors. Bouncing around like a child with candy Pike asked, "What brings you here today? Did you catch something or find something?"

"Pike leave them alone. Would you at least let them talk?" shouted Aged Sir Oak. "Come friends."

Once they were all sitting around Aged Sir Oak, Piper brought out a small bag. As she unwrapped it Pike and Aged Sir Oak watch with anticipation. Holding the spider crystal up so that all could see it Aged Sir Oak's eyes got huge, and he asked, "Where did you get that?"

"We found it lying on the ground by the Shady Brook during our picnic today. We know a bit about it too. Piper read us something out of an old book she took out of the library in the village." answered Decklyn.

As they told Aged Sir Oak what they knew about the spider crystal from what Piper had told them he said, "If you hold it in the light just right you can make out the spider inside. Not everybody can see it. If you are looking for it, you won't find it. It's when you aren't looking for it that you come across it. Queen Vespera was good at hiding her possessions. She became as evil as Empanvic wanted her to become. It hurt her however when he died. I guess because she couldn't defeat him that way. Whatever you do, don't show this crystal to Balfour or any of the villagers."

With a curious look on her face Piper asked, "Why can't we show Balfour or any of the villagers?"

"They fear the spider crystal. Years ago, when it was made, they thought it was a way for Queen Vespera to read into their minds. Mind reading is a dangerous thing. It took years for any of the villagers to talk to anyone mythical. Whereas the villagers fear this crystal others like Sorsha and Lady Morphana cannot wait to get their hands on one. It is said that the queen only made one of them, but others believe because of her greediness to take over the throne she made more than one of them. The old protectors managed to take the one that we all knew about and hid it before their untimely deaths. I almost wonder if this is that crystal that they hid so many years ago." Aged Sir Oak said.

"So, what exactly does this crystal do? I mean we know where it came from and what the purpose was when it was created, but what we don't know is how its powers really work. Did the other protectors ever use it? asked Phoenix.

"The protectors never used it from what I knew. They just hid it so that nobody could ever find it. I believe that is why they all came to their deaths too. None of them would give up where it was and Lady Morphana got extremely mad. The crystal lives off of the powers deep inside of you. If you are truly good then it will do only good things to help you along the way. If you are pure evil it will help you bring havoc and destruction to all that you do." Aged Sir Oak said while watching another one of his leaves fall to the ground.

"Aged Sir Oak, I am surely going to miss your leaves in a few more weeks." Piper said while picking up one of the leaves that fell from his branches.

Looking down at Piper he said, "As am I my child, but it all comes with the changing of the seasons. If I were you protectors, I would put the spider crystal somewhere only you four know about. Don't even tell me. If someone were to capture anybody and try and pry information out of them about the crystal, they could do it. If they didn't know where the crystal was at least it would be kept safe and out of evil hands."

 measure

Back at the castle Lady Morphana can sense a neutral power. Going over to her cauldron she made up a potion to find out what the power was and where it was coming from. To her surprise the power was coming from the fort of the protectors. Thinking that this had to be the journal that they kept Morphana knew she had to get her hands on it. "Why it must hold powers that I could use against them. I need that journal so I can read all about the secrets that they hold so dear. Slobbo!"

Walking into her potions room Slobbo appeared to have smoke coming from all over his body. Looking up at him Lady Morphana asked, "Why is your body smoking?"

"I was trying to feed Scales my lady and he has a nasty cold." Slobbo said while patting one of his burnt arms.

Laughing just a little Lady Morphana said, "Oh, my poor baby. Make sure he is taken care of at once, but before you go, I want to run this by you first to see what you think. The protectors journal. Is it real or fake?"

"Legend has it my lady that Prudence was the first one to write down their adventures and that she was the first one to come up with a potion to make the book take the thoughts right from their heads. I don't know how it works, but all the protectors must do is touch the book and their adventures for the day would be recorded in the book" replied Slobbo.

Pacing back and forth Morphana began to smile. "I really must get my hands on that journal. If that is true and it does tell their thoughts and adventures, it must hold the thoughts and adventures of the protectors before them. I really would like to know what Prudence was thinking right before she died. I want that book. I don't care how you get it. I want it here tonight. I must know what it holds."

Slobbo was out the door and walking fast towards the barn. He needed to make sure Scales was taken care of first and then he would have to think of a way to get the protectors journal.

☙❧

Back at the fort Decklyn and Phoenix were sitting at the table in the kitchen trying to figure out where to hide the spider crystal. "I personally think we should hide it under the bed. To an average Joe back home it would make sense to look under there first, but here everybody seems to think of other things first. They would never think to look under the bed." Phoenix said.

"Do you realize how stupid that sounds? We cannot hide the spider crystal under the bed. I say we take it to Sparuxe and have them hide it in the caves of the unicorns. If unicorns are so precious and hard to get a hold of it's the perfect hiding spot for the spider crystal. I am sure they wouldn't mind helping us out either. What do you think Piper?" Decklyn asked.

As Piper was finishing writing in a book she turned to Decklyn, smiled and said, "I agree with you Deck. It would make more sense than hiding it under the bed. That and Sparuxe would love to help us out since we helped them out the other day with the dragon."

"Ok, fine. We do it your way. By the way Piper what are you doing?" Phoenix asked while giving Piper a weird look.

"I am writing down false information about today's adventure in this ratty old book I found in an alley way in the village the other day." After seeing Decklyn turn around and give her a weird look she replied, "Well, we need a fake journal. I would feel safer if I knew that the fake book was lying open in the fort while we hid the other one in our day packs. Doesn't it make more sense if Lady Morphana were going to steal our journal with our adventures in it to steal the wrong one? This is the decoy."

"She is right you know. Lady Morphana had said that she always wanted to know what we were thinking and always doing. Looking through her crystal ball she would never know that this is the fake journal. It makes sense." Tiffany said while taking a seat next to Phoenix.

"Women, they think of everything." Phoenix said while twirling a pencil through his fingers. Just as he said this the book in front of Piper vanished in thin air. Jumping up from the table Piper said, "I didn't do that. Where did the book go?"

But before any of her friends could answer her there was a loud bang and a purple smoke cloud filled the ceiling of the kitchen. Before all of them was Lady Morphana and through an echo like voice she said, "Sniveling brats! You think you can fool me? I am Lady Morphana and I know all the tricks in the book."

Thinking they were busted, the four friends just stood there and listened to Lady Morphana. It was to their relief though when she said, "I have your journal now and I will soon know all of what you have accomplished here in Shelvockwood. You think you can keep your secrets from me? Hahaha! Don't bother trying to get it back either. My castle grounds are heavily guarded." And with that she vanished just as quickly as she had come.

"Is she that dense? Even if she did get the right journal we still wouldn't go and try to get it back. I mean seriously. We would at least make sure that everything we did in the future would be done with caution." Phoenix said while picking up the chair he had knocked over when they had all heard the loud bang of Lady Morphana's entrance.

"I don't think we have anything to really worry about. There wasn't much in that book anyways. I do think we should worry about the spider crystal though. If Lady Morphana knew that we had it she would have stopped at nothing to get it. I mean after all she did kill the other protectors. We just don't know how she did it. I certainly wouldn't want to find that out either." replied Decklyn while picking up his jacket from the hook by the door. "Let's go and give the unicorns this crystal to hide for us. I wouldn't want it to fall into the wrong hands anytime soon."

The other three grabbed their coats and headed out the door. The walk to the caves of the unicorns was rather far, but it didn't take them as long as they thought it would. The caves were just past the Shady Brook, down amongst the entrance to the Whispering Wood. On a nice fall day like today you could see the forest floor covered with different colored leaves that had fallen from the treetops above. As the protectors made their way across the forest floor, they saw the caves just ahead of them. These caves didn't look like ordinary caves; big rocks with dark holes in the center of them. No, these ones looked like the forest in the background. In fact, if Piper hadn't pointed them out Phoenix would have walked right into one without noticing it. "I think they have them this way to blend in with the forest background, so it is harder to find them. Makes sense since the unicorns are the most sought creature in the forest." Piper said.

"Well, it is a good thing you did say something Piper. I think Phoenix would have hurt himself and given away their cover." Tiffany said while chuckling just a little.

"Ha-ha, laugh at my expense, but you all can't tell me that you wouldn't have done the same thing if Piper hadn't opened her big mouth; again." Phoenix said while ducking Piper's out reached arm.

"Should we knock or just enter at our own risk?" Decklyn asked wondering a little bit.

"I doubt they will hear a knock, but we can at least enter and let them know we are here." Tiffany answered as she entered the caves first. "Hello, Sparuxe? Chanbo? It's the protectors. We have come to ask you all a favor. May we come in?" she yelled through the caves.

To their surprise not just Sparuxe and Chanbo came, but many, many more of them. Before they knew it, they were all surrounded by unicorns. Some of many different sizes. Finally, one of them spoke and it wasn't Sparuxe or Chanbo, but an older looking unicorn. "Yes, friends you may enter our home, but I for warn you that if you are here to endanger us be prepared, we will put up a nasty fight."

"Oh, heavens no! We have come in peace and have come to ask you all a favor if you will." Piper replied.

"Well, in that case follow us. And stay close because only a unicorn knows how to get around in these caves. If you venture off, you will be lost till one of us finds you. And you will never be able to find your way out of here. One of our many tricks is in case Lady Morphana's goons come and try to take off with one of us. They wouldn't know how to get out and we sure wouldn't tell them. By the way, my name is Sunpolis." replied the unicorn.

There were a lot of turns and twists that they went through.

Finally, what seemed like ten minutes later, they came to a clearing. In this clearing there was fresh grass and a running river. Amazed by what they saw their thoughts were interrupted by Sparuxe. "Amazing, isn't it? We unicorns cannot survive in the wintertime, so we put our magic together and came up with this. Fresh air, all the grass one could imagine, and fresh running water. This dome is what is magical and keeps everything hidden from the outside."

"We need one of these things to keep Morphana out of Shelvockwood for good. I wonder if that would work?" Phoenix said jokingly, but kind of serious at the same time.

"No, that wouldn't work. We have all thought of that before and it would take must power to get one that strong. Besides she is much too evil for that." Sunpolis said.

Just as Decklyn was about to say something another unicorn came up to them. This one was much prettier looking for a unicorn. It had long wavy white locks with purple and pink roses in its hair. This one had to be female. Walking up to the protectors the unicorn said with a light airy voice, "What has brought you down into the depths of our caves?"

Being a bit brave Decklyn answered, "We have come here to ask a favor of the unicorns."

"What is the favor dear boy?" the unicorn asked.

Looking right into the eyes of the unicorn Decklyn replied, "My friends and I have found a rare crystal that cannot get in the hands of evil. Will you keep it here in your caves and protect it for us?"

Thinking for a minute the unicorn nodded its head and said, "We can hide the spider crystal for you."

Shock fell on all their faces. How could this unicorn know about the spider crystal? "Excuse me for being rude, but how did you know that is what we wanted to hide?" Piper asked.

"My dear, I am Vailtorcles. Before any of these younger unicorns came around it was just myself and my husband Sunpolis. We have faced many adventures and dangers in Shelvockwood. One of them being the spider crystal."

Upon seeing Piper's confused face, Vailtorcles went on. "When Queen Vespera created the spider crystal it was to overthrow the power of the kind, King Empanvic. When the protectors had killed Empanvic that outraged the queen. The spider crystals powers became evil and brought hardship to Shelvockwood. It wasn't until Prudence, the guide of the protectors, had gotten the spider crystal that the hardships stopped. Once the protectors had the crystal, they overthrew the queen and killed her as well. It wasn't until a few years later that the protectors were in danger. Lady Morphana may seem evil, but she is a sweetheart compared to her aunt. Her aunt was the sister of Vespera and when she found out what had happened to her sister she went into a ball of rage. It was Demetri the defender who came to us with the spider crystal. He was the last one alive out of the four protectors. Poor Theresa had gone first and when Phillip had lost her, he went after the aunt and got himself killed in the process. Prudence was much harder to kill she put up a great fight and almost killed the aunt in the process. When Demetri was the only one left, he made sure that the spider crystal was taken care of and then he himself went off to fight in the honor of his friends. It was after the aunt killed Demetri that she was defeated and run out of Shelvockwood. Sorsha was the one that in the end ran her out, but she didn't know how long it would be until Lady Morphana or her aunt would try and rule Shelvockwood again."

In silence the protectors sat. This was the first time that any of them had heard some of what happened to the other protectors. Finally, Piper spoke, "If Demetri had given the spider crystal to you how did it end up out of your protection?"

Stepping up next to his wife, Sunpolis said, "A few years ago a young man came into our caves just as you did. He said he wasn't here to cause trouble. He wanted to get rid of all the evil in

Shelvockwood for good. With him he carried a large dragon egg. When asked what he needed from us to change Shelvockwood he answered the spider crystal. Of course, our defenses went up, but when he said that he meant to turn Morphana's heart to pure good we had Vailtorcles read him. My wife can read anyone and anything. If she senses that they are lying its to the death. This young man wasn't lying, and he had a glow about him that told us he will accomplish just what he came for. We gave him the spider crystal and told him to hold onto it dearly. How it got out of his grasp we don't know, but it is back now so no harm done."

"Did this young man give you his name?" Tiffany asked with curiosity.

"As a matter of fact he did." Vailtorcles said. "He said his name was Perlangitis. Do you know of him?"

"Yes, we do." Decklyn answered. "That is Lady Morphana's long lost love."

Chapter 12

All Hallows Eve in Shelvockwood

The protectors had learned a lot about Lady Morphana and the old protectors while they were visiting the unicorns, but they had other things on their minds right now than old stories. It was the day of All Hallows Eve and there was to be a big celebration in the Whispering Wood. As the four friends were headed to the forest to help Queen Lavinia and her fairy friends with the festival preparations, they couldn't help but talk about Lady Morphana. "I know that she is always on our minds and not usually for good intentions, but don't you kind of feel sad for her in a way?" Tiffany asked while walking over a fallen log in the path of the maze.

"Not in the least bit do I feel sorry for her. She and her entire family are nothing but trouble. Look at what happened to the old protectors. I wouldn't want to see any of you killed. I would go crazy like Demetri did." Decklyn replied.

"I personally think it is weird that the old protectors resemble us." Phoenix said. As he noticed the looks, he went on with, "Well, the defender was Demetri. Our defender is Decklyn. Demetri's girl was Prudence. Decklyn's girl is Piper. Same with Phillip and

Theresa. We just must make sure our ending doesn't have their ending."

"Wow Phoenix. I never looked at it that way. It does make sense. I agree with you on that one, but I agree with Tiffany on the other. I feel bad for Lady Morphana. I think she is good on the inside like her mother used to be. I don't see a shred of evil in her like her father Empanvic. I bet if Perlangitis was able to get to her heart he would have melted it for good." Piper said as they came through the maze finally and entered the Whispering Wood.

"Maybe you are right. I think we could find out more though if we got a chance to talk to Lady Morphana." replied Tiffany.

"That's it! We will go and talk to Morphana tonight." Decklyn said.

"Ok now I know he has lost it. Decklyn has gone bye-bye Piper. Say hello to your new boyfriend, the whack job." Phoenix replied.

"Decklyn don't be silly. How could we ever get a chance to talk to Morphana without her realizing who we were?" Piper asked.

"That is easy." answered Decklyn. "I was talking to Balfour the other day about the festival, and he had mentioned that every year on All Hallows Eve, Lady Morphana throws a party in her castle. Balfour said it isn't like our festival where we all just show up in regular clothes. Balfour said her party is like one we would have back home. They all dress up so that nobody knows who anybody is. I had questions too and Gabriel said that some of the villagers who go to her party the ones that are daring, and she doesn't even know who they are. We could all dress up and go talk to Lady Morphana herself."

"If we did that, we wouldn't be able to tell anybody about it. Aged Sir Oak and Queen Lavinia wouldn't allow us to go at all. They would think it suicide. And what would we dress up like? I am sure they don't wear masks." Tiffany said.

"We can talk about it later. Aged Sir Oak is watching us." Phoenix said while nudging Tiffany in the rib cage.

"Why hello friends. Isn't today a lovely day for a festival?" Aged Sir Oak asked as the four friends approached him.

Smiling up at Aged Sir Oak, they didn't have time to talk to him for Queen Lavinia buzzed up to them and started putting them to work instantly. Before long the forest floor was covered with fallen leaves of all shapes and colors. Aged Sir Oak was dressed in lots of acorns that sparkled and long berry strings. Everybody showed up. Unicorns, sprites, nymphs, villagers, all were there to enjoy the festivities. In one corner next to Aged Sir Oak there was apple bobbing and across from him Balfour was pumpkin carving and face painting with the children. There were many fun games with magic and enchanting music. All was going well until there was a big bang in the sky and a huge purple smoke cloud appeared. Walking in front of the crowd Piper, Decklyn, Tiffany, and Phoenix stood there staring at the head of Lady Morphana. Before Lady Morphana could speak Phoenix leaned into Decklyn and said quietly so that only Decklyn could hear him, "I feel like we are in a story on tape, and this is the part where someone has to stop everything to flip over the tape."

Decklyn started chuckling and instantly stopped when he saw Morphana wasn't amused. "Hello Shelvockwood. Enjoying your All Hallows Eve festival? I have brought a gift that I thought you all might enjoy."

"We don't want anything you have to offer us." replied Phoenix.

Chuckling Morphana responded with, "Oh, but I do want to give you this gift. I hope you all like it." And before anybody could say anything she started to speak again. "Erta, octa, mierper luxe boco!" And with that she was gone.

There would have been a lot of commotion and talking going on, but nobody could move! Whatever Morphana had said wasn't good. It appeared that she had cast a spell on everybody, and the spell wasn't a pretty one. Nobody could talk. And it's probably a good thing that it wasn't raining out because everybody was moving in slow motion like in a cartoon.

○×○

"Hahaha! That ought to put a damper on their festivities. Don't you think so boys?" Lady Morphana asked Slobbo and Gumbo.

"That was pure evil my lady. I like it." Gumbo said.

Leaning in so only Gumbo could hear him Slobbo said, "Quit sucking up to her. If she promotes anybody it is going to be me. I was with her the longest and I know her better."

Starring evilly at Slobbo, Gumbo was about to reply to him when Morphana began to speak. "That spell has to be one of the most hilarious ones I have come up with yet." Whipping tears away from her eyes she said, "But we have a party of our own to get ready for. How are the preparations coming along?"

"If I may ask my lady without getting in trouble, I thought parties in the castle were forbidden." Gumbo said through gritted teeth.

Taking a deep breath as if to hold in yelling Morphana looked down at Gumbo and said, "They were forbidden years ago by my aunt, but unlike my aunt I have a sense of taste and adventure. I don't always have to stop everything I am doing to make sure I rule Shelvockwood. My time will come, but in the meantime, I can enjoy myself. Now leave my throne Gumbo and attend to the kitchen."

Looking a little upset Gumbo gave Slobbo another quick glare and was off towards the kitchen. Turning back to Slobbo, Morphana seemed to have lost it. "How dare he ask me that! I have forbidden anybody to mention my family in this castle and he dared to ask me about MY parties? Slobbo, you have not defied me. You have always been there for me, and I will not forget that. Go and make sure everybody; the ogres, goblins, trolls, and scales know not to cause any mayhem tonight. Tonight, is a night everybody parties and I don't want the protectors thinking I would ruin that for them."

With a bow to Lady Morphana, Slobbo was out the door of the ballroom and down the main hall of the castle. Turning back to her crystal ball to watch the protectors in action. Lady Morphana knew that they were smart. She knew that the day she took the journal from them. It was a fake and to plant a fake has nothing to do with luck but with common sense. She must see how they would get out of this spell because she knew that they would be able to.

☙❧

It had only been a half hour, and everybody was already bored with the spell. What could they do about it though? Phoenix was about to signal something to Decklyn when he realized that it would take him forever just to get his point across. Out of the corner of his eye he noticed Tiffany started to run; or at least that is what it looked like she wanted to do. She must have moved her leg wrongly because before she knew it, she fell on the ground. Phoenix, Piper, and Decklyn slowly started to move their way towards her. When they got close enough to her, however, Piper who was behind the two boys tripped over whatever Tiffany tripped over and fell forward. In doing so she fell on top of Phoenix, who fell on top of Decklyn, and they all landed on Tiffany. This would have looked like a sight to see, but once they all landed on each other there was a big blinding flash of light. Whatever happened broke the spell. Everybody was confused as to what happened. The four friends lying on the ground were all sore from the fall. Buzzing over to them Queen Lavinia said, "Are you all ok? That looked like a nasty fall. We need to hold an emergency forest committee meeting over by Aged Sir Oak."

Once all assembled around Aged Sir Oak, Balfour was the first to demand what happened. "She has some nerve coming here and casting a spell on even the children! How did the spell break? What do we do now?"

"Calm down Balfour. We are all fine, even the children. Yes, they are a little shaken up, but that is normal. How did the spell break Queen Lavinia?" Sorsha asked while brushing dried leaves off her dress.

"The protectors broke the spell." Noticing that they all were going to ask how Queen Lavinia answered them. "When your crystals touched, your inner thoughts broke the spell. You all were thinking the same thing, or at least close to the same thing. Once the crystals got that signal from you all their power combined broke the spell. I am assuming you had to be touching each other too. As for what to do though I have no idea."

"I think we have an idea what to do Queen Lavinia." Piper replied.

Looking down at her Aged Sir Oak said, "As long as it doesn't involve you getting hurt or killed you have my vote."

"We cannot tell you what we are planning on doing because it is dangerous and risky, but it must be done now that this has happened." said Decklyn.

"What are you planning on doing exactly?" Balfour asked.

"We are going to disguise ourselves and go to Lady Morphana's party." Tiffany replied.

Before any of the committee could object, they were interrupted by a man's voice. "I think it is a good idea and I can help them get into the castle."

"Who are you stranger? And what are you doing walking into our meeting?" Balfour asked.

"I my friends am Morphana's long lost love, Perlangitis. I want to win her back and I can't do that on my own. We both need each other. You need me to get disguises and I need you to help me get back in her heart. Do we have a deal?" asked Perlangitis.

Shocked wasn't the right word for everybody. Stunned was more like it. Piper was the first one to speak up. "You have yourself a deal. When do we get started?"

✺

After a lot of objecting from Aged Sir Oak, the protectors and Perlangitis left the festival and headed to the village. While everybody was enjoying themselves at the festival Perlangitis took the four protectors to a shack in the village where they wouldn't be seen from Morphana's eyes. Throwing ratty old costumes at them Perlangitis told them to change into them. "You have got to be mad? These things won't fool my grandmother and she is crazy!" Phoenix said.

"I realize that these don't look like decent costumes, but they are magical. Put them on and the costume takes over. I gave the ladies witch ones and you boys got vampire ones. I must warn you though that you won't look like yourselves once you put these on. You will look like vampires and witches." Seeing that there was some concern Perlangitis said, "We won't stay long, just long enough to get some good information."

"What are you going to be?" asked Piper.

"I am going to be a warlock. Of course, I won't have the powers that a warlock would have, but I will look the part. That is all Morphana's party really is about. Dressing up and being someone, you aren't normally. She will probably dress up as a Sorceress. You see her aunt forbids her to have any fun. It was all about business. Taking over Shelvockwood and not falling in love. I am hoping to change all that." Perlangitis replied while throwing the cape over the rest of his costume.

Before Tiffany could respond to him, she noticed that he really had become a warlock. He didn't have that charming personality anymore but had a rough and nasty look about him. Decklyn and

Phoenix couldn't wait to put on their costumes now. Once they did, they grew a bit taller than they normally were. Their faces became pale, almost a whitish color and they grew fangs. The girls, however, were a little bit scared to see what they would change into. As they put their dresses on their hair grew long and black. Reaching up to their heads to notice their hair they also noticed their nails had grown a bit longer and were black as well. Everybody looked the part, and you couldn't tell who they were after they put the costumes on.

Looking out through one of the windows Tiffany commented, "How are we ever going to get to the party in time? It is already after ten o'clock and by the time we get there on foot the party will be almost over with."

"Not to worry my dear. That is where you ladies and I come in hand." replied Perlangitis.

Decklyn and Phoenix gave weird looks as Perlangitis brought out three long wooden brooms. Handing one over to each of the ladies Phoenix said, "Ok they get one and you get one, what about Decklyn and me?"

Chuckling a little bit Perlangitis said, "You my friends fly."

Not believing a word that came out of the man's mouth Phoenix ran outside and threw out his arms with his cape. Instantly the wind picked him up and he was airborne. Decklyn followed him and the other three took off with the brooms right behind the boys. Flying was much quicker than walking that whole way. It didn't seem like they were the only ones in the air either. A distance away from them were more witches and warlocks on brooms. And just up by the towers of the castle were humans flying around. They must be vampires. Perlangitis signaled the others to follow him. Flying down to the castle grounds they landed inside the courtyard. Perlangitis motioned them to come in close and as they all did, he said, "Now is the time we must all stick together. Do not lose each other. These creatures are not friendly like the ones you are used to. We have come here for one thing and one thing only. To speak to Lady Morphana herself and get answers. Let us not make our stay here long for it will become dangerous."

They all walked up to the castle doors. Taking deep breaths, they walked inside the Castle of Terror.

◂❤▸

Just as they entered the castle there was a flash of lighting followed by a crash of thunder. It made Tiffany jump and Perlangitis just gave her a look of be careful not to be so jumpy. Once they got their eyes adjusted, they noticed that it was very dark and gloomy inside. There were long twisty stairs straight ahead of them. Off to the right was a long corridor leading to the kitchen and to the left was the entrance to the ballroom where the party was being held. Straight back on the back wall of the ballroom was a throne and sitting on the throne was a woman who looked nothing like Lady Morphana. She had bright red flaming hair with black streaks in it and a dark red and black velvet dress. She appeared to be very happy sitting up there looking down at everybody. Leaning in so that only the four of them could hear him, Perlangitis said, "That is Lady Morphana dressed in her Sorceress outfit We can mingle for a bit but let us make this night quick. Some of these people even give me the creeps."

Nodding at him the four friends played their parts well. The girls gave looks like they were disgusted with life, but at the same time wanted the world to notice them. The boys looked around with wide eyes and made sure that they noticed every blood related thing in the room. Perlangitis threw his shoulders high in the air like he was holding up the world and he even walked that way to make it look like he was in charge. Nobody noticed anything different in them. They appeared to be like all the other witches, vampires, and warlocks there.

As the music began to play Lady Morphana got up from her throne and walked amongst the crowd. Laughing and appearing to have a good time, she didn't seem to notice anything different or strange about the five intruders. Walking up to them she said, "Welcome friends. How did you find your travels?"

"The sky is a thing for creatures. I myself am not really a flyer." Perlangitis replied.

Giving him a look of pure interest, Lady Morphana asked him if he cared to dance. Taking her hand and winking at the protectors, Perlangitis walked her out onto the dance floor. Following them Decklyn and Piper went next. Then Phoenix and Tiffany followed. Perlangitis said that they all should stick together so they made sure they were in ear shot of the conversation. "I have this want that makes people happy. Don't know why I still have it, my father forbid me to keep it, but it was my mother's. And I have these magical rocks that if you hold them in the palm of your hand you can walk through stone walls. Those come in handy when you want to cut someone off or get away from someone. I myself have used them many times to get away from my aunt. The old hag that she is. Why do you ask about anything magical that I had when I was a child?"

"I am just making conversation. What better way to know you than to get to know your past as well. When I was younger one of my brothers used to turn our grandmother's ogres into toad stools." Perlangitis replied.

Laughing just a little, Morphana seemed to be having fun. The protectors couldn't believe that this was the same woman who a few months ago had Piper, Phoenix, and Pike locked away in the towers. "This thunderstorm we are having isn't a good sign." Lady Morphana said. "It shows a sign of trouble on the way. I believe that thunderstorms are pure evil."

Giving her a confused look Perlangitis asked, "But I thought you were pure evil?"

Shaking her head Morphana answered, "My mother was born

good hearted. When she met my father, he was pure evil. He converted her heart to evil as well and then they had me. I have a bit of both in me, but I am more like my mother than my father. My mother's heart has always been good since the day she was born. Just covered up with an evil blanket. My mother's sister, however, is pure evil. She went evil the day she found out my mother was born. I am nothing like her either. I try to be evil because I know that is my mother's dying wish, but somehow inside I am told that wasn't so. What makes me evil today is all the good I have seen has come out bad. The protectors." She started to say evilly "They killed my father and then they killed my mother. So, my heart is black because of the deaths of my parents."

The protectors couldn't believe how easy it seemed for Perlangitis to get all this information out of her. It almost seemed like Lady Morphana was enchanted. As Perlangitis caught Piper's stare he knew he must ask Morphana why she cast that spell on Shelvockwood earlier. Taking a deep breath, he leaned down to her ear and asked, "I must know why you cast that spell on all of those creatures and people earlier today?"

Stopping suddenly Morphana looked up at Perlangitis with wide eyes. "How did you know I did that? I didn't tell anybody in my castle that I did that. Who are you?"

Thinking quickly, he said, "I saw it in my travels to Shelvockwood today. I knew it had to be the work of an evil Sorceress and that must be you. Do I have the wrong person?"

Smiling with a cute half grin she said, "Oh, yes that was me. I did that to amuse myself. I don't mean any harm to any of them really. I just must keep up my appearance. Shelvockwood thinks I am evil, so I must live up to that."

"You don't always have to be strong." Perlangitis said.

Morphana was about to comment on his remark when the music stopped. As she turned to face the band and clapped along with everybody else the band picked up another tune. While her back was to him Perlangitis gave the signal to the protectors to head to the door. Walking fast through the crowd of evil creatures, Perlangitis and the others managed to make it to the ballroom door before Lady Morphana turned around. Once they were outside in the courtyard the boys took off in the air. Perlangitis and the girls jumped on their brooms and were right behind the boys. It wasn't until they were all back in the shack that they could breathe a sigh of relief. Once out of the costumes they were all back to their old selves again. "What I don't understand is why Lady Morphana was acting like a love-struck teenager. Why wasn't she evil?" Tiffany asked.

"That is easy." Perlangitis replied. "She has always had a heart of good. It's just covered by a thick sheet of ice. Once melted though she will be just as good as you or I. That was one reason why her aunt Sigcerlaw had me thrown out of Shelvockwood. Little did she know that I would be back. Alright protectors, this is where I say goodbye, but only for a little while. Things may get worse before they get better. Be safe on your journey home."

The protectors were out the door of the shack and walking home on the path through the Whispering Wood. They had so much they wanted to talk about, but they knew that being out in the wide open like that was not the time or the place to be talking about what they had learned that day.

Chapter 13

Good Nymphs, Bad Nymphs

A few days after the All Hallows Eve festivities the protectors were still stuck inside the fort. It had started raining that night while they were at Lady Morphana's costume party and hadn't stopped yet. The fort however wasn't as boring as it had seemed. The girls managed to get the entire thing clean the first day stuck inside and the second day they all played card games and told stories. It was on the third day that they started to get a little cabin fever. "Ok no offense, but I hate being cooped up all the time. Is this rain ever going to let up?" yawned Decklyn.

"It's not so much the rain, but the thunder and lightning that has been going on the whole time too. I have never seen anything like that before. It does creep me out a bit." shivered Tiffany.

Before Phoenix could make a comment there was a knock on the door. "Who in their right mind would be out in this mess?" Piper asked as she went to the door and opened it. Standing shivering at the doorstep was Pike and some of his sprite friends. They ran inside and Piper shut the door behind them. While Phoenix put some hot water on the stove to heat for hot coco, Tiffany and Piper went and got blankets for Pike and his friends. "Why on earth would you venture out in this mess Pike? You should know better than that." Decklyn said.

Between shivers Pike replied, "Sprites aren't fond of thunderstorms. Most of our kind went hiding in caves throughout the Whispering Wood, but me and my friends would rather be with you all or Aged Sir Oak. Unfortunately, Aged Sir Oak shuts down until the storm blows over." Upon seeing the worried faces of the protectors, Pike went on, "Oh, he isn't hurt or nothing. He just becomes non magical, like a common tree when storms roll in. Doesn't want to be left out in them alone."

"Do you know why it is storming so bad? I mean it has been going like this for days. What could it be from?" Phoenix asked Pike and his friends.

"The only thing we can think of would be some crazy magical spell of Lady Morphana's. Why else would it be this bad for days?" answered one of the sprites.

"Believe me or not, but I don't think Lady Morphana had anything to do with this storm. I think it is a darker magic that even she doesn't know. You are all more than welcome to stay until the storm lets up. It's probably safer in here anyways than out there in the woods." Tiffany said.

So, to make them all a little calmer, the boys set up a small table in the living room for board games. The girls went into the kitchen to make some hot chocolate for everybody and then go and join in the fun. Only a few hours later the storm let up rather quickly and the sun came out to dry everything. "That must be one of the ugliest storms I have seen in a long time Just look at it out there now. Not a cloud in sight." Piper said while looking up at the sky through a now open window. Seeing the sunshine made the sprites excited and restless so they rushed out of the fort to enjoy the fresh air. The girls were cleaning up all the games while Decklyn and Phoenix were discussing the outcome of the storm. Phoenix was just about to motion the girls over when there was a rather small knock on the door. "What was that?" asked Phoenix. "It sounded like pebbles being thrown at the door."

161

"Tiff, be careful when you open the door ok." Decklyn said with concern.

Tiffany went to the door and cracked it open enough so she could peek outside and see what the noise really was. She couldn't see anything until she looked down towards the floor of the cabin floor. Standing a few inches tall was Nefertiti and some of her friends. "Oh, come on in neighbors." She said to Nefertiti and her friends. "I hope you weren't caught in that awful storm."

Speaking towards the sky so that Tiffany could hear her Nefertiti said, "Oh, no. We stayed underground in our tunnels and walked here that way. It wasn't until we got to your fort that we had to come outside and when we did it was sunny out."

One of the other nymphs replied with, "We came to discuss the storm actually. Some things we thought you all should know."

"Well, then please do come in." Decklyn said.

Opening the door wider for Nefertiti and her friends, Tiffany gave her friends a worried stare. Once they were all inside and seated around the table in the living room, that is when Nefertiti's friend started. "I am Melvincia. Daughter of Guillian and cousin to Nefertiti. We have come here to tell you whey we believe the storm was a bad sign of things to come."

As everybody watched tiny Melvincia pace back and forth across the table. Nobody could utter a sound. Turning towards the four friends that sat silently on the floor watching her with every move she took, Melvincia continued. "Nefertiti and I may look young, but we are over one hundred years old." Even with the shocked looks from the protectors Melvincia went on. "We are young for nymphs, this is true. Maybe we live so long because we are narrators for those who pass on. Or maybe Shelvockwood is magical, and creatures, people, sprites, unicorns, and trees live for long periods of time. This we do not know, but what we do know is that there is a reason we have lived this long. Nefertiti and

I believe that we are destined to tell the new protectors how the other ones died."

"You know how they died?" Phoenix asked. "I thought that was a mystery and nobody really knew how they died."

"We know how the protectors died." Nefertiti replied. "We were there."

At the same time Piper and Tiffany dropped their mouths. Decklyn hung his head and shook it rather slowly while Phoenix started coughing like he was choking on water. Once she was finally able to close her mouth Piper looked at Melvincia and said, "Will you please tell us how they died."

"Before I tell the sad tale of how they came to their untimely deaths I must first tell you where they came from." Taking a seat on the table so that her legs hung over the edge, Melvincia went on. "Prudence, Demetri, Theresa, and Phillip came from the same land that you four have come from. Time there stands still while years go by here. When I asked Theresa a long time ago where she came from all she told me was that there were many trees like Will the Willow around."

As soon as she had said this, Tiffany gave a huge gasp. "Oh my! You guys realize who she is talking about don't you?"

"Actually, I have no idea who she is talking about." Decklyn said while giving Tiffany that look of, please continue.

"I know what she is talking about." Phoenix said softly. "If you remember about ten years ago, our time those high school kids that disappeared and nobody could find them. All they could find was their campground site a few miles into the national state park. That is where we went camping and stumbled across Shelvockwood."

Piper looked like she was ready to throw up. The other's weren't that far off either. They all looked like they had eaten some bad Chinese food. Not knowing if she wanted Melvincia to go on with her story, Piper choked out, "Please continue Melvincia. We must know the story if we are to survive in the end."

163

"Well, before I get into how they died I must first tell you a bit about Morphana's mother. As you know she was good until she met Empanvic. In fact, she used to be good friends with Sorsha's mother." Looking at the mouths hit the floor again Melvincia said, "Please let me go on or this will take all day. Sorsha's mother and Vespera were the best of friends. They did everything together. Then one summer Vespera went away to visit some family and when she came back Elizabeth (Sorsha's mother) wasn't here. Elizabeth had gone into hiding because of Empanvic's family. They had taken over and run everybody into hiding. Vespera didn't know what was going on and was not even in Shelvockwood for five minutes when she was captured by one of the ogres that was on duty. She was thrown up into one of the towers and left there till her sentence was to be carried out. Empanvic was the one that gave those orders. His father and mother were so proud and wanted him to carry out what happened to the captured. When he got to Vespera's cell however, he became enchanted by her beauty and her attitude. He thought she would have a lot of potential to rule with him, so he began his little project of turning her evil. It didn't take long though because she fell in love with him rather quickly. Years went by after they had Lady Morphana. She was in her twenties when she met Perlangitis. Morphana's parents were furious. Especially her mother, her mother knew that love conquered all. If it can change her from good to evil, it certainly can change Morphana from evil to good. Perlangitis had to go. Vespera had become eviler than Empanvic over the years. When the protectors had killed both of Morphana's parents, some say she had gone mad. Vowed that she would get revenge for their deaths, but it wasn't Morphana that did away with the protectors. It was Sigcerlaw, Vespera's sister."

"Ok, I must ask now. I thought Vespera's sister was pure evil because Vespera was born?" Tiffany asked.

"Yes, that is true." Nefertiti said.

"Ok, so then why would she kill the protectors for her sister's death? If she hated that Vespera was born, why would she even care if she died? Wouldn't she have been thrilled that she met her death?" asked Decklyn.

"Sigcerlaw may have hated her sister and become evil because of it, but she felt that blood was thicker than water. Nobody could kill her sister, but her. She became so outraged that she decided the protectors needed to vanish for good." Nefertiti said through the quiet atmosphere.

Nodding her head Melvincia went on, "Theresa was the one to go first. She was caught just outside of the Whispering Wood. Sigcerlaw had poisoned the canteen Theresa had packed earlier that morning. Out of all of them though, she had the mildest death. When she didn't come home that evening, Phillip went out looking for her. What he found was her body. So enraged he went and stormed the castle by himself and got attacked by all the ogres and swamp goblins. He was ripped to shreds. After finding out what happened to their friends, Demetri and Prudence knew that they were next. They knew that the spider crystal couldn't fall into the hands of Sigcerlaw. So, Demetri said he would hide it. Before he left, he told Prudence to stay put and that they would find a way to defeat her together. Not to go for her alone. Prudence was too proud not to face Sigcerlaw alone. She was also upset over losing her two good friends. Right after Demetri left Prudence headed straight for the castle following in Phillips footsteps. Sigcerlaw was waiting for her in the courtyard. This was one of the biggest battles that Shelvockwood has had. Nobody knows if it was Prudence's anger or her courage that caused her crystal to defend her that way, but it did. She had thrown out a few white lights towards Sigcerlaw and hit her. They didn't do much damage but knocked her on her back. Furious, even more that this protector was stronger than the other two were, she threw huge boulders at Prudence. She missed all of them, but one. It caught her from the right side and threw her to the ground. Pinned on the ground where she fell Prudence was stuck. As Sigcerlaw advanced towards her she had the ugliest smile on her face. Right before she smashed Prudence's head with a rock, Prudence said to her, "I have seen the future and you will NEVER defeat the protectors of the ice crystals. You will lose and your niece will be the one to take you down." Sigcerlaw was even more outraged than she had been when she found out about her sister. Without pausing to take a breather she smashed Prudence in the head with a boulder and then walked off the grounds of the Castle of Terror. Upon finding Demetri exiting the Whispering Wood, she threw a huge lightening bolt at him. It hit him directly in the back. Crawling on the ground and trying to get up Demetri demanded she tell him how she killed the other two. Before throwing the last lightning bolt at him, the one that finished him off she said, "You are the last protector here in Shelvockwood. I just killed the guide and now I am going to finish you off." Demetri was in tears at this news and before he could even utter two words, she finished him with an even bigger lightning bolt."

Noticing that there wasn't anybody who wasn't crying Nefertiti said, "Sigcerlaw thought that what Prudence said about Lady Morphana was true, but she didn't think she could do it on her own. She gave Perlangitis the chance to leave or be killed. He left because he knew one day, he would be able to return. Sigcerlaw waited a few years before she left Lady Morphana in charge. To this day Lady Morphana thinks that Perlangitis left because he didn't love her. That is what her aunt told her so that she wouldn't accept him even when he did return. We believe that the storm is a sign that Sigcerlaw is returning to Shelvockwood to finish off the fortune Prudence saw years ago."

Nobody said anything for a long time. Then Piper spoke up, "The storm as "mad" as it has been for days signifying Sigcerlaw's evilness and that she is close? I thought she ran from the kingdom after the protectors killed Empanvic and Vespera so she wouldn't be killed. All that was not true."

"She wanted the protectors to think she left. She was outraged. Wanting revenge and picking them off one by one. We don't know if she is close or not. Aged Sir Oak would be able to sense her because they had a few encounters before and he can just tell when she is near. He hasn't said anything to us or anybody else for that matter, so we think that everything is ok for now." Said one of the quieter nymphs.

Just as Phoenix was about to say something there was another big flash of lightning that lit up the whole room; followed by a clap of thunder loud enough to shake the ground. As everybody jumped all the candles that were lit from earlier in the day blew out from a huge gust of wind. It became very dark in the fort. Decklyn and Phoenix got up off the floor and started shutting the windows while the girls ran around to re-light the candles. As the friends were relaxing from the sudden scare of the new storm, they were all hit from behind.

☙❧

"Excuse me, Lady Morphana." Gumbo said.

Turning to look at him from her vanity she asked, "What is it Gumbo?"

"Some of the goblins were just wondering how much longer Scales was going to be roaming around in the castle. We were wondering if he may find it more interesting to chase around ogres instead of goblins."

Smiling with a crooked smile she replied, "Scales has more fun chasing around goblins who fear him. Ogres are dumb and don't put up much of a chase. Besides he is inside because of the storm. Will you go fetch Slobbo for me. I need to speak to him at once."

Throwing his head down Gumbo nodded his head yes and then was out the door of her chambers. It wasn't long before

Slobbo entered and shut the door behind him. Walking up to Lady Morphana he said, "Gumbo said you wanted to see me my lady."

"Yes, Slobbo, he was right. I must ask you a question and I want your honest opinion." Noticing that he was kind of weary she added, "You have my word that I won't yell at you."

Nodding in approval Lady Morphana continued, "Scales is cooped up in the castle because of the nasty weather outside. I rather enjoy watching him chase around the goblins. Its very amusing, but this is the second storm we have had that is rather nasty. I usually enjoy thunderstorms. They remind me of the fun times I had with Perlangitis and the few times that I shared with my mother. Don't get me wrong, I am enjoying it very much so, but I can't help thinking that it may be my aunt returning to Shelvockwood. I don't really have the power to conjure up a storm with this magnitude. Do you think that Sigcerlaw is nearby?"

With a horrified look on his face Slobbo answered, "Do YOU think your aunt is back?"

Lady Morphana may have been born evil, but she didn't really have it in her. She even had a scared look on her face when Slobbo asked that question. "I believe she is a very powerful sorceress and that she somehow knows that Perlangitis is back. Between you and me Slobbo, I don't know how she does it. I have seen Perlangitis battle with good and evil and somehow, he makes good seem a lot better. I understand that the protectors had killed my parents, but my parents brought me up to not care about anything, but myself. So really their death means nothing to me. I am grateful that the protectors did away with them. I wish Perlangitis was here so I could talk to him though."

"Lady Morphana, if I may speak to you as if you were a friend. I think that is the best thing you have said since your reign. I am willing to stand by your side through whatever your decision may be." Slobbo replied.

"Slobbo" she started, "I am a little confused right now. I may be speaking out of confusion, but that is good to know that my trusty minion is with me till the end. Now go make sure Scales is having a good time chasing the goblins around."

Pleased that Morphana has chosen him instead of Gumbo, Slobbo almost skipped out of her chambers. Once alone Morphana took out the letter Perlangitis had left when he left her the dragon egg. Opening the letter again she read:

"If you decide that you want to work things out and melt that icy heart your mother has given you let me know. I will be around. Take care my love and remember you can change who you are. You don't have to be like your father...pure evil."

And for once Lady Morphana smiled for all the right reasons.

The protectors found themselves bound and gagged on the floor of the fort. Furious because he couldn't talk Phoenix was giving the intruders the evil eye. Piper and Decklyn were also glaring at them. Tiffany was the only one who seemed nervous or scared. The intruders were more nymphs, but the protectors figured out that they were the bad ones because all the nymphs like Melvincia and Guillian were tied up as well. All except for Nefertiti. Piper caught her out of the corner of her eye. She was hiding behind one of the table legs. The bad nymphs were all over the table slapping hands and smiling that they had done such a good job. Nefertiti was quick. She dashed right next to Decklyn's side. He looked down, but then quickly looked back up so as not to draw attention to her. Decklyn knew that he didn't have much time once she untied his hands. Closing his eyes and thinking hard, Decklyn wished that the bad nymphs would be stunned. Opening his eyes nothing happened. *"Darn"* he thought, *"that should have worked. Now what am I going to do."*

Before he could answer himself, Nefertiti was in his head as well. *"I got it. Just start untying the others and find something to put the bad nymphs in till we can get them over to the forest committee."*

It all happened so quickly nobody knew what was going on. One minute the bad nymphs were talking and having a good time and the next they were all lying stunned on the table. Decklyn didn't waste any time untying the others. Finally able to talk Phoenix started pestering the stunned nymphs. "Can't move, can you? Not as funny now, is it?"

"Phoenix! Don't do that!" Tiffany yelled at him. "You didn't like it when they did it to you."

"Oh, come on Tiff. You can't tell me you didn't want to tell them off when you were bound and gagged up. Let me just get all my jollies out." he said.

"No!" Tiffany answered looking rather annoyed. "Besides we should be finding something to put them in. Come and help me look."

"Fine." Was all Phoenix could say.

Laughing at him, Decklyn gave Piper a hug and then went to help Guillian and Melvincia tie up the other nymphs. Piper sat back and watched the bad nymphs. They didn't look so happy. In fact, they looked rather irritated that their plan didn't go the way they wanted it to. Guillian and Melvincia were rather fast at tying them up, but Decklyn was finding the task rather difficult because his fingers were much bigger than the nymphs were. "Here let me get that for you." Guillian said.

"Thank you. I was having a difficult time with it." Decklyn said while blushing a little. Coming down the ladder with a small cage in his hands was Phoenix. "We found something to put the little brats in."

"Phoenix." Tiffany shouted in a whisper.

"What?" asked a confused Phoenix.

He brought it over to the table and set it down so that they could all walk into it. Well, Nefertiti and her other friends had to escort them into it, but once they were all inside Tiffany shut the cage and locked it. "It is too late now to bring them to the forest committee. What are we going to do if they escape in the night?"

"That's easy." Replied Piper. "We are each going to take turns watching them."

"In that case, I would LOVE to take the first shift." Phoenix said through a wide-eyed grin.

"Uh, actually Phoenix, I think I will take the first watch. Why don't you get some sleep, and I will wake you up in a few hours or so." Decklyn said while giving Phoenix a shake of his head.

With a disgusted look on his face Phoenix said, "Yeah, sure. Whatever floats your boat."

The night for everybody wasn't as long as they all thought it would turn out to be. Everybody took turns watching them. Even the other nymphs watched them so that nothing bad would happen all night long. The next morning Nefertiti, Guillian, and Melvincia followed the protectors to the Whispering Wood to meet with the forest committee. When they all arrived there the forest committee was just getting ready to finish up their meeting and head out when Balfour noticed the group walking towards them. "Good morning, friends. What do we have here?"

Looking at Balfour Piper said, "Good morning yourself. We had an encounter with some of the bad nymphs last night and we thought that we would bring them here to your meeting so that they can have some sort of punishment."

It didn't take long for the protectors and the good nymphs to tell the story of what happened the day before. Phoenix was giving a full detailed description of what happened, or what he thought happened. When all was said and done Balfour took the cage from Decklyn and started walking towards the village. Queen Lavinia turned towards the young friends and said, "Hopefully nothing else comes of this storm, but just in case it does everybody should be on full alert. Keep your eyes and your ears open for trouble friends."

Chapter 14

The Lost Letter From Prudence

"It turned out to be a nice day after all." Phoenix managed to say through mouthfuls of food. Since the horrible storms weeks before the protectors were bound and determined to enjoy the sunny weather while they still could. They didn't know when there would be another horrible storm or even worse yet, when it would start snowing. The weather in Shelvockwood was just like the weather in their own world. It had the same seasons and everything. The only difference it seemed to hold was the magic that roamed throughout the land.

After hearing the long story of how the old protectors died, everybody wanted to know how it would end for them. Would they get to go home in the end and live their lives like nothing had happened? Or would they meet a sticky fate just like the other ones did? On their way back home to the fort however, they ran into Sorsha. "Hello, Sorsha. Why what's going on? You have a look on your face like you just found out that you've become queen or something." Tiffany said.

Walking to the protectors Sorsha leaned in and whispered, "Actually I have wonderful news. Can you all come to my cottage so we can talk in private?"

Nodding their heads, the four friends followed Sorsha back

to her cottage. Once the door was shut Sorsha offered them seats around her table and started to tell her news. "Like I was telling you, I have the most wonderful news. I was cleaning out some old trunks that Anastasia had, and I stumbled across a letter." Pausing in her story Sorsha looked at the bewildered faces in front of her. "What are you looking at me like that for?"

Chuckling just a little, Piper answered for everyone. "It's just that we have no idea who Anastasia is. The only time we have heard that name was in a story book back home and she was a lost princess."

"Oh, I am sorry. By now I figured you would have known who she was and what she had done for Shelvockwood. Anastasia was my older sister." Even though there were shocked faces again, Sorsha continued. "We all grew up with Lady Morphana and Perlangitis. It wasn't until the protectors had kill Morphana's parents that things got worse. My sister and I were devastated when we found out Sigcerlaw had killed our mother. She did so because Vespera was good friends with our mother and Sigcerlaw wanted to hurt her sister. Anastasia lost it. She came up with a great potion to end Sigcerlaw's powers for good, but before she could even minister it Sigcerlaw had killed her as well. I don't know how my sister died, but I know she died trying to save Shelvockwood. Which is what my mother always wanted us to do. Make sure Shelvockwood is always safe from evil."

"So sorry to hear that, Sorsha. How long have they all been dead now?" Piper asked.

"It has been over one hundred years since the deaths of the protectors and my family. They have been dead for years, but in your time, it may have been only a short while that they have vanished." She replied.

"Yeah, ten years in our time." Phoenix said.

"So, you said you have found a letter. Who's the letter from and what is it about?" Decklyn asked.

"Well, you see that is the great news. The letter is from Prudence." When she didn't get the reaction, she was hoping for from the protectors, Sorsha went on. "Prudence wrote the letter to you."

"What do you mean she wrote the letter to us? She wrote it for the new protectors in the future?" Phoenix asked.

"Well, yes and no. Prudence did write the letter to the protectors in the future, but she addressed it to Decklyn, Piper, Tiffany, and Phoenix." replied Sorsha.

Now she got the response she was looking for. Each one of them dropped their mouths to the floor. "Are you kidding me?" Decklyn said.

"You must be joking." said Phoenix.

"No way possible." Tiffany replied.

"It makes sense." Piper said. Her three friends all turned to look at her in shock. "Well, it does. Prudence was the only one of the protectors who could read and see into the future. So why wouldn't she be able to see our names?"

"And just how do you know that?" Phoenix asked in a smart voice.

"Simple really." answered Piper. "I read it in a book from the village library."

"Of course, you did." Phoenix said kind of sarcastically.

"AND the nymphs told us she saw into the future. If you remember that story." Piper replied with a snotty look on her face. "Sorsha, do you mind if I read the letter out loud?"

"Of course not. Here you go." Sorsha said while she handed Piper the letter.

The letter was on parchment paper and looked old. As Piper carefully unfolded the paper, she took a deep breath and began to read the letter out loud to her friends.

To my dear friends: Decklyn, Piper, Tiffany, and Phoenix,

If you are reading this letter, then that means my friends and I have died, and you are the new protectors of the ice crystals. I have been able to read the future since I battled with Kind Empanvic. When I killed him, I ended up taking his power to see into the future. My dear friends there are a few things I must tell you, but first I will tell you about how I know who you all are. We all grew up down the street from each other back in Willow. In fact, I used to babysit for you Phoenix. Our mothers were good friends and will be extremely upset when my friends and I don't return. Shelvockwood for years and years has had protectors of the ice crystals. The very funny thing that I read about in a book is that the protectors have always had names that started with letters just like ours. There were always two boys and two girls. One of the girls has a name with a P and so does one of the boys. I can't explain why. I just know that is how it has worked for years. There is no way you guys can go home and tell our parents what happened. They won't believe you and will have you locked up and committed. So, friends, I must tell you a few things that have happened before I tell you a bit about your future to come.

Demetri and I had another encounter with a very old and dear friend of Lady Morphana's. It was hard to even get a chance to talk to him because he hardly leaves her side. We were having a stroll one day through the meadow and we ran into Slobbo. Piper, you will know him as Lady Morphana's right hand man or rather right-hand ogre. He has been with her since she came into reign years ago. He was very careful with what he said to us, but he did manage to tell us that Morphana isn't as evil as she may want to be.

He said there were many times that she could have had his head, but she never followed through with it. Demetri and I believe deep down she isn't evil like her father and mother. Theresa and Phillip believe that she is a faker, but I beg to differ. Morphana was nowhere to be found when Theresa and Phillip were killed. I have seen all our deaths and no matter how much I tried to avoid them, they all appeared to be the same. You can't cheat fate or death. It happens to everyone, but maybe with my help and advice you can have Morphana on your side in the end.

Sigcerlaw will come back. She will try to kill you all and Perlangitis, but Morphana is the key to your survival. Take it or leave it, you will need her help. I have seen that her heart melts and she will go into hiding. Find her and you will defeat Sigcerlaw. Don't find her and try to do it on your own, you will die. I have seen two futures for the four of you. One ends badly while the other ends happily. Choose wise my friends for you only get one chance.

Some other friendly advice Phoenix, listen to Tiffany. She knows what she is talking about. Tiffany, Phoenix means well. He just likes to have a good time and ease up the atmosphere every now and then. Take care of each other. Decklyn, Piper may get bossy and irritating sometimes, but she doesn't mean to be. She is thinking of everybody else and putting them first. And Piper, don't be so proud. You can ask for help occasionally. That is what friends are for. Take care of each other my friends and good luck! Sincerely, Prudence

When Piper was done reading the letter, she folded it back up and set it down on the table in front of her. Silence filled the room. Nobody knew what to say. What could be said? The other protectors died trying to save Shelvockwood and it appeared to everybody in the room that that was the fate of the four friends as well. "I don't think we have to worry about Lady Morphana." Chocked out Piper.

"And why not?" asked a bewildered Phoenix. "She has done nothing, but cause mayhem since we came into Shelvockwood. Why should we trust her at all? She comes from an evil messed up family."

"Because..." Piper replied, "she isn't the one that killed the protectors, and she isn't the one that banned Perlangitis from Shelvockwood. When she had me captured, she could have done away with me right then and there. It would have been really easy to pick us off one by one after killing me. Decklyn you would have gone insane with furry and been after her for what she had done to me. Morphana didn't though. That leads me to believe that she is trapped between good and evil, or rather right and wrong. She wants to be evil to please her mother and father, but she would rather be good to be with Perlangitis."

Taking into consideration what Piper just said, Decklyn shouted out, "You are right! Lady Morphana isn't the one we should be worried about. Both of her parents are dead, and she couldn't hurt a common house fly. I think we should be worrying about her aunt, Sigcerlaw."

"I don't know as if I believe it." Phoenix said while he crossed his arms.

"We could at least give her a chance, I guess. I mean what do we have to lose?" Tiffany asked.

"Only our lives." answered Phoenix.

ଔଓ

After reading the letter the friends and Sorsha decided to clean out some more trunks, boxes, and bookcases. Maybe they would be lucky enough to find another letter. Sorsha's cottage may look small from the outside, but like the fort it was enormous inside. What seemed like hours later, Sorsha called the protectors over. "I found something." she shouted with glee.

"What did you find now?" asked a curious Decklyn.

"Just some old pictures, but I think you can benefit from them." replied Sorsha. As soon as all the protectors were seated around her, she opened the box of pictures she had found in one of the trunks. "This one was taken before the festival took place. See how Aged Sir Oak's half dressed."

"He would uproot himself if he saw this picture." Phoenix replied. "Can I show him this?"

"PHOENIX!" shouted Tiffany. "You don't really mean to do that! You could cause serious damage to Aged Sir Oak if he uprooted himself because of a silly..."

But she was cut off by Phoenix who picked her up in his arms and jokingly said, "Now you have known me for a few years now and you can't tell I am joking around?"

Blushing so that her whole face practically turned red, Tiffany answered, "Oh, I guess not. We are all being serious right now and you must joke."

"Remember what Prudence said in her letter." Decklyn said while turning to his friends. "You have to take it easy on Phoenix he means well."

Looking almost disgusted, Tiffany turned back to help Piper sort through some more pictures. There were pictures of Pike when he was much smaller than what he was now, some of Queen Lavinia and her fairies and even a picture of Balfour when he must have been just a teenager.

"These pictures say a lot about the friends we know now." Piper said while looking at a picture of Prudence and Theresa with Sorsha sitting by Vailtorcles the head female unicorn.

"Not one of us has really changed from back then." Sorsha

replied. "We all got older, but none of us really are different in the way we act or think."

"Oh, here is Theresa's old journal. This should give you some insight to what they had to deal with in their battles." Sorsha proclaimed.

"I don't really understand how the journal works. I mean how are we to know about all their battles if Theresa was the first one to die? She couldn't have written in her journal after that." Piper said.

"Well, that is easy Piper. The journals are connected to not just the writer, but all the protectors thoughts. The journal keeps writing down what happens even after the writer is dead. It stops however, when the last protector dies." answered a sad Sorsha.

"How sad, but good to know." Decklyn replied.

They all went on to discover old pictures of the other protectors outside of what appeared to be Willow High and the Willow Library. It seemed that digging any further would just upset the protectors, so Sorsha decided to call it quits.

"I think it was a good day to go through trunks. What are we going to do with the letter from Prudence though? I think that everybody should know what really happened." Tiffany said through a yawn.

"I agree. I was going to take it to Aged Sir Oak, read it to him and see what his thoughts were on the matter." Sorsha piped up.

"Well, if you don't mind, I would love to go with you to see his reaction to the letter from Prudence." Piper replied.

"You are all more than welcome to come if you would like. I just have to get a few things together first before I head out the door." Smiled Sorsha.

Watching Sorsha like they had never watched her do magic before, the protectors were amazed at what they saw. Sorsha had gone over to her cauldron and poured what looked like grape juice into the bottom. She then closed her eyes and said over the cauldron, "A new meeting is upon us. Meet by Aged Sir Oak."

When she opened her eyes there was a big bang and a cloud of smoke. Turning to look at the horrified faces of her friends, Sorsha couldn't help but laugh.

"Why are you laughing?" Decklyn asked.

"I am laughing because Phoenix is on the floor yet again." Sorsha said through chuckles.

Turning around Piper, Decklyn, and Tiffany all saw that Phoenix was on the floor again. Not able to hold in their laughter the three friends burst out laughing at the sight of their friend on the floor of the cottage.

છાજ

Arriving at the Whispering Wood where Aged Sir Oak was eagerly awaiting the arrival of the forest committee, there was a silence that carried a chill with it. The whole forest committee was there; Balfour, Queen Lavinia, and even Sunpolis and Vailtorcles. After everybody was settled Aged Sir Oak spoke first, "Protectors, I am told that you have some news on Lady Morphana. Don't keep us waiting any longer. Please inform us of what the news is."

"You should be sitting down, but since you can't just don't shed too many leaves, ok?" Phoenix replied.

Piper then took out the letter from Prudence. "This friends' is a lost letter from Prudence. What I am about to read to you may be very difficult to understand, but you must take everything I say and think about it hard before passing judgment." After she got a bunch of nods from everyone, she went on with reading Prudence's letter. Finishing up the last part of the letter, Piper then turned to the forest committee and asked the terrifying question she and the other protectors were desperately wondering, "So, what do you think?"

Sunpolis was the first to answer, "I always knew that Lady

Morphana wasn't evil at all. Isn't that right my dear?" he asked, turning to Vailtorcles.

"Yes, you have always told me you know deep down in your heart that Lady Morphana couldn't hurt a fly. I myself believe you as well. She has the heart of a unicorn." Vailtorcles answered.

"Are you all mad? This is the woman who put an end to life in Shelvockwood as we know it and you are going to go based on some letter that you "think" you got from Prudence. What if Lady Morphana made the letter up herself and placed it in a spot, she knew you would find it? Did you all think of that?" Balfour practically yelled.

"Balfour does have a point. I know that Lady Morphana has deep magic, and she could have made the letter up." Queen Lavinia spoke.

"Yes, but why would she go to great measures as to say things about the protectors and where they grew up? As far as I know she had no idea where they came from." Sorsha blurted out.

"To solve all your questions and to prove to you all that Lady Morphana is indeed good, there is a way we can tell if the letter is a fake or not." Vailtorcles started to say. "Many years ago, when Queen Vespera ruled, she needed a potion to determine the truth. Living with Empanvic one would have to have a truth spell. Afraid to be seen around us unicorns, Vespera sent an elf into our layer. The elf begged us to give him the truth spell so that Vespera could use it on Empanvic to find out when he was telling the truth and when he was lying. We had no idea that Vespera even knew about us, let alone the truth spell. Sunpolis was skeptical, but I myself trusted Vespera. She after all was good at heart from the beginning. We ended up giving the elf the truth spell for her, but it was too late. By the time the elf got to her she was dead."

The whole forest committee looked shocked, as did the protectors. Nobody knew what to say. Maybe it was because he was older, but Aged Sir Oak spoke first. "If what you say is true, then you could somehow use the truth spell on this letter to see if it is real or fake is that correct?"

"Yes, that is correct." Said Sunpolis. "My dear wife is right when she said Vespera was good at heart. We know this because we used the truth spell on her when she first became Empanvic's wife."

"Well, let's get on with it then. I want to know it it's a fake or not." said an impatient Phoenix.

Sunpolis got up and went over to the letter that was in Piper's hands. "Put it down over there by the stream and then back away from it."

Piper did as she was asked. When she was away from the letter Sunpolis nodded to his wife Vailtorcles to come over. Together they bent down on the letter and rubbed their horns together to create magic dust. When the dust particles fell on top of the letter it started to glow gold. "That proves it then." said Sunpolis.

"Proves what?" asked Phoenix. "Just because it glowed a golden color proves what exactly?"

"It proves that this letter is original and not a fake." Vailtorcles replied.

"I'm so confused. So, the dust from your horns tells us if it's a fake or not? How?" asked a curious Decklyn.

"Well, you see Decklyn, that's simple. If the letter was indeed a fake, then when the dust from our horns had fallen on it the letter would have turned blood red. Unicorn horns are the most magical of all magic combined. If Sigcerlaw knew how powerful our horns were, she would have had us all killed years ago to get the magic inside." said Sunpolis.

"The magic inside your horns can't last that long though after you're dead, can it?" Piper questioned with concern.

"You are right Piper. Our magic lives within us. If we are alive, so is our magic. Once we are killed though the magic only stays strong for maybe an hour at the most and then it is as gone as we are." Sunpolis replied.

"Now that we know this is in fact a letter from Prudence what should we do? Do we show it to Lady Morphana, or do we try to find Sigcerlaw?" inquired a very curious Tiffany.

"I think we should leave Sigcerlaw alone for now. As for Lady Morphana, I think it would be best to leave a copy of the letter in her castle somewhere so she can read it for herself." answered Vailtorcles.

"Agreed." said Aged Sir Oak. "Morphana should know what really happened. Maybe she will fight for our side, if she is good as you think she is Piper."

"Then let us get a copy of this letter written out and over to her castle soon." replied Tiffany. "I would rather get this all out of the way as soon as possible so we aren't worrying about her anymore."

Chapter 15

Perlangitis is Summoned

I t didn't take long for Lady Morphana to find the letter in her castle and read it. She at first thought it was some sort of cruel prank from the protector's, but as she worked her dark magic on the letter, she soon began to discover that it was in fact not a prank. Morphana was furious. How could her aunt be this evil? Morphana didn't even seem as evil as she thought she was. Reading this letter has really made her think about her family more and whether or not she wants to practice in the dark magic. The only one she would be able to talk to without being thought of as a weak sorceress would be Perlangitis. But would she be able to talk to him without completely melting her heart of ice? Morphana was beside herself and she didn't know what to do, as she paced up and down her dark room. Then there was a knock on her door. "Who is it?" she shouted.

"It is just me my lady. Slobbo. I couldn't help but notice that you are walking with heavy strides across your floor. Is there something wrong?" Slobbo asked.

"As a matter of fact, there is." Lady Morphana said as she opened the door to her chamber. "Come in dear friend. I need to run something by you without it getting out that I'm too soft."

Looking around to make sure that Slobbo was the only one

in sight, Lady Morphana quickly shut the door behind them. Taking out the letter so she could read it to Slobbo (because she didn't know if ogres could read) Morphana began. When she had finished Slobbo surprised her by saying, "I did have an encounter with Prudence and Demetri before Sigcerlaw got to them. And I did tell them that you are not evil my lady."

Still in shock as to what came out of Slobbo's mouth, Morphana stood by her bed with her mouth open. Before she could say anything though Slobbo continued, "You can cut off my head for betraying you if you are truly evil, but deep down I think you are like your mother. She was born good and married into evil. You are half good and half evil, but I think the good in you will overcome the evil."

"How do you know I am not evil? How do you know I won't cut off your head as we speak?" asked a still shocked Lady Morphana.

"That's simple my lady, because you would have done it without asking by now." Slobbo replied. "If you ask me though my lady, I think we need to go find Perlangitis immediately. I have this bad feeling in the pit of my stomach that your aunt Sigcerlaw is on her way back to Shelvockwood."

"After all of these years that you have been by my side, you have never once spoken to me like you are my equal." Morphana replied.

A bit nervous that she was going to hit him for talking to her like he was her equal Slobbo asked, "Does that make you mad my lady?"

"Slobbo." she started, "I've always wanted someone to advise me when I took over for my mother and father years ago. You are my best friend and closest advisor that I trust. And you are right. I am not evil as I thought I was. If I was as evil as my father or my aunt, I would have done away with those protectors the minute that they got to Shelvockwood. How do I go about and find Perlangitis?"

"That's the easy part my lady. He hides inside the waterfall. We must make haste though and see him tomorrow before the sun

185

breaks. If my gut feeling is right, then we don't have till tomorrow night before your aunt is here."

∞

She couldn't get much sleep that night. Tossing and turning all night long, Morphana was having the worst dreams imaginable. She had no idea that she soon would be awakened by her mother. It was her mother's loud screaming that woke her out of a restless slumber. Sitting bolt upright in bed Morphana was staring into the eyes of her dead mother. Just a white ghost hanging above her bedpost was her mother, Vespera. It didn't take Slobbo and Gumbo long to come rushing into her chambers. Both were shocked to see Vespera's ghost floating above Morphana's bed. Gumbo said, "Why your majesty. Welcome home."

Turning to face Gumbo, Vespera said, "Don't be sucking up to me. Leave my daughter's chambers at once!" Turning to look at Slobbo she said, "Both of you!"

And with that both Gumbo and Slobbo left in a rather hurry from Lady Morphana's chambers. Left alone with the ghost of her mother, Morphana could do nothing but stare up at her. "Well don't just give me that dumb look. You know why I have come back from the grave. You are mad if you think I am going to let you give up what's rightfully ours. This land belongs to Empanvic and I. Don't screw it up by throwing it all away to those protectors of the ice crystals. My sister would be furious if she knew. I bet that's why she's on her way here now!" shouted Vespera.

"Aunt Sigcerlaw is on her way here?" asked a nervous Morphana.

Rolling her eyes towards the ceiling Vespera said, "Of course she is on her way here. She can sense there is something out of place in her blood. Evil runs through your veins and the minute you start thinking along the good side of things your blood shifts.

186

Sigcerlaw felt the blood shift in her veins. You want to go back to Perlangitis don't you? Well, Morphana I forbid it!"

"My heart has always belonged to him though. And how can you say you are so evil when you come from good blood? You weren't evil till my father turned you that way. And you did it because why?" asked Lady Morphana.

"I became evil because I loved Empanvic. He made me see things differently and I fell hard for him. That's why I turned evil." replied Vespera.

"Then you know why my heart may be melting away from the evil blood that runs through my veins. I love Perlangitis. I always have. He shows me things differently than the way you and father raised me. By the way, how did he die" Morphana asked while staring at her mother in the smoky eyes.

"Empanvic died by the hands of one of the protectors." answered Vespera.

"Well, according to the fables of the unicorns, you were trying to save father. You wanted to change his heart to good, but one of the protectors got to him first and that outraged you enough to get killed in fighting for him." Morphana said.

Shocked that her daughter was right on target with this one Vespera said, "That is true. I was trying to fight for the good side. My heart never went evil. I loved your father so much though that when I had found out he had died by one of the protectors I went insane with rage. Love does funny things to the heart."

"So, why are you here then? If you are fighting for the good, why are you mad about the blood line changing that way?" asked a curious Morphana.

"I made a deal with death. If he gave me this one shot at changing your life, he could have my evil soul. There isn't much left of my evil soul, but he sealed the deal. I'm here tonight to warn you. If you want to live and carry on our blood line you must side with the protectors against your aunt." said Vespera.

Looking rather confused as to why her mother said this after she said she didn't want her to turn good, Morphana asked, "What? But I thought you said…"

She was cut off as her mother said quietly, "I said that loudly so that Gumbo wouldn't think I was trying to give you a hint. He is your aunt's right-hand ogre. He's been spying on you for her and reporting back to your aunt. She is on her way here to put an end to your madness. Whether that is to keep your heart evil or kill you before it turns good. You must get out of the castle before dawn. Take your trusty ogre with you. I left Slobbo with you when you were little because he was my right-hand ogre growing up."

Whispering so that she was sure Gumbo wasn't listening Morphana said, "How do Slobbo and I get out of here without Gumbo seeing us leave or be suspicious?"

"That's easy. Perlangitis left you a rather large present did he not?" Vespera smiled as she asked.

"You mean Scales? I thought you never wanted me to have a pet dragon?" Morphana asked.

"Your father never wanted you to have a pet dragon because he knew that trained right, they could be very good-hearted creatures. He wanted you to have the most vial evil thing at heart. There are things you don't know about your father and me." said Vespera.

"Tell me while you still have time mother. I know that you aren't here long, and I must get packing to leave the castle grounds for good." said Morphana.

"Alright, but you may be disturbed by what you hear." said her mother. "Your father was in love with my sister, Sigcerlaw. She was born with an evil heart. My parents never knew why, because she came from a family with no evil in it. Empanvic loved my sister because she was so evil. He met her after he married me. I don't know if it is because of his evil heart, but he fell out of love with me like what we had was nothing. I knew I had to change him otherwise I would lose him forever. When I went to the unicorns for the spider crystal, the head female, Vailtorcles and informed me that Sigcerlaw was planning on killing me so that her and Empanvic could be together. I knew I had only a few hours to change him, so I hurried. It was too late. By the time I got to him Prudence had killed him. And in my anger for love she had killed me too. Sigcerlaw was outraged because she didn't get her chance to kill me and live her life with Empanvic. She killed the protectors and then swore she would be back if others came in replace of the old ones. You my darling daughter are caught right in the middle of the big family mess."

Stunned, Morphana just sat on her bed staring up at her mother. Not upset towards her mother anymore, or even her father. She was furious with her aunt for what she had done. Sigcerlaw was the reason Lady Morphana had lost both her parents years ago. Something had to be done. At dawn she was going to start taking action against her evil aunt Sigcerlaw.

∞

After the restless night and the encounter with her dead mother, Morphana was up before sunrise. She hadn't gone back to sleep after her mother vanished through the night air. Instead, she had started packing up her most treasured items. There came a quiet knock on her door.

Walking over to her door she opened it ever so quietly. Standing outside her door was Slobbo with a small bag in one hand and a bucket of food in the other. "For goodness sakes Slobbo, why are you bringing food with us?" Lady Morphana asked.

"It's not for me my lady. It's for Scales. He doesn't like to get up in the morning so I figured a little pick me up would get him up and moving around. We must make haste Lady Morphana. Are you almost all packed and ready to go?" asked Slobbo.

Looking rather sad, Morphana said, "I'm as ready as I'll ever be to leave my parents home. Let's go."

The two of them walked down the hall of the castle. Passing the ballroom where her thrown sits, Lady Morphana hung her head in shame. Once outside they just had to cross over to the stables to get Scales and they would be in the clear. Unfortunately, around the corner of the barn came Gumbo. "Why my lady, why are you up so early? That's not like you to be up this early."

Thinking quickly, she replied with a snotty tone in her voice. "I don't believe I asked you to keep track of my daily activities. I'm simply helping Slobbo move his stuff into the barn to be closer to Scales. I don't need him around me all the time like Scales does. I was thinking when I got back to the castle, I was going to ask you Gumbo to be my right-hand man, but since you are so ignorant in the morning bout certain things maybe I will reconsider my offer."

With wide eyes Gumbo said, "Oh no, I'm sorry my lady. I was just curious. I wasn't trying to interfere with your activities this morning. Please forgive me and my head. I'll be waiting for you in your chambers then."

And before she could yell at him some more, he bolted around her and Slobbo. Once out of sight Lady Morphana and Slobbo gave each other looks of relief as they had just missed almost not making it off the grounds of the castle.

Hurrying to get Scales up and moving (it didn't take them long thanks to Slobbo's quick thinking on the bucket of food) Slobbo threw on a saddle and strapped their belongings to it as well. Quickly helping Morphana up on Scales, Slobbo quickly followed. At full speed Scales ran towards the end of the castle grounds and took a big leap into the air and was gone. Making sure she told Slobbo they needed to find their own hiding spot and not with Perlangitis, Morphana noticed the dark hooded figure standing in the middle of her courtyard. Starring up at the sky, looking straight at them was Lady Morphana's aunt Sigcerlaw.

∽

Landing in the open meadow, Morphana climbed down off Scales. When her feet touched the ground, she came face to face with Perlangitis. Slobbo must have told him where to meet. Jumping into his arms Morphana began to cry. "She is going to kill me! I couldn't see her face, but I know she was giving me the look of death. We barely made it out of there. She got there as Scales was taking off. Oh, what am I going to do?"

Holding her tight, Perlangitis said, "It's alright dear. I came back for a reason. The stars have all aligned in the sky and I knew fate was sending new protectors. Now is the time to defeat your aunt. You can't do it alone, but most of defeating her must be done on your part."

"I'm not going to stay with you for a while. I don't want Sigcerlaw finding your hiding spot. I'll move from different spots if I must and use different disguises. I am after all a sorceress. I have done stuff like hiding before, but it was usually to spy on the protectors." said Morphana.

"There is an old building inside the village. Sigcerlaw won't look for you there for a while. She will first look at the protectors fort and then Sorsha's cottage. Plus, if you are in a disguise, she won't even suspect it right away. Let's go while we still have the time." replied Perlangitis.

Chapter 16

Tis the Season

It was months after Lady Morphana and Slobbo had left the castle. The protectors didn't know about her leaving the castle ground for good. So, they all went on about their business like nothing had changed. It was after all the Christmas season and the four friends had two parties to get ready for. The first party was to take place before Christmas in the village. The villagers felt that parties should be held before Christmas. That way you stay home with your family on Christmas. As for the second party, that was to be held in the afternoon in the Whispering Wood. "Are you ready to celebrate the holidays in Shelvockwood?" asked Piper.

"Yeah, I don't see why I wouldn't be excited." replied Tiffany.

"Well, we always have Lady Morphana to worry about. She could ruin a good day in a matter of seconds." Phoenix said under his breath.

"Phoenix does have a point. Whenever we have a special day planned out Morphana finds a way to ruin it somehow." Decklyn said.

"How long has it been since we've heard from her?" Tiffany asked.

"A while, actually. I wonder what she is up to." answered Decklyn.

Weeks went by rather quickly and then it was time to get the forest ready for the Winter festival. The Christmas party in the village was short and sweet. The villagers would rather stay away from the protectors. They don't believe in magic and forbid their children to believe in it as well. There was a table set up for food and a table set up for gifts. There were a few gifts on the table. Most of them were for the kids, Balfour had told them. Clara was very glad to see the protectors at the party though. She never left their sight the whole night and threw a fit when it was time for them to go home.

Earlier in the day Decklyn, Piper, Phoenix, and Tiffany were helping the forest committee get the Winter festival ready. Queen Lavinia had covered the clearing in front of (and around) Aged Sir Oak with a magic dome. This kept the wind out (there was however, still a little bit of snow on the ground for decoration purposes) so that it was not as chilly as the winter air was. Queen Lavinia also had put clear see through drains around the area of the forest to get rid of all the melted snow as the festival went on.

"This dome keeps people out right? How does it work exactly?" Piper asked the queen.

Flying over to where Piper could hear her, Queen Lavinia answered with, "Only woodland creatures and magical folk can enter the dome. They are the only ones that can see the dome itself too. No villagers can enter or see it. As cold as it is outside and dark as it gets during the evening the villagers are very content with staying in their homes in the village. They wouldn't be out in this and even if they were they wouldn't be out long for they fear the dark magic from Lady Morphana. That is why I believe they all hate magic all together. As for Lady Morphana and her minions it is magically protected from them as well with charms."

"If you say no villagers can enter this dome and they don't know magic at all, then how come that villager over by the pine tree is doing magic to put decorations up high on the top of the tree?" asked a very skeptical Tiffany.

Everyone instantly looked over towards the cloaked village woman. She was dressed like a villager, but she was doing magic. This was very weird and disturbing. Sorsha walked over to her with haste and with the wave of her hands threw the cloak off of the woman. Hunching down by the pine tree the woman didn't move an inch. Walking a bit closer to her, Sorsha sternly said, "Turn around."

Slowly turning around, everyone there came face to face with Lady Morphana. Not expecting to see her out in the open like that everyone instantly got mad. Decklyn and Phoenix stepped in front of the girls to protect them. Sorsha and Queen Lavinia were getting ready to strike when Morphana spoke, "Please hear me out. I've come here as a friend and not as an enemy. I would like a truce."

"Since when do we believe what comes out of your mouth?" shouted Aged Sir Oak.

"Please, you must believe me. I come with news. I was visited a month or so ago from my mother, Queen Vespera." Noticing that some of them were about to interrupt her, Lady Morphana said, "Please let me finish. She came to give me a warning. Her sister was on her way to Shelvockwood to end my reign for good and take over the land. I've learned horrible news about my father and my aunt that turns my stomach."

Walking over to her, Tiffany put a hand on Morphana's shoulder and said, "Tell us what you have heard about your father and aunt."

After a rather long story about her family Lady Morphana asked, "Will you help me defeat my aunt Sigcerlaw?"

Whispering to Piper, Tiffany said, "How can we not help her? She came to us for help, and I believe her story. If she was evil or going to harm us, she would have done so by now."

"I agree." Piper whispered back to Tiffany. Then turning to face Lady Morphana, Piper said, "You have my word that I will help you. I can't speak for everybody else, but I believe you."

Rolling his eyes towards the sky, Phoenix says, "Oh, give me a break. After all she has put us through you are going to switch sides like that?" Smiling just a little through the corners of his mouth at Piper's expression on her face he replied, "Well, I was just curious; wanted to make sure before I signed up to die is all."

Tiffany and Decklyn agreed as well that Lady Morphana needed their help. Aged Sir Oak was not happy one bit, but he agreed to at least be there for moral support till he knew her intentions were for real. With everyone on the same page, Queen Lavinia and Sorsha got to work with spells and charms to make sure they rid Lady Morphana of her evil for good. While they were doing that the rest of the magical community got back to decorating for the festivities.

☍☍

The layout was beautiful. Aged Sir Oak was decorated in tons of stringed popcorn that sparkled in the sunlight. He had what appeared to be red berries all over his branches. Pike was scampering around Aged Sir Oak and driving him batty. "Will you go find someone else to pester." shouted Ages Sir Oak.

With a gay laugh, Pike replied, "How can you be so miserable today of all days?"

"Because if you must know I do not trust Lady Morphana as far as I can throw an acorn and that isn't very far." grunted Aged Sir Oak. He was watching her very carefully as she sat with Piper, Tiffany, Sorsha, and Vailtorcles down around the base of his tree trunk. Leaning in to hear the conversation a bit better Aged Sir Oak gave Pike a smack of his branch to send him off towards the direction of Phoenix. "Go play with the boys." he whispered to him. With a frown on his face Pike was off to play with the rest of the boys.

"I never really had a problem with you Morphana. That was until you decided to take over the land of Shelvockwood. We were in the same spells and charms classes together." Sorsha said as she turned around to give Aged Sir Oak the raised eyebrow look.

"Mother never wanted me to really hang out with you Sorsha. I believe that was because she was too busy trying to save father from his evil ways that she didn't want to risk losing me too." Morphana replied.

"How do you figure she would have lost you?" Piper asked with curiosity.

"Well, my father would have been so outraged that he lost his only heir to his thrown, that he probably would have killed me had my heart gone to the good side. You see I was born into an evil family; even though my mother's heart was good. Father changed her heart to evil. Being born into an evil family like that can make your heart evil from the beginning. Mother loved me just as much as she loved father. She didn't want to chance losing me in the process of saving him." Morphana said, turning to look in Sorsha's direction for some sympathy.

"Well, if you ask me." Sorsha said to Morphana. "You may have been born into evil, but you are not evil. I think you were born with your mother's heart and your father's looks. He was a very charming man to look at. Just like Perlangitis is." She said, giving Morphana a wink.

"I can see the twinkle in your eyes whenever someone mentions his name." Sorsha continued even when Morphana started to blush. "If your heart melts for him like your eyes do then you truly are in love."

"Well, Perlangitis was very happy when he found out Slobbo and me needed an escape from the castle. He has begged and pleated with me to change for years. Even after I kicked him out of Shelvockwood, he never gave up. I know he'll stop at nothing to see that my heart really and truly does melt away from the evil." said Lady Morphana.

"He's a man with a good heart and soul. He is also a man who is determined to get what he wants out of life. Just in case you didn't know Morphana, he wants you." said Tiffany.

"How do you know that he does?" asked Morphana.

"Well," Piper started, "when you had your All Hallows Eve party in the castle, we all dressed up with Perlangitis and crashed it." Not giving Morphana a chance to yell or talk, Piper went on. "You see Perlangitis may not have come right out and said anything to us the night of the party, but I can tell by the way he was looking at you and the way he danced with you."

"I don't know." Morphana started to say but was interrupted by the loud noise coming from over by the table with all the gifts. Decklyn, Phoenix, Pike, Sparuxe, and Chanbo were all on the forest floor laughing. Rushing over to them the girls came to a halt when they saw the mess that they were all in. Decklyn was tangled up with Sparuxe, and Phoenix was in a bind with Pike and Chanbo. All laughing over what looked like spilled cider.

"Do we even want to know what happened?" asked a somewhat annoyed Tiffany.

Through gasps of air, Decklyn managed to say, "Phoenix was in the middle of drinking a cup of full cider when Pike out of nowhere came running and ran right into him. Before Phoenix knew what was going on he inhaled the cider, and it came out of his nose." Not getting much of a response from the girls he replied with, "Well, I guess you just had to be there."

"Oh, lighten up ladies, we are having fun and not killing each other." Phoenix said while cleaning off his face.

"Well, let's get back to work so we can have an enjoyable holiday before Morphana's aunt has a chance to ruin it." Sorsha chimed up.

The boys helped each other up and continued with setting up the rest of the forest for Christmas.

ॐ

The festivities went on without an interruption from Sigcerlaw. However, that didn't stop everyone from still being on their toes.

They all had to come up with a game plan to put an end to the evil in Shelvockwood for good. Sitting around the table in their fort, the four friends were figuring out ways to get rid of her. "I have an idea on how we can beat Sigcerlaw." Tiffany said one morning.

"And just pray tell. I would love to know how we can defeat the greatest evil next to Empanvic." said Phoenix.

Giving him a rather disgusted look, Tiffany continued with, "Lady Morphana has to be the one to put an end to her madness."

"That's not a bad idea, but how is she supposed to do that? The evil is melting away from her heart. She won't be able to overcome her aunt." Piper replied.

Just when Phoenix was about to put in his two cents, there was a knock at their door. Opening the door, the four friends were visited by Perlangitis and Lady Morphana. "We have come over to help figure out how to get rid of my aunt for good." Morphana said while greeting the four friends.

After taking their seats at the table, Tiffany looked at Morphana and with a serious face said to her, "I think you have to be the one to put an end to your aunt."

With huge eyes, Morphana slowly said, "You've got to be kidding me? How am I supposed to defeat my aunt who we all know is worse than my father ever was?"

Resting his hand on Morphana's shoulder, Perlangitis said with kind words, "You can do it. You've always had it in you to come out on top of all your family. Your aunt knows this. That is why she is hoping that you will cower down to her so she can end it herself."

"Well, what are we all waiting for? Let's end this nightmare." Decklyn replied.

The four friends, Perlangitis, and Morphana sat down and came up with a plan to defeat Sigcerlaw for good.

Chapter 17

The Reign of Sigcerlaw

Months went by without a concern or fear or Sigcerlaw. All the woodland creatures were out of their homes now that the winter months were gone, and the unicorns were enjoying the warm weather more so than any other creature. It is known throughout the land that unicorns carry tons of wisdom. The magic lies within their horn and only when they lose it do they lose all their powers. It is also known that unicorns have the most magic, even more than a wizard or sorceress. If one possesses the power of a unicorn, they become unstoppable. Even though they are very magical, unicorns are also very trusting. Even the most untrusting person (to some extent) is trusted. One of the many things a unicorn loves to do is frolic and play. Everybody knows this; however, it is very dangerous because they get playing and forget about being in the open.

One day Fairtices was minding her own business and frolicking with the other small unicorns when suddenly, she looked up and asked her friends, "What is that?"

Noticing right away that it was an evil witch walking towards them, all the unicorns began to panic and run in all directions. Frozen in fright, Fairtices stood watching this evil get closer and closer. Sigcerlaw was now nose to nose with the small unicorn. "Aren't you going to run like the rest of them?" she asked Fairtices.

"I should be, but I am not afraid of you. I know that even if you capture me the protectors will come to my rescue." said a scared but determined Fairtices.

"My time is near, and I can't count on my swamp goblins to do anything. Time is very precious, and they are not succeeding well." The witch said. With that she snapped her fingers and magically rope appeared out of nowhere and wrapped around the poor unsuspecting unicorn. Snapping her fingers again, Sigcerlaw looked towards the entrance to the Whispering Wood and magically there appeared five swamp goblins. They picked up Fairtices and followed Sigcerlaw towards the Castle of Terror.

Standing at the base of the waterfall, Perlangitis looked up at the sky worried. Meeting up with him Lady Morphana put her arms around him and asked, "What is it my love? What troubles you on this lovely morning?"

"You've been out of the loop for awhile my dear. There is something wrong; the wind is not the same warm breeze it should be. It's got a cold chill to it and I'm afraid you are used to that cold chill." He said with a sad tone.

Knowing he was right, for Morphana has had a heart of ice for so long that the cold breeze of trouble to her was enjoyable. "My aunt is up to something. It's written in the breeze this morning. I wouldn't trust her. We must go warn the protectors." said a worried Morphana.

Morphana and Perlangitis hopped up on Scales and took off into the cold cool day, headed to the protectors.

The four friends met up with Morphana and Perlangitis in the forest. "We have to defeat her for good this time." Phoenix said.

"Agreed. We cannot let her win this time. We all must stick together though." Decklyn said while shooting a quick glance over at Morphana.

"I've seen my aunt in action, and I know what she did to the protectors. She will not win this time. You all have my word." Morphana replied.

As they all sat there going over their ideas of how they could all come out of this battle alive, they were quickly interrupted by a very small, scared unicorn. "Please, help us." said the unicorn.

"What's the matter? You look like you've seen a ghost?" Tiffany said.

"We were just playing in the meadow; the weather is so nice today. We haven't had weather like this in a long time since winter. Out of nowhere she came. She took our friend." cried the unicorn.

"Who came? Who took your friend?" demanded Phoenix.

"The evil witch. The one that has been gone for so long. She came and took Fairtices." Sobbed the unicorn.

"I know what she is doing." replied Morphana. "She's tapping into the dark magic. Or at least trying to."

"What do you mean she's trying to tap into the dark magic? What could she want with a unicorn?" Piper asked.

"Unicorns have magical powers in their horns. It's known throughout the land that unicorn horns hold the most magic. If one wanted to tap into dark magic, they would need a unicorn horn." Perlangitis informed the group.

"We can't let her do that. We must go save the unicorn right now." Piper said while standing up and grabbing her things.

"No, this is something that I must do on my own." said Morphana.

"We can help." Piper replied.

"No, that's what she is expecting is a big fight. She wants all of us there to stop her. If it's just me she will think I have come back to my senses and evil ways. I will be fine. Scales will be hidden from view so that if I need to get out of there in a hurry I can." Lady Morphana said while climbing up on Scales.

Taking off up in the air, Lady Morphana looked down on her newfound friends as they comforted the small unicorn and waved bye to her. Nervous that she must go and face her aunt alone, Morphana patted Scales and said in a whisper, "Fly me home Scales."

ⲟⲭⲟ

Sitting in her chambers preparing for her dark magic ritual, Sigcerlaw had no idea her niece was on her way to the castle. She was brushing her long dark purple hair and looking rather smug. Talking to herself she says out loud, "Only a few more hours my dear and I will be able to hold you in my arms again." Starring at herself in the mirror there came a knock on the door. "Come in." she said in a soft evil tone.

Slowly the door opened and in walked Gumbo, and right behind him was her niece, Morphana. Opening her eyes wider in shock and disbelief, Sigcerlaw stood up from her chair and said, "Well, well, well. It's a pleasure to see you my dear niece. Whatever are you doing back in your father's castle?"

Gracefully walking over to her aunt, Lady Morphana's dark cape swept the floor of her old bedroom. Holding her chin up she replied to her aunt, "You didn't think I was going to let you have all the fun in destroying the protectors, did you? I simply gave them a little hope that I had changed my ways and let them all think that I was on their side. I want nothing more than revenge on them for killing my father and mother."

Tilting her head to the side and smiling evilly, Sigcerlaw chuckled and said, "Yes, you must get revenge on them for killing your parents. I have a way of bringing your father back to help us destroy them."

Giving her aunt a shocked look, Morphana asked, "How is it that you can bring my father back from the dead? He's been dead for years and who's to say he will have any knowledge of what's going on."

"You are still a silly girl, Morphana. If you were my daughter, I would have taught you a long time ago about the evil magic you so should know by now. There is deeper magic than even Sorsha knows." Sigcerlaw said while walking towards her chamber door. "Come with me child, and I will show you just how evil you could be."

They walked, it seemed forever, through the castle. When they finally got to the dungeon door Morphana's aunt turned to her and said, "This way my dear." Opening the door to the dungeon they started to descend the many steps to the bottom. Once they reached the bottom, Morphana saw the unicorn caged up in the corner of the dungeon.

Trying to make her aunt think she wasn't here to rescue the unicorn, Morphana started laughing. Turning to her aunt she said, "A unicorn? What on earth would you want with one of those silly things?"

"Stupid girl! Don't you know anything?" asked a very agitated Sigcerlaw. "Unicorns are very precious creatures. Using any part of a unicorn will make someone pure evil. That's all your father ever wanted was his only child to be pure evil like him. But my stupid sister was born with a pure heart, not an evil one. You have always been on the fence and tonight my dear you will become pure evil."

Morphana stood in shock. This wasn't a plan to get the protectors here to start a war, this was a plan to turn Morphana pure evil. She walked right into a trap. Smiling evilly at her, Sigcerlaw said, "Not what you expected is it my dear? Let's tangle you and me."

Before Lady Morphana could react, she was hit by a purple smoke cloud that threw her up against the wall. The purple cloud split and formed smoke chains that wrapped around Morphana's entire body binding her to the wall. This is NOT how this was supposed to go. She came here to save the unicorn and prove her love to Perlangitis.

As her aunt was preparing the ritual table for the unicorn, Morphana was suddenly hit with a vision. Perlangitis comes crashing into one of the dungeon windows and starts battling with her aunt while Morphana struggles with the purple smoke cloud. She is almost freed from the purple smoke chain when she watches her aunt kill her true love. Morphana snaps out of her trance when she hears a crash from the back wall. Turning towards the noise, she is horrified to see Perlangitis standing up facing her aunt.

"Well, if it isn't the great Perlangitis." Chuckled Sigcerlaw.

"I hope you are ready to die. One of us isn't making it out of here alive today." said Perlangitis.

"NO!" screamed Morphana.

Turning to face her niece, Sigcerlaw said, "He's here to save you, how cute. Enjoy watching him die my dear." She threw a lightning bolt at Perlangitis.

He jumped out of the way, and it missed him by a split second. Outraged at what was playing out in front of her, Morphana held her breath and busted out of the purple smoke cloud chains. Before she knew what was going on she threw her hand up in the direction of her aunt and threw out her own lightning bolt. It connected with her aunt and sent her flying towards the opposite wall. Rushing to her side Perlangitis said, "We have to get the unicorn and get out of here before she comes to." Looking at the evil look in Morphana's face he said, "And before you become pure evil. It's starting to take its toll already."

Whipping around, Morphana sent another bolt towards the unicorn. Perlangitis shouted, "Morphana! What are you doing?"

Facing him she said, "Saving the unicorn and getting the hell out of here." Rushing over to the cage she threw off the broken door that she hit with the bolt of lightning. Perlangitis was right behind her and pushed her aside to scoop up the shivering unicorn. Taking a quick glance in the direction of her aunt, Morphana said to Perlangitis, "I don't know where that came from, but I had a vision of you dying and I can't imagine losing you. The only way I set foot back in this castle is when I become a good queen."

They climbed out the broken window that Perlangitis came crashing in. Scales was already outside waiting for them and once they were all safely on him, he took off in one quick leap: leaving nothing but dust behind him.

☙❧

Coming to, Sigcerlaw slowly rose from the ground. Looking around the dungeon room she instantly became furious. "GUMBO!" she yelled.

Throwing open the door Gumbo appeared in the doorway. Looking around the messy dungeon he asked with a shocking tone, "My lady, what happened? I thought you were finishing off your niece and the unicorn. Where are they?"

Bruised up and hair all matted, Sigcerlaw walked over to Gumbo and replied, "I underestimated my niece. Her heart melted for good. She is no longer evil. I would have killed her love Perlangitis and that unicorn too, but she broke through my evil chains and hit me with my own lightning bolt. They escaped through that window. Where is that unicorn horn that I had saved from years ago?" she asked while rubbing her left side.

"You told me that you hid it in Empanvic's tomb. This way you know that it would be safe." Gumbo said while dusting dirt off her cape.

"We need to go get it. Tonight, I bring Empanvic back from the dead to take revenge on his own daughter." said a determined Sigcerlaw.

Chapter 18

The Cottage Behind
the Waterfall

After the encounter the night before, Morphana didn't sleep well. The protectors had insisted that she stay the night with them while Perlangitis took the shaken unicorn back to Sunpolis and Vailtorcles. Everyone was still sleeping. The sun hadn't risen yet. Morphana was sitting at the table trying to gather her thoughts when there was a huge bang and a big dark evil-looking purple smoke cloud appeared. Another bang followed from upstairs, so Morphana knew that the protectors were awake. Rushing downstairs to join their new friend the protectors came face to face with the purple cloud and what must be Morphana's evil aunt.

"You may have outsmarted me this time Morphana, but remember I am as evil as they get. You will not be making it out alive the next time we have an encounter." Sigcerlaw said evilly.

"What makes you think dear aunt that I will allow you to live yourself? Who's to say I don't kill you in the process of you killing me?" Morphana said proudly.

"Hahaha, oh child you do have A LOT to learn. I never said I was going to kill you." Sigcerlaw said through a chuckle.

Morphana was about to ask her who was supposed to kill her then, when there was a second voice that spoke. One that she hadn't heard in years. "Your aunt speaks true child. You have much to learn from the dark arts, but I'm afraid that you will never learn. I my dear am the one that is going to kill you." said a cocky, but much alive Empanvic.

With a very shocked and confused look on her face, Morphana turned to her new friends for help. Piper couldn't take any more of this malarkey and spoke. "You may think you are going to kill your daughter sir, but I'm here to tell you that you are dead wrong."

"And by dead wrong she means that you will die again since you are somehow alive right now." Phoenix added without joking at all.

"If you protectors think for one second, I'm going to let you kill me a second time you are sadly mistaken. I will enjoy every second of battling you and watching you die. Till we meet very soon, enjoy your last few days alive." Empanvic said and with that the purple smoke cloud vanished.

"I NEVER thought I would have to fight my dead father!" screamed Morphana. "This is getting ridiculous. What are we going to do? You all can't fight him either. If my aunt did bring him back and this isn't a trick, he would be much stronger than he was before. We have no chance."

"And that my dear is where you are wrong." Perlangitis said as he was walking in. "Your aunt just proved her weakness. She needs Empanvic to battle you. You scared her last night by fighting her. She can't defeat you on her own. You leave Empanvic to me. Once he is dead again is when you can defeat your aunt and Shelvockwood will again be safe from evil."

"That sounds all great, but how am I supposed to let you go and fight my father? He is evil and worse now. I don't even know how to defeat Sigcerlaw." a worried Lady Morphana said.

"We're going to be with you every step of the way. You are not alone anymore and with our help we will come up with a plan to defeat both and get you back on the throne. But you know on the good side this time." Phoenix said while patting Morphana on the back.

"I wish I had a good feeling about this, but I don't see how this going to end well." Morphana sadly replied.

"Just wait my dear and you will see." smiled Perlangitis.

Even though their day started off rocky with the news of Empanvic being back, the friends made the best of it. They packed up a few picnic baskets and headed to the meadow to have a lunch with Sunpolis and Vailtorcles.

Meanwhile back at the castle, Sigcerlaw was having the time of her life with her long-lost love. "Empanvic my dear, this is our moment to rule together. Finally, we are together at last."

Smiling with a cocky evil grin, Empanvic replied, "You are brilliant for summoning me back from the dead. I cannot believe my daughter is ruined because of this thing. What's his name again?"

"His name is Perlangitis. He has won her heart over and melted it before my very eyes. I'm sorry that I was not able to turn her evil. I came back as soon as I felt the blood shift in my own veins." sighed Sigcerlaw.

"Well, to get my daughter to even think about fighting me, we have to take the one thing from her that means the most." Empanvic replied while he poured himself a glass of wine.

Turning her head ever so slightly to the side and smiling evilly, Sigcerlaw nodded her head. "That is the best thing I have heard all day. What's your plan?"

"Before we get to that I need to know how you got me back here. I've done some dark magic in my time, but I've never actually brought someone back from the dead before. It's intelligent." replied Empanvic.

"It was very simple really." She said while walking around Lady Morphana's old room. "After your stupid naïve daughter somehow got out of my smoke chains and hit me with my own lightning bolt I was infuriated. I knew I would never be able to defeat her myself. That the only person who would be able to put an end to her would be you. I started talking to myself and pacing the dungeon floor. Outraged from everything and still irritated at losing you years ago, it hit me like a ton of bricks. Why didn't I think of it before? Waving my hand towards the back of the dungeon wall I quickly reviled your secret layer. I remember you taking me down there when you were with my stupid sister. Now I realize where Morphana gets it from. She is just like my sister Vespera. Walking over to your table I opened your book of spells to the back of the book. Years ago, I was told one day I would need it to bring you back to life. So, in a way I knew you were doomed to die by the hands of the protectors."

Looking shocked Empanvic asked, "You knew all along and didn't tell me, but why?"

"The only thing I got from my parents was this great piece of advice. Never mess with the future. You had to die so that I could bring you back. Everything happens for a reason. Now let me finish my story so we can plan our attack on your retched daughter." Sigcerlaw said with glee in her voice.

"Continue darling. I want to know everything." he said while leaning towards her neck and running his hand over her cheek.

Smiling just a little, she continued. "I cut the back of the book open with my fingernail. Inside was a spell to summon you back. I had everything I needed right in the room with me. The summoning spell asked for eye of newt, a lock of your hair, a few different herbs, crow's feet, and finally some of my own blood. As soon as the first drop of my blood hit the potion a big black cloud of smoke started to crawl out of the caldron. It crawled across the floor and started to come back around to where I was standing. Out of the black smoke you started to crawl and then you were standing in front of me; starling at me as if no time had passed from the last time."

"I haven't stopped thinking about you. Even in death, I've thought of you. Vespera meant nothing to me after we had Morphana. She was never pure evil. I think she wanted to turn me good. I married the wrong sister, but she had me under a spell. We have got our second chance, Sigcerlaw. Let's have some fun, shall we?" Empanvic responded.

Turning to face him she said, "The only thing I can think of is capturing Perlangitis. Making her want to come and save him. She won't come here alone, and you know that those protectors will be with her. I don't see how this is going to end well for us."

"My dear, you have underestimated me. We must separate them. Like you did years ago. That's how we are going to end them all. And you leave my daughter to me." Empanvic said. "Let's just capture Perlangitis."

＠＞＜＠

Perlangitis thought it would be best for not just Morphana, Slobbo, and Scales to hide, but the protectors as well. So, everybody packed up what they could and made the long walk to the waterfall. Perlangitis's cottage was hidden behind the waterfall itself. With the rush of the water nobody would have thought to look for them behind the running water. With just a wave of his hand the water parted like a curtain; giving them all room to walk through without getting wet. Once the last person was through, the water went back to running fast and loud. They only walked for another five minutes and then they came upon the cottage. The cottage looked like it had been abandoned for years. There were vines and flowers growing all over the place. Just behind the cottage was a stable big enough for Scales to stretch in. Perlangitis had built the stable knowing that Morphana would soon be moving in with him and he knew she would not be able to give up Scales.

"We should be fine in here." Perlangitis replied. "I have cast a few protection spells so that nobody can find us. Make yourselves at home."

"We need to sit down and come up with a plan to defeat both Sigcerlaw and Empanvic." Decklyn said.

"Agreed." replied Piper.

Morphana, Tiffany, Phoenix, and Piper started to walk into the cottage, but Decklyn grabbed Perlangitis by his arm and nodded his head in the direction of the stable. "Morphana, Decklyn and I are going to settle Scales in his new stable. We'll be right back." Perlangitis said.

Smiling at him, Morphana and the others went inside and left Decklyn and Perlangitis alone. As they headed towards the stable Perlangitis turned to Decklyn and asked, "So, what's up my friend?"

"We both know that Morphana won't battle either her aunt or her father without a little push. We can make a plan with the others, but I think secretly part of the plan needs to involve you being taken captive. This won't really upset the plan that we all make but will help Morphana want to fight her own blood."

"That is very risky, but I have full trust in her. I believe she will defeat her aunt and father. It should be very easy to get caught, but we have to make that look like I wasn't trying to get captured." Responded Perlangitis.

"If we don't give her the push to want revenge on her love, she will crumble at their mercy." Decklyn said. "I've seen Piper get very heated over the thought of losing me. I can just imagine her fury if I was captured, and she thought for the slightest chance that I was going to die."

"Well then. That's it." said Perlangitis. "Time, I work on getting captured."

☙❧

Back at the cottage everybody was sitting around Perlangitis's table. Not a single person was quiet. They were all throwing in their ideas of how the battle should go and take place. "I think we should just storm the castle grounds and catch them off guard." Phoenix replied.

"That's not going to work. They will know we are coming. Sigcerlaw is a sorceress remember?" Tiffany responded to him. "Besides I think we should just wait them out in hiding."

"Hiding never did anything; just prolonged the execution." Piper said.

Running his fingers through his hair, Phoenix says, "We have to think of something and soon because the longer we sit here arguing about the plan the sooner those crazy two come after us."

"He's right. We need to come up with a plan and now." Morphana says.

"We need to split up." Piper replies.

"Are you out of your mind? That's exactly what they want us to do. They want us to split up so that we are vulnerable and easy targets." Tiffany says with worry in her voice.

"I know that. This is what they will be expecting which will give us all the opportunity to fight on our own ground so to say." Still getting worried looks, Piper continued. "If we are by ourselves, we start thinking the worst. What if they got the others? What if they got my partner? Then we start to get mad and revengeful. Which puts us in the defense mode, and we start to think for ourselves and fight back. I'm sure there is in some way a little fighter in all of us. Yes, even you Tiff, if pushed enough."

"She's right. That's what they want, so I say we give it to them.

212

Let's split up and meet on the grounds of the castle. Bring the fight to them." Perlangitis says.

"I hope you guys are right. I'm worried." Tiffany says with concern.

✪

Entering the dungeon, Empanvic stumbles upon Sigcerlaw casting another one of her many spells. As she chants, she throws things into the caldron, "Adplica quoque ad inferos deducentur. Ex cinere ut ossa. Surge carcere terram. Surgite! Then there was a loud bang. She looks up at Empanvic and an evil smile starts to form across her face. "Let the fun begin." She snarls.

"What have you conjured up my dear?" Empanvic asks with joy in his voice.

"Come my dear and see for yourself." Grabbing his hand, she leads him up and out of the castle to the grounds. Waving her hand, Empanvic notices the ground is moving. Dirt starts to rise and through it comes skeleton hands. Before they know it there is an army of dead skeletons. "They look hideous. I love it!" Empanvic states.

"Let our army of skeletons capture Morphana and her new friends." Turning to face her new army Sigcerlaw says, "Capture Perlangitis and Morphana. Kill the protectors!" Her army starts to move through the gates of the castle towards the forest.

✪

Not liking Piper's plan at all Tiffany sets off towards the meadow with Perlangitis. As Piper had suggested they all split up, but into groups. That way if someone was caught the other could let the rest of the groups know. At least she was with Perlangitis. He seemed to know what he was doing. Piper had gone with Morphana, which left Decklyn and Phoenix to go off together. At least they each had a pair. They were all within ear shot as well so that at least if someone did get taken, they would know about it. Turning to face Perlangitis as they were walking Tiffany asked, "Is this plan going to work?"

Noticing her concern, he replies with, "Tiffany, I've spoken to Vailtorcles. She's a future reader with the stars. Nobody really knows that, but a few of us. From what she tells me we all will make it through this in one piece. Just remember don't give up the fight."

"Well, that makes me feel a little bit better, but not by much. I just want everything to work out. I'm worried." She replies.

"As you have every right to be, Tiffany." He turns and looks at her all serious. "Just so you know. Decklyn and I have a plan to get Morphana to fight against her father and aunt. I'm going to get taken, so you need to protect yourself as best as you can."

Shocked that this was even going to happen, Tiffany responded with, "In a messed-up way that makes sense. If I knew that Phoenix was taken, I would fight for his life in a heartbeat."

"I hope you're ready because here comes Sigcerlaw's army. I was wondering what she was going to send our way." Perlangitis said while pointing off in the distance.

Slowly making their way through the trees were nasty looking skeletons. It was hard to see them as it was dusk out. Tiffany held her crystal high in the air and instantly a lavender light emerged and shot up into the sky. This was the warning shot that was to let the other groups know that danger was lurking close.

She barely had time to shoot off the signal when out of nowhere a skeleton grabbed her arm. She gave a blood curtailing scream as the skeleton raised its other hand with a sharp looking blade and swung at her.

એક

Piper and Morphana saw the light in the sky. "That's our signal. Something is coming." Morphana said.

Before Piper could reply she heard a scream. Running towards the direction of the light, Piper almost ran right into Phoenix. "I swear to the all mighty Piper, if they hurt Tiff, I'm going to go ballistic."

"Let's get moving." Decklyn called as he raced past Piper and Phoenix.

Arriving in the open meadow where Tiffany and Perlangitis were, what they saw was shocking. Perlangitis was fighting off three skeletons and poor Tiffany was fighting off two. And off in the distance there were more coming. "How do you kill something that is already dead?" Tiffany was yelling towards Perlangitis.

"This is the work of dark magic. Only another dark spell can put them back into the ground." Perlangitis called out.

Just as the words were out of his mouth he was hit on the head by a big rock. Knocked unconscious, two skeletons grabbed him by his feet and started dragging him off towards the woods.

"NO!" screamed Morphana. "We can't let them take Perlangitis!"

As she tried fighting her way through the skeletons, more came. She couldn't make her way to Perlangitis. The skeletons were way into the deep forest with him now. Trying to fight back tears Morphana looked around at her new friends. Decklyn and Phoenix were fighting a gang of skeletons and poor Tiffany was still fighting off two of them. Nervously looking around for Piper, Morphana noticed that she too was being dragged towards the woods. Furious she bent down to her knees, bringing her arms up with her hands held out high she said these words, "Ex resurrexistis cinis, sed cades in cinerem revertetur. Aliquam non recepert vos. Et cadite!" After her words she threw down purple smoke powder. There was a loud boom and then a big clash of thunder. Seconds later every one of the skeletons turned into ashes and blew away in the wind.

Decklyn ran towards Piper who was laying just outside the

border of the forest. Phoenix was helping Tiffany up off the ground and making sure she wasn't hurt. Once Decklyn and Piper were back with the group Lady Morphana said, "That is the last time I use dark magic." Turning to look at her friends she says, "And that is the last time we split up. We work together and end this tonight."

∽◯∾

The only two remaining skeletons entered the castle grounds dragging Perlangitis with them. "Wonderful work, but where is Morphana?" Sigcerlaw asked.

Facing each other the skeletons shrugged their shoulders and put their hands up in the air. Furious at their answer, Sigcerlaw waved her hands and instantly the skeletons became dust. Turning to Gumbo she says, "Take Perlangitis to the dungeon until his welcome party arrives."

"Yes Madame." Gumbo replies while throwing Perlangitis over his shoulders.

"You think they'll come tonight my dear? I'm sure they want a good nights rest." Empanvic says while rubbing Sigcerlaw's shoulders.

"If I know my niece, she's as predictable as my sister was. She'll want to avenge him tonight." Sigcerlaw said while shrugging Empanvic off her.

"Then we must prepare for battle, come my dear." Empanvic stated.

With that Empanvic and Sigcerlaw entered the castle.

Chapter 19

Empanvie's Vicious Lie

"**I**f you want to help me defeat my family, there's something you all should know." Morphana said while walking through the forest. She was walking fast and as if she was on a mission. Everybody had to practically run to keep up with her.

"Morphana, slow down a bit. I can't keep up." Piper said.

"I'm sorry, but I must get back to the waterfall and get Scales. Only he can help me defeat my father. I'm not worried about my aunt. She's easy enough to defeat." Morphana said while slowing down her pace.

"Tell us what you know about your father. What can help us in battle?" Decklyn curiously asked.

"I stumbled upon a letter addressed to my aunt from my father while I was rummaging through old spell books in the dungeon. It was telling my aunt how my mother Vespera had me to trap him, and he couldn't stand to look at her anymore. She wasn't evil enough for him, her heart was pure good. No matter how much she loved him he couldn't be with someone who was purely good. He wanted to be with my aunt." Getting no reaction from the protectors, Morphana went on. "Prudence didn't kill my mother."

Now there was shock. All the friends looked dumbfounded.

"Wait, I thought Prudence killed both of your parents. That's how the story goes." Tiffany said.

"So, the story is told, but in the letter to my aunt, my father says that for them to be together she had to kill her sister. He would somehow make it look like one of the protectors killed her so that I would turn pure evil and take over the throne." Morphana stated. Looking down at her feet she said, "Sigcerlaw killed my mother. She was dressed like Prudence and was to meet up with my father later that night, but in doing so found out that Prudence killed my father."

"And from there the story went on to the protectors meeting their untimely deaths." Piper replied.

"It's very hard to wrap my head around that my father never wanted a child like me. That he never loved my mother because she wasn't evil enough. That he planned her death and in doing so got himself killed instead." said a sad Morphana.

"Your aunt can't beat you without the help of your father. We defeat your father; we defeat your aunt. Let's just get there first and go from there." Phoenix replied while walking even faster now.

"Tonight, we either die trying or we end them for good. Someone is not making it out of this battle alive." Morphana said through gritted teeth.

"Then let's get there." said a determined Phoenix.

ᴏᴋᴏ

While the friends were walking to save Perlangitis, Sigcerlaw and Empanvic were in the dungeon preparing for his death. "Don't worry Perlangitis, it will all be over soon." Sigcerlaw said through a wicked smirk.

"Oh, I'm not worried. Morphana is going to end you both. She isn't alone." said a rather enraged Perlangitis.

"Haha, silly boy. What makes you so sure that my daughter has it in her to defeat her aunt, let alone me?" laughed Empanvic.

"Good ALWAYS triumphs over evil." shouted Perlangitis.

"My dear boy" started Sigcerlaw, "don't you remember the other protectors? I do recall they all died. And if I'm not mistaken good didn't win that day."

"We have to hurry my dear." Empanvic said. "They are almost here."

"Oh, how I love that you can see into the future. Do tell, is it a happy ending for us my dear?" asked Sigcerlaw.

"Victory, once again." Empanvic said while smiling towards Perlangitis.

Just as Sigcerlaw was mixing up her last potion there came a big rumbling and shaking of the ground. Once it stopped the dungeon was brightened up with an orange glow from the grounds outside, followed by screaming. "What on earth is going on?" shouted Sigcerlaw.

Running into the room came Gumbo yelling, "They're here! And that dragon of theirs is burning all the goblins up. What are we to do?"

"WHAT?" screamed Sigcerlaw.

"Let the battle begin." Empanvic said and with a wave of his hand Perlangitis and himself vanished in thin air.

"Call in everybody you can get." Sigcerlaw ordered as she threw down a potion and in a cloud of purple smoke she vanished too.

⊗⦶

Scales was doing a wonderful job of burning up the grounds of the castle. He had just finished off the last of the goblins when Morphana and the protectors reached the castle grounds. Phoenix was about to say something when out of nowhere a dark black cloud of smoke formed on the ground. Emerging from the cloud was Empanvic and Perlangitis. "Let him go father!" shouted Morphana.

"What makes you think for a second child that this is going to end well for all of you?" asked Empanvic evilly.

"And what makes YOU think that you are going to walk away from this alive still?" Decklyn shouted back.

"Silence!" Empanvic yelled as he hit Decklyn with a bolt of lightning.

Decklyn fell to the ground and didn't move. "NO!" screamed Piper.

As Phoenix ran over to heal Decklyn, Piper made her move towards Empanvic. Holding up her ice crystal she shot out a white ball of light that hit Empanvic dead on. He toppled over. Just then a purple cloud of smoke appeared behind Perlangitis and out came Sigcerlaw. With a dead look on her face she emerged and stabbed Perlangitis in the back. Looking over at her niece she said, "Let's finish this."

Morphana was outraged and waved her hands up from the ground and threw a boulder at Sigcerlaw. That battle had begun. Phoenix and Tiffany were attending to Decklyn and watching in horror as Piper was fighting Empanvic. She was throwing great big balls of light at him left and right and wasn't slowing down. It looked like she had him backed into a corner. Morphana, however, wasn't doing so well. Sigcerlaw was hitting her with every potion she had. As the tears were coming from her face Morphana looked like she was about to be defeated. Sigcerlaw had one last potion to throw at her niece to finish her off. She was about to throw it when she happened to look in the direction of Empanvic. To her horror he was on the ground all bloody and bruised. "I don't think so!" she shouted.

Sigcerlaw threw her potion in the direction of Piper. "Piper lookout!" screamed Tiffany.

Piper moved just in time for the potion to hit the castle wall near Empanvic and explode, throwing both Piper and Empanvic towards Sigcerlaw and Morphana. Grabbing Piper by her ponytail Sigcerlaw said in a dark evil voice, "I don't think you'll get the chance to kill him this time!"

Piper didn't let up, she hit Sigcerlaw with a white light; enough to free her from her grip. Getting up off the ground Piper went over to Empanvic and with one last ball of light from her crystal struck him in the chest. He let out a scream and exploded into dust. "NO!" screamed Sigcerlaw.

With a dark purple cloud of smoke, she vanished back into the castle walls. Piper helped Morphana up and ran over to Decklyn who was slowly getting up from the ground. "Are you ok?" asked a worried Piper.

"Yes, but I don't know about Perlangitis." Decklyn said with a worried gesture towards Perlangitis's body.

Phoenix had gone over to Perlangitis and was working his green ice crystal on him. Morphana was sobbing over his body while Tiffany was comforting her. Just when Phoenix was about to give up, Perlangitis gasped for a breath of air. Looking at Morphana he asked, "Did we win my love?"

"My father is back in the land of the dead, but I fear my aunt is going to be looking for revenge. We must get out of here and go back into hiding and fast." Morphana stated.

Phoenix and Morphana helped Perlangitis up. The friends started walking towards the forest; wounded, but alive.

ᗧᗧᗤ

Back in the dungeon Sigcerlaw was throwing a huge fit. Things were flying across the room, books were being thrown, and the big cauldron was dumped onto the floor. "I lost him again!" she screamed.

Gumbo walked into the room and asked, "Are you hurt my queen?"

"Yes, my heart is broken again. That little protector killed my beloved Empanvic. This is NOT how this battle was supposed to go. I want blood!" said a still outraged Sigcerlaw.

"There must be a way my queen, to get what you want." replied Gumbo.

"I've thought of everything you little twi..." just then an evil smirk formed on Sigcerlaw's lips. "Why of course. Why didn't I think of this before. I'll just send them back to where they came from. Then I'll have my revenge on my niece."

"Send them back, but won't they just come back and defeat you, my queen?" asked a confused Gumbo.

"There is a way I can send them back and close the portal for good. They won't be returning, and no new protectors will be able to get in ever again! Quick we must get the ingredients I need. Pick up the cauldron, we have work to do." Sigcerlaw said with glee.

ⓔⓧⓔ

Once everybody went through the waterfall and headed to Perlangitis's cottage. Tiffany was just about to head through the door when she got a sharp pain in her head and fell to her knees. "Tiff are you ok?" Phoenix asked.

Tiffany didn't hear him, while she was on the ground, she got visions of Sigcerlaw's plan. "Oh, no." she said looking at her friends. "We have a problem."

"What's the problem?" Decklyn asked.

"Sigcerlaw plans on sending us back home. Back to Willow and then closing the portal to this world. Then she will be able to kill Morphana." Tiffany said with bulging eyes.

"There must be a way to stop her. We can't go back just yet.

222

There is too much to do here. We can't leave till we've helped you all." said a worried Piper.

"There is a way you can get back here." Morphana said.

"Oh, and how is that?" asked Phoenix.

"When she sends you back to your world, you must get to the door to this world before she closes it. You have only 20 minutes to get to it otherwise it closes for good." Perlangitis said.

"But if it closes while we are back here, how are we to get home again?" asked Tiffany.

"That I don't know. You may be stuck in our world forever." Perlangitis said while hanging his head.

"Well, I guess that's a risk we are willing to take. Who's with me?" Decklyn stated.

"I am." answered Piper.

"Me too." Tiffany replied.

"Oh, well then, I guess that I must agree too. Can't live in a world without my main girl." Phoenix said while looking at Tiffany.

"Well, then it's settled then. When she sends you back, you have exactly 20 minutes to get back to the door. Hopefully you are not that far from the door itself." Morphana stated.

With worried looks, the four friends continued back into the cottage.

Chapter 20

The Reign and Fall of Sigcerlaw

The next day the friends were expecting Sigcerlaw to send them back to their world, but it didn't happen. A week had gone by, and nothing had come about from the battle at the castle grounds. It was a nice sunny day in Shelvockwood, and the protectors were outside the hidden waterfall with Morphana and Perlangitis enjoying the refreshing crisp water. Scales was curled up on the bank of the creek soaking up the sun, while Perlangitis and Decklyn were having a discussion next to him. Morphana and Piper were wadding in the water, while Tiffany and Phoenix were splashing about. All seemed right with the world when suddenly, the water started to swirl, and the winds picked up. Running from the water Morphana, Piper, Tiffany, and Phoenix ran up next to Decklyn and Perlangitis. The water was forming into a hurricane and dark storm clouds started rolling in. Just when the winds were at their worst, up came Sigcerlaw from the waters below. Hovering over the water the hurricane died down, but the winds still blew with fury. Looking at the scared faces of her enemies below, Sigcerlaw started chanting, "Sit amet mundum et potestatibus tenet erras mittam ad pristinum. Expelle eos quoniam in aeternum!"

"She's sending us back!" shouted Piper.

"Remember you only have 20 minutes to find the portal." yelled Morphana.

Before anybody else could say another word, a dark deep red smoke cloud appeared around each one of the protectors. Encircling around them, the cloud started rising over their bodies; and then with a big bang they were gone.

As soon as the guardians vanished in thin air, Sigcerlaw threw a lightning bolt at Morphana knocking her to the ground. Scales was up and throwing fire towards Sigcerlaw, but she threw out smoke chains that slithered up and around Scales pinning him to the ground. Perlangitis jumped behind a boulder just in time, missing one of her lightning bolts. "You think you have won by getting rid of my love? You are sadly mistaken." Sigcerlaw growled.

She was still throwing lightning bolts in his direction, one right after another. As she was advancing up to him Morphana got up and threw a lightning bolt at her and knocked her down. Furious Morphana said, "This ends Sigcerlaw! You think by sending the protectors back to their land that you will win?"

Getting up off the ground Sigcerlaw said, "You are just as wounded as I am dear. If you think you can stop me then by all means come and get me, my dear." Sigcerlaw said and threw down a potion at her feet and vanished from the waterfall.

⊘⊘

The four friends fell hard onto the woodland floor. Turning to look at the girls Phoenix asked, "Where are we? Is everyone ok?"

Rubbing her head Tiffany replied, "We're only a few feet from our tent. See it's just over there."

Turning to look where she was pointing, Piper jumped up. "Come on guys we don't have much time. We need to get back to that cave and fast."

As the rest of the crew jumped up and brushed themselves off, they started to run in the direction of the cave. "Didn't it take us like 30 minutes to get there?" asked a worried Tiffany.

"Don't think about it. Just keep running!" said a pumped-up Decklyn.

Dodging trees and jumping over fallen logs the friends kept on running. "We're almost there." said Piper.

The trees were just a blur as the four friends sprinted through the woods. Up ahead Phoenix was the first to get to the cave. Waving his friends on he said, "Let's go get this witch!"

It didn't take the friends long to enter the cave and find the hole they needed to jump down. Phoenix was the first to enter. Tiffany was right behind him. Piper turned to look at Decklyn and said, "Hurry up Deck!" Then she too jumped into the hole.

Reaching the hole Decklyn noticed a dark purple and blue smoke cloud start to form. He didn't wait any longer and jumped down the hole. After he jumped the hole closed and there was no trace of one ever being there.

 exo

Sorsha was making a potion in her kitchen when she heard a huge crash. Rushing over to her broom closet she saw the door open and on the floor Decklyn, Piper, Phoenix, and Tiffany. "Why are you crashing through the portal to other worlds?" Sorsha asked.

"We made it! I didn't think we would make it." said an out of breath Phoenix.

"We don't have much time. We were at the waterfall with Morphana and Perlangitis enjoying our day. Out of the water came Sigcerlaw. She sent us back to our world and closed the portal. We made it back here in time before the portal closed. We must get back to Morphana and help her." Decklyn replied.

"Morphana summoned me and said she needed a powerful

potion. One that was not made of dark magic, but that would defeat her aunt. She is on her way here right now with Perlangitis." Sorsha said.

"Oh, thank goodness." Tiffany said while she got up off the floor. "Maybe we can come up with a plan before we just go after this crazy lady."

Sorsha was about to say something, but there was a knock on her door. Opening her door Phoenix greeted Slobbo. "Hello, where is Lady Morphana?"

"She is coming. Must help Perlangitis hide Scales in the Whispering Wood. I am glad to see you all made it back. Morphana was very upset that Sigcerlaw sent you all away. They battled a bit after you left, but I'm afraid Sigcerlaw wants Morphana on the castle grounds for this battle. If that happens Morphana may lose or use dark magic. We cannot let that happen."

"We will talk with her Slobbo. She isn't alone this time." said Piper.

The protectors, Sorsha, and Slobbo were just sitting down at the table to discuss options for battle when Morphana burst through the door with Perlangitis. "I'm going to end her! Poor Scales is shaking with fright from those smoke chains. I swear I am gonna ring her neck!" Looking at the table of friends Morphana stopped yelling and through sobs said, "Oh, thank the stars! You all made it back. I was so worried you wouldn't. I am afraid I cannot do this alone."

"Sit down Morphana and have some water. We are gonna come up with a plan. And in case your aunt is watching Tiff put an invisible shield over the cottage so she can't find us."

Taking a seat next to Piper, Morphana said, "Ok. What do you all think?"

"I think we should just show up and end this, but that is what happened to the last protectors. I mean in a sense they all did it alone, but charging in and battling is what she wants us to do.

She is gonna be waiting for us. We must think of something else." Decklyn stated.

"What if there were more of us?" Piper asked.

Everyone looked confused. Decklyn said, "Piper, babes, what do you mean? There isn't much more we can do with who we have."

"I mean what if we get the spider crystal and use it to our advantage. Get more help from unicorns. Vailtorcles and Sunpolis may be able to help us in this battle. I wouldn't dream of asking the villagers, although I know Balfour would love to help if he could."

"That's it! Piper is right." Morphana shouted. With the whole room looking confused Morphana continued. "You all have your crystals, but maybe with the spider crystal I can tap into its magic and use that to our advantage. It's gonna take a miracle to defeat her."

"We have a plan. It's not solid, but it's a plan. Tiff, you think you can keep us all invisible long enough to get us to the caves of the unicorns. We can't let Sigcerlaw know what our plan is until we are in front of her." Phoenix said.

"Piper you and the rest of the protectors go and get the spider crystal. Perlangitis and I must get Sigcerlaw out in the open away from the castle. If she sees any of you its over. She thinks she is gonna win because you all got sent home. She has no idea you are all here." said a determined Morphana.

"Ok, let's try and get her to go to the meadow. It's wide open and no surprises. Give us like an hour to get to the caves and talk to the unicorns. We won't be far behind." Piper said.

Smiling for the first time in a long time Morphana said, "Now the real battle begins."

 exo

"Why do we always have to run through the woods? I am not in shape for this kind of exercise." Phoenix said while he was jumping over another fallen log.

"Keep up Phoenix." Decklyn yelled while dodging a tree branch.

"We are almost there. I see the clearing up ahead." Tiffany said excitedly.

It was hard running through the forest this time because they all had to hold hands for the invisible shield to work. If one of them let, go then they would be seen by Sigcerlaw. Rushing to the cave Phoenix slid in front of the cave like he was sliding into home plate. "Safe!" he yelled.

"Phoenix only you can make a smile form on my face in a time when we should be serious." Decklyn said while smacking Phoenix on the back.

"Times a ticking. Let's go talk to Vailtorcles and Sunpolis." Phoenix said while getting up from the ground.

Entering the cave, the friends were greeted by Sparuxe. "Hey friends, what brings you to our cave?" he asked.

"We need to talk to Vailtorcles and Sunpolis. It's urgent." replied Piper.

"Vailtorcles knew you were all coming. She wants me to give you this and said use it wisely." Sparuxe said as he brought out the spider crystal.

Looking a bit puzzled Decklyn asked, "Why didn't they give it to us?"

"Sunpolis and Vailtorcles are the oldest unicorns around. If they even thought for a second you would need them, they would be here. They must have faith in you that you can do this on your own." Sparuxe said while scrapping the ground with his hoof.

Grabbing the spider crystal from the unicorn Tiffany said, "We got what we came for. Let's go meet Morphana."

Upon arriving at the meadow, the friends could see Sigcerlaw and Morphana throwing purple electric bolts at each other. Morphana wasn't blocking them very well. "We have to help her." Piper said, turning to her friends. "You get her the spider crystal. I'll handle Sigcerlaw."

Not giving them a chance to react, Piper took out her ice crystal and aimed it at Sigcerlaw. A white light shot out and hit her on the side knocking her to the ground. Piper kept advancing towards Sigcerlaw. As she was ten feet away Sigcerlaw got up and shot a lightning bolt towards Piper, but it was deflected by a green light. Phoenix was right by Piper's side. "You are not taking her on alone." He spoke.

Phoenix and Piper were battling Sigcerlaw. This gave Decklyn and Tiffany time to get to Morphana and hand her the spider crystal. "Are you ok?" Tiffany asked Lady Morphana.

"I will be. This ends today." Morphana said while taking the crystal and placing it around her neck. The spider crystal started to shine a black and purple color. Turning to face her aunt Morphana threw out her right hand and out shot a black and purple spiral bolt. It hit her aunt with such force that it threw her 20 feet away.

Sigcerlaw got up in time to be hit with more bolts. This time green, white, and the black and purple spiral all hit her. Sigcerlaw smiled evilly. She knew what they were all up too. Looking at her niece she threw one last electric bolt at Morphana. She didn't realize that Decklyn and Tiffany had gone invisible to get closer to her. When she threw out the bolt towards Morphana, Decklyn appeared next to her and stabbed her in the heart with a knife. Sigcerlaw looked at Decklyn in shock before she took her last breath. Smiling because they had won Decklyn didn't know that the bolt, she threw out didn't hit Morphana, but had hit Piper instead. Turning around, he saw his girlfriend lying down on the ground not moving. "What happened?" he shouted as he ran over to her lifeless body.

Phoenix was already over Piper when Decklyn and Tiffany got there. Morphana said, "Sigcerlaw threw that bolt at me, but Piper shoved me out of the way, and it hit her. My body could have taken the hit, but you guys are different."

"What do we do?" Tiffany started to say in panic.

Before any of them could say anything, else Phoenix threw his green ice crystal over Piper's heart and started chanting in another language. The crystal lit up and sent a shocking green light through Piper's body. Phoenix was still chanting when Piper gasped for air and her eyes bulged open like she was in shock. Phoenix then came out of his chanting state. "Piper?" he said.

"Phoenix, what happened?" Piper asked.

He threw his arms around her and brought her in for a tight hug. Decklyn and Tiffany also got down on the ground and hugged their friends. Looking at Morphana, Piper said, "Get in here and get a big hug."

Smiling, Morphana got down on the ground with the rest of the friends and they all hugged. "This is what it's like having family?" Morphana asked.

"This is exactly what it's like to have family." said a very happy Piper.

"My lady! My lady! Oh, thank the stars. You're ok!" shouted Slobbo as he and Perlangitis were running towards the group of friends. "I was so worried about you."

"Slobbo! I am so glad to see you." Morphana said as she got up off the ground. "Perlangitis, my aunt is gone. Decklyn put a knife through her evil heart."

Perlangitis picked Morphana up and swung her around in circles. "I knew you could do it. This calls for a celebration! Let's go home, tomorrow we celebrate."

Chapter 21

Not the End, But Only the Beginning

The next day Phoenix rolled too far and fell out of the hammock. "Son of a…"

"Watch your mouth." Tiffany yawned.

Decklyn sat up and looked around the room of the fort. "Where is Piper?" he asked.

Getting up the friends made their way down the ladder. Piper wasn't in the fort. There was a note on the table in the kitchen. The note read: *Couldn't sleep. Went for a walk in the Hidden Garden. ~Piper*

"Is she mad? I mean yes, we defeated all the evil in Shelvockwood, but doesn't she know that more evil could happen?" Phoenix blurted out. "It's not like we have cell service out here."

Snickering at his comment Tiffany said, "I'm sure she will be ok. We still have our ice crystals."

"Let's go find her." Decklyn stated.

Leaving the fort Tiffany locked up like she usually did, just out of habit. The friends started walking in the maze. "Marco!" Phoenix shouted.

"Phoenix, you really think that that is going to…" Tiffany started.

She was cut off because in the distance they all heard. "Polo!"
"That must be Piper." Decklyn smiled.

Rounding a turn in the maze the friends found Piper sitting on a bench by some flowers. "What's up Pipes? You scared some of us to death not being in the fort?" Decklyn said.

"I couldn't sleep, and I was just thinking what we are going to do now. How are we going to get back home? I know this is the kind of adventure that I wanted, but are we all going to be ok to never see our family and friends again?"

"Pipes, that's a chance we took to help Lady Morphana defeat her aunt. If it wasn't for us all Shelvockwood would be in the hands of Sigcerlaw. Think of Sorsha, and Queen Lavinia, Aged Sir Oak and Balfour, all the sprites and unicorns; everyone we have met in this land would be in so much trouble without us. Some of our own from back home died protecting this land. Back home we are just everyday kids, getting ready to graduate and start our lives. Whoever gets to live in a fantasy world and mean something?" Phoenix stated.

"Ya, I know. I guess I just don't know what we do now." sighed Piper.

"We go to the Whispering Wood and celebrate with everyone else. If we can't get home, we make this our home and become legends here and missing persons back home." Decklyn answered.

"I guess you're right." Piper said. "Let's go celebrate."

 exo

The Whispering Wood was decorated like it was Christmastime. Everybody was there. Balfour was there with a ton of villagers, and they were all dancing and playing with the unicorns and sprites. Queen Lavinia and all her fairies were flying around Aged Sir Oak. Pike was just sitting at the bottom of Aged Sir Oak and letting Clara braid his fur. The forest floor was crawling with nymphs, good and bad ones. The bad ones hovered around Lady Morphana and Perlangitis waiting for her next move. Slobbo was there trying to get Scales to settle down. He was wide-eyed, looking at all the little creatures like they were fast food to go. And in the distance towards the unicorn caves, Sunpolis, Vailtorcles, Sparuxe, Chanbo, and Fairtices were walking towards all the fun. As soon as everyone saw the protectors there was a huge cheer. "About time you joined us. We want to hear all the details of the battle." Stated Aged Sir Oak.

"First thing first." Decklyn started. "Lady Morphana, will you come join us please."

Looking shocked she walked over to the protectors. "What are you doing?" she whispered to the friends.

"What we should have done in the beginning." Tiffany whispered back.

Looking at all the villagers and creatures Piper shouted, "Lady Morphana has a melted heart, she is no longer evil. If it wasn't for her great wisdom and help Sigcerlaw and Empanvic would have killed us off like the other protectors. This celebration is not just for us all winning the battle, but Lady Morphana is now the true heir to Shelvockwood!"

The crowd went wild. Morphana was shocked. Looking around her eyes landed on Perlangitis who had a huge smile plastered on his face and was clapping along with everyone else. Morphana spoke, "I am truly sorry that it took me this long to realize that you are all I have ever needed." Noticing Sorsha walking up to her Lady Morphana said, "Sorsha I am so sorry I ever doubted you."

Smiling at her Sorsha replied, "I knew one day you would get here. I never gave up hope." She then grabbed Morphana in a big embrace. The crowd went nuts again. It was so loud you could hear it echoing through the Whispering Wood.

The crowd finally went back to dancing and mingling with others. The friends were left with Aged Sir Oak, Sorsha, Lady

Morphana, Queen Lavinia, and Balfour. "I guess we can have a quiet forest committee meeting." Chuckled Balfour.

"Good. We want to know how we are going to get back home now that the portal has been closed." said a worried Tiffany.

"I have been wracking my brain and I think we need Morphana's help." Sorsha said.

"Random question, but what happens with all of the ogres, giants, and swamp goblins now?" asked Phoenix.

Lady Morphana chuckled and said, "When I go back to the castle, I will put them to use for good and not evil. They are dumb creatures and need a leader. Shelvockwood doesn't need to fear them anymore. I will have their heads if they are mean." With worried looks she replied, "I'm kidding. I'll have Scales eat them."

"You're joking again, right?" asked Tiffany.

Smiling at her she shook her head yes. "No worries. They won't be a burden again. I will make sure they do their part in making up for all the bad I have done. And I believe I have a way of reversing my aunts way of closing the portal. Sadly, it involves a little bit of dark magic." She said while looking in Perlangitis's direction.

"I can do it if you are worried about going evil again." Queen Lavinia said.

Perlangitis turned to the queen and said, "Yes, that would make me happy if you could do that. It's not that I don't trust Morphana, but I'm afraid she may get a taste of the evil again and I don't want that."

"Neither do we." Decklyn said.

"After the celebration let's go to Sorsha's cottage and get this show on the road. As much as I love being here, I'm ready to go home." Decklyn said.

The friends celebrated well into the night. Today was a good day.

ಲൂ

The next day the protectors got up and got ready for the day. They packed up all their belongings and headed out the door of the fort to Sorsha's cottage. They told Sorsha they would meet up with her and Lady Morphana and Queen Lavinia. Upon arriving at her cottage, the other ladies were already there. "We think we have figured out how to open the portal back to your land. Are you ready to go home?" asked Sorsha.

Looking kind of glum, the friends all shook their heads yes and each one of them handed Sorsha their ice crystal. Sorsha took them and put them in the trunk that contained all the old pictures and letters. "Till the next time we need the protectors of the ice crystals." She spoke.

"Let me take a picture of all of you for us to remember you by and one day tell our next generation." Queen Lavinia said.

The friends got together with Sorsha, Lady Morphana, and Queen Lavinia. Waving her magic wand, a flash of light brightened the room and was gone. Magically a photograph appeared with them all together. "Thank you all so much for doing what you all did." Sorsha said.

Lady Morphana looked at each one of the protectors and said, "Yes, thank you. I know when you first got here, I wasn't the most welcoming person. I kind of made your lives miserable to be honest. If it wasn't for all of you, I probably would be either ruling with my aunt and father or dead. I wouldn't have Perlangitis and the life you have given me now. Thank you."

Piper and Tiffany hugged Morphana and Sorsha. "We will never forget you all." said a sad Tiffany.

With a sad smile Piper said, "You have all become amazing friends and we will miss you all."

"Yes, thank you for the adventure we were all looking for." Decklyn said.

Phoenix was rubbing his hand through his hair. "Yeah, thanks for torturing us and all the fun. It really was a good time."

236

After all the hugs the friends waited patiently by the closet door for the portal. Queen Lavinia started by the cauldron adding things that some of the friends knew what they were and some of them had no idea what she was putting in there. Instead of blue and purple smoke like when Sigcerlaw closed the portal there was green and gold smoke coming from the cauldron. It crawled on the floor and slithered to the closet going up under the door. Sorsha opened the closet door and right where the back wall used to be the portal to their world was open. "This potion will keep the portal open when it needs to be open." Queen Lavinia said. "Sigcerlaw tried to close it for good, but with a little bit of dark magic it's now open. You all can go home. Thank you, protectors of the ice crystals!"

Grabbing Piper's hand Decklyn led her to the portal, and they walked through. Tiffany smiled up at Phoenix, took his hand and walked through the portal. Then the door closed behind them, and they were gone.

⚬⚬

Coming out into the dark cave, the friends walked out into the entrance of the cave. Looking at the bright sky Decklyn said, "Well, we made it home. What should we all do now? We still have to finish camping."

"I don't know about you Deck, but I'm beat. I want to walk home and nap for the rest of the weekend." Phoenix replied.

Chuckling at him, Tiffany said, "I am ready to head home. It is summer break, so we have all summer for another adventure."

"You know what Tiff" Piper said with a huge smile, "we do have all summer to find another adventure."